MR. BREATHNACH CAME INTO SIGHT on the staircase, staggering forward, propelled by his own unbalanced weight. He reached the landing, bracing himself on the facing wall briefly, with one hand, before he started headlong down. Kevin Conlon raced toward him, watching in horror as the man's bare feet slipped and slid on the wooden stairs. Clutching at the navy blue toweling robe covering his ▨▨▨ body, Breathnach began to fall ▨▨▨▨▨▨▨▨ Kevin reached him, tryin▨▨▨▨▨▨▨▨▨▨▨▨▨ st. But Kevin was ov▨▨▨▨▨▨▨▨▨▨▨▨▨▨, and the two of them ▨▨▨▨▨▨▨▨▨▨▨▨ ence to the stairs an▨▨▨▨▨▨▨▨▨▨▨ ther, sprawled on the ▨▨▨▨▨▨▨

Breathnach's eye▨▨▨▨▨ up and his gasping mouth opened and closed, in what seemed, and indeed was, his dying breath. . . .

PRAISE FOR ANN C. FALLON'S JAMES FLEMING MYSTERIES

BLOOD IS THICKER

"Fans of Elizabeth George, P.D. James, Martha Grimes, Caroline Graham . . . should rejoice at this new entry. . . . It is certainly to be hoped this is an author we will hear more from . . . and soon!"

—*The Mystery News*

WHERE DEATH LIES

"As provocative as any murder you'll find in Agatha Christie or P.D. James . . . Fallon's Mr. Fleming will be welcome with mystery lovers for a long, long time."

—*Irish Voice*

Also by Ann C. Fallon

Blood Is Thicker
Where Death Lies

Published by POCKET BOOKS

DEAD ENDS

A
JAMES FLEMING
MYSTERY

ANN C. FALLON

POCKET BOOKS

New York   London   Toronto   Sydney   Tokyo   Singapore

An *Original* publication of POCKET BOOKS

POCKET BOOKS, a division of Simon & Schuster Inc.
1230 Avenue of the Americas, New York, NY 10020

ISBN: 0-671-75134-4

First Pocket Books printing December 1992

10 9 8 7 6 5 4 3 2 1

POCKET and colophon are registered trademarks of
Simon & Schuster Inc.

Cover art by Richard Ross

Printed in the U.S.A.

For Frank,
who loves Halloween

DEAD ENDS

Chapter One

Kevin Conlon leaned back against the thick tapestry cushions and stretched his long legs along the length of the window seat. He pushed his glasses to the bridge of his nose in an old unconscious habit as he riffled the sheets of thick paper in his hand and settled comfortably to his task.

The large but cozy sitting room was empty, silent save for the sonorous ticking of the schoolroom clock, whose burnished pendulum now caught the light from the flickering fire. Kevin was rather surprised, but nonetheless pleased, to see that his guests had chosen to brave the wild weather of County Sligo on this late October day. He glanced idly out the mullioned window, his attention distracted by the increasing roar of the wind. The bare sycamore trees were swaying under its force, their branches writhing like so many arms and hands against the dull gray sky. Kevin leaned his head against the cold glass and let his eyes rest on the view—one of which he never grew tired, one that restored his spirit no matter what the season.

The windows fronting the hundred-and-fifty-year-old house known as Cromlech Lodge commanded a sweeping view of the black humpbacked Ox Mountains on the left across to the sea that surged on Rosses Point and around to the right to the lonely mountain of Knock-na-Rea. He noted that low cloud was already covering the great stone cairn—Queen Maeve's ancient tomb atop Knock-na-Rea—and he could see, like an Olympic god from his high and lonely vantage point, the rain falling in shining silver sheets. It was moving towards the sea, and towards him.

Smiling to himself, he judged that the wind and the rain might well drive his assembly of lodgers back to the warmth and creature comforts of afternoon tea in the very room in which he sat.

He bent his head to proofread the menus: fourteen for his full house of guests and eleven more for casual diners who might drop in for dinner at his justly renowned restaurant.

It was simple but nourishing fare tonight. He mused that Sean must be feeling homesick again, for this evening's meal was composed of comfort food. Coarse goose liver pâté (misspelled again by Bridie, the local woman who wrote out his menus for him in an admirable hand but with execrable spelling). Parsnip soup, a personal favourite of his, and cod in a cream sauce. The *boeuf en crochette,* with boiled and mashed potato, was hardly exciting but the diners would be rewarded with Sean's amazing carrot and leek casserole dressed in a delectable glaze. Kevin tapped his pencil on his teeth. It was a pity he hadn't managed to get the oranges at the fruit market that morning. Blackberry tart could be just that—tart, unless Sean was going to be wildly inspired at the last minute.

A log disintegrated on the fire and startled Kevin. He looked up and watched in fascination as the rain approached, in seconds sending streams down the glass an inch from his nose. The natural light in the room grew dim, throwing the chintz-covered sofas, the easy chairs, the chaise longue, the wine velvet curtains, deeper in shadow than before. But Kevin was reluctant to move from his position to stir and stoke the fire.

This had been Mary's favourite time of day. How often she had sat here, doing just what he was doing now. He closed his eyes to see her more clearly, sitting clad in her thick navy sweater and cords, patiently, quietly writing out the evening menu. Always so quiet yet her hospitality was immediately perceived by all who crossed their well-worn threshold. Mary, so young, so strong and so quiet. He opened his eyes as if she'd just walked in; the hair on his head lifted slightly as he imagined she was touching his arm. The pain of her loss was diminishing. He could think about her now without the searing pain. He could now, after a year, even talk to her again.

"It's raining, Mary. You would have been curled up here, hugging your knees. The view is just as it always was." His voice grew thick and soft. "I'm not so bitter now. . . ."

His thoughts wandered to his only child, Miriam, safe at her boarding school in nearby Sligo Town. He glanced at the clock. Classes would be over and now it would be time for all her clubs and activities. He sighed, looking forward to hearing her lovely girlish voice on the weekend, as she ran to his car. She was so glad he'd started to drive again. Her father driving again was a return to normalcy for her, he supposed. But for him it was a triumph over horror and loss. When Mary had died alone on the road, where black ice had risen up like a demon and tossed her car into a ditch, he'd said he'd never drive again, his nerve gone with his heart.

Time heals after all, he thought. And now the time was right too, to put his affairs in order. He was glad when his old school friend, Madigan, now a famous Dub-

lin barrister, had been able to recommend a solicitor to
do the job.

But what a weekend to choose! With Halloween cele-
brations and Miriam coming home, scheduling the writing of his will with this Fleming character had been poor
planning on his part. He shrugged. "Not to worry,"
Mary would say. And for the thousandth time he resolved not to.

In the quiet of the house the loud slamming of the
outer front door startled him. He strode quickly to the
open stone flagged lobby, where the old oak accoun-
tant's desk served as a point of greeting. He straightened
his white shirt and flecked woollen waistcoat.

"Mr. Breathnach," he said heartily to his guest of a
few days.

"Conlon!" said the large red-faced man sourly. "I've
had a bloodyawful day . . ."

"I'm sorry, if . . ."

"Not your business, Conlon, not your business." The
man was wiping his face, wet from both rain and heavy
perspiration. He tossed the keys on the desk. "Have
one of your people put my car around back, will you?"
Kevin stopped the scowl on his own face.

"Anything else?"

"Yes, indeed. I'll be wanting the afternoon tea that's
so bloody famous around here. And send one of the
maids up to draw me a bath. I've got to get out of these
clothes."

Kevin silently agreed as he observed the man's shirt
beneath the heavy overcoat.

"We'll see to it, Mr. . . ."

But his courtesy was wasted on the man's back as he
trod heavily up the wide uncarpeted wooden staircase,
gripping the newel post and the banisters as though haul-
ing his great weight up an incline. As Breathnach
mounted from the first landing, virtually out of sight, he
called over his shoulder the single word "Now."

Kevin was much puzzled by Mr. Breathnach. Part of the Lodge's charm for him, and for Mary too, had always been the interesting guests that chance and word of mouth had brought. Guests from all nations, especially the Continent. Lots of Irish-Americans over the years. Their small share of celebrities—actors, writers, artists. Irish people from every county. One and all, they were prosperous guests able to afford the high rates needed to pay for the kind of quiet luxury once inherent in an earlier age. But Breathnach seemed not to appreciate the quiet solitude, or the excellent cuisine, or the purity of the air, the fine local stable, or even the peace for which others sought, often so assiduously. He seemed instead, to Kevin, to have some mocking intent behind his unwelcome questions about the Lodge itself and Kevin's own plans.

Kevin pulled on the old bell rope and vivacious Caitlin appeared through one of the many doors off the foyer. As he gave the instruction she nervously straightened her white apron over her black dress and then took the stairs two at a time.

Kevin himself moved Breathnach's Volvo estate car, outfitted with every option, to the rear parking lot and as he did so he glanced nosily around the interior of the car. Spotless. There was no clue to Breathnach's intentions or even his profession. Kevin locked the car and ran through the rain, back to the hotel, regretting as usual that they'd been forced to alter what had been a wonderful kitchen garden in order to house the much more mundane car park. However, the huge yew hedges successfully screened the cars from view and with that he could not quibble.

He resumed his place on the window seat and finished writing in the prices for that day's meals. But the earlier stillness was now broken by the amusing sound of the dour Mr. Breathnach in the room immediately above. When Breathnach had phoned for his booking he'd asked specifically for a room with a view fronting the house and on a lower floor. Kevin now knew why. Without an elevator the man would have had difficulty reaching a guest room on one of the upper three storeys.

At first the sound of Breathnach's voice softened Kevin's opinion of the man whom he now pictured singing happily if raucously in his bathtub. But as the monotonous lines of the popular song "My Way" rose in volume, Kevin's impression of the man as some sort of obnoxious business shark was reinforced. He was glad to finish his writing and begin to move the small side tables away from the walls and corners and near to the sofas and chairs, preparatory for the four o'clock tea.

Mrs. O'Neil bustled in and began switching on the standing lamps and the low table lamps. On hearing the singing she glanced quizzically at the high ceiling and then shrugged discreetly to herself.

"Desperate weather, Mr. Conlon," she said in her rich soft Sligo accent.

"It is surely," answered Kevin. "Do you think there'll be many in for the tea?"

She heard the anxiety there, that never seemed to leave him. Kindly she assured him there would be.

"After all, Mr. Conlon, the guests that's come hardly do be comin' for good weather at the shank of October. They've come for rest and food and a bit of brisk air. I'm going now to see to the trays and such." She stood in the arched doorway and glanced again at the ceiling. They smiled at one another conspiratorially. "Seems he's cheered up then," she said without naming Breathnach.

"Indeed," said Kevin, "but I wish he knew more than one song. By the way, what about the barmbracks? Did you come to an arrangement with Sean?"

"Ah, God, he's been in a mood ever since but, Mr. Conlon, I prevailed. That man knows nothing of baking. Hasn't a clue how to make the barmbracks for Halloween and he was forced to admit it. I've asked Mrs.

McGrory in the town and she's doing us twenty with a few in reserve. At a good price too.''

"Grand, grand. She'll remember all the little bits to put in?"

"Don't you be worrying. She well knows what to do. Mr. Conlon, you've checked on that other 'arrangement'?" Mrs. O'Neil winked broadly as yet again Kevin smiled conspiratorially.

"Yes. I'll be picking them up in the morning, all going well." He reached into his back pocket and took out a bit of crumpled paper, reading through the list of needed items for the Lodge's Halloween celebration on the next day.

"They say the weather's to be fine and clear," Mrs. O. called over her shoulder as she moved off. The dumbwaiter had landed with a loud thud in its housing in the foyer. "That'll be some of the tea trays now."

The outer door opened and Kevin greeted four local people well-known to him as they often arrived for Friday tea, elderly women whose hardiness was invariably brought to the fore by the challenge of inclement weather. They nodded and smiled in triumph as they walked on through to the lounge—at home as if visiting an old friend.

They were quickly followed by an odd assortment of the hotel's guests, flushed red and bright-eyed from a long tramp across the fields that abutted the hotel grounds. Their feet were muddied and there was much laughter as they scraped their boots and shoes on the ancient iron boot scrape at the granite threshold and then crowded happily, hungrily, into the lounge.

Kevin glanced out the door to watch as two cars pulled into the gravelled drive, disgorging more guests before moving around to the rear. This time it was a party of girls from Barclay's Bank in the town, celebrating their monthly paycheck with a gorgeous cream tea. Kevin felt his anxiety that they might have no one for tea be replaced by a fear they'd have too many. He pulled on the bell rope again, and again Caitlin arrived, breathless with enthusiasm.

"Go on, child," he said kindly. "It's time to take the orders and I know you'll get things right, now, sure you will."

To his embarrassment she dropped a curtsy and he turned away.

"Caitlin, go on, go on."

Lodgers continued to arrive, and they seemed content with how they'd spent their day: hiking, shopping, touring, and in one case, pub-crawling. Part of the ongoing satisfaction for Kevin in running the hotel was the incongruous pairings of guests he'd witnessed over the years. Many a friendship had been fostered at Cromlech Lodge and engagements were not unknown.

And so it was now that one tall angular woman, visiting from New York, a widow used to travelling alone, was waxing enthusiastic about her visit to the Yeats Museum in the town.

Entering the Lodge at her side, and just as enthusiastic, was her companion, a fellow guest, a retired college professor from England who'd spent his summers in Sligo and who'd returned for a nostalgic and lengthy visit to the happy scenes of his youth. Yeats, Kevin noted, was a common bond here, but so too was loneliness. He clucked and murmured as they displayed their careful purchases of fine Irish woollen lap rugs in colours spun from the translucent shades of sedge and heather, of dry stone walls and agate seas. They thought him a splendid host, but he knew how much better at this had been his Mary.

He was totting up numbers at the tall desk when Caitlin appeared by his side.

"Oh, Mr. Conlon, I'm sorry to be tellin' you, but there is a drip."

"A drip?"

"Indeed, sir, a drip. Now, it's not a drip of great size. Yet. Or great speed. But now, I know drips, I do, sir. And this one's buildin' up."

"Lord, where is this drip?"

"Why, in the lounge, over near the far corner, it's just missin' that lovely little round table with the red lamp on't."

"Right, go on there and take the trays from the dumb-waiter. I'll take care of the drip."

Kevin walked casually into the lounge and chatted briefly with the diners here and there, moving slowly towards the spot. Yes, indeed, a drip: the water now being absorbed by the old Persian rug on that side of the room. He pondered as he moved away. No one seemed to have noticed it yet, but they would in time.

He hustled down to the kitchens and found a large round pot. Sweeping it away from the protesting chef he placed a bunch of crumpled tea towels in the bottom, to deaden that giveaway *plink-plonk* of the drip, and ran upstairs. He could hardly disguise what he was doing so he walked instead purposefully across the room to the drip and placed the pot under it. It made the slighest of noises. Then he returned to chatting with the guests, helping to set out the individual trays, pouring tea, stoking the fire before he moved again to the foyer to draw breath with Caitlin.

"Tell me, Caitlin, that's surely Mr. Breathnach's room?"

"Oh, yes, sir, the big man. Indeed. I drew the curtains in the bathroom and ran the water. 'Hot' as he said. And, sir"—she dropped her voice to a whisper—"he asked me to put in some bath oil. Did you ever? It had a real boggy smell."

Kevin pondered the vision of a slick and slippery Breathnach. "Bath oil? Caitlin, are you sure?"

"Yes, indeed, one of them little sachet things, like a packet of baking soda."

"Bath salts then, Caitlin."

"Whatever you say, sir," she said demurely.

Kevin realized with a shock how much of the world was a mystery to young Caitlin, and realized for the first time that she was barely older than his own daughter.

"Miriam's coming home tomorrow," he said more gently.

"For the Halloween. Oh, that's marvelous, Mr. Conlon, marvelous! I do miss her about the place."

"Marvelous," he said, repeating Caitlin's favourite word. "I think we'll all have a bit of fun. That reminds me, will you tell Jim and Pat I'll be wanting them at midday? There's loads of boxes in the attics I want to bring down and they can help. Bits and pieces for the costume party. You'll remember now?"

"Ah, the brothers'll be happy to oblige." Caitlin ran off to answer a call for more strawberry jam and Kevin stole over to view the now heavier drip.

If only Breathnach would come down for tea . . . he thought to himself . . . I could get in there and have a look without a lot of fuss and explanation. He glanced at his watch impatiently and returned to his post at the desk.

"Ah, here he is at last," he said half-aloud as he heard movement on the upper landing. But some note of discord struck him and he looked up sharply.

Mr. Breathnach was emerging into sight down the staircase, staggering forward, propelled by his own unbalanced weight. He reached the landing, bracing himself on the facing wall briefly, with one hand, before he started headlong down. Kevin raced towards him, watching in horror as the man's bare feet slipped and slid on the wooden stairs. Clutching at the navy blue towelling robe covering his huge body, he began to fall, and he sagged as Kevin reached him, trying to hold him around the waist. But Kevin was overwhelmed by the man's weight, and the two of them slid and fell against the wall, thence to the stairs and on down until they fell together, sprawled on the parquet flooring.

Breathnach's eyes rolled up and his gasping mouth opened and closed, in what seemed, and indeed was, his dying breath.

—— *Chapter Two* ——

"Oh, my God," said a voice from the doorway, cutting through the shrieks and cries of both the staff and guests who had poured out into the foyer. "Quick, get help, get help! Ring for an ambulance!" The stranger flung his leather gladstone bag and his Donegal tweed coat to the floor in haste, and rushed to lift the heavy body up and off Kevin, who lay pinned, entangled and bruised on the wood floor.

"Thanks, thanks," Kevin said automatically. He spotted Caitlin's white and stricken face. "Caitlin, get Mrs. O. Now, child!" he shouted as he staggered to his feet.

"You, Sean!" he yelled to his elusive chef. "Get some blankets from upstairs."

He became conscious of mumbling voices, some tearful, some horrified, more curious. And he turned, only then aware of the forty or so people crowded in the doorway of the lounge.

He stared at them and said nothing, and a heavy silence fell. He turned to grab the blankets and help the stranger who was working to ease the body into some

12

more human, less grotesque position. Together the two men pillowed the head and covered the body.

Mrs. O'Neil and the pale Caitlin reappeared with towels and smelling salts, which they administered in vain. Caitlin said that she'd phoned for the ambulance and Mrs. O'Neil said she'd rung them as well. But they all knew—even the guests visiting for the first time—what a long and winding journey an ambulance would have to reach the Cromlech Lodge. Kevin knelt down and put his ear to the man's chest but could detect no heartbeat.

"What about CPR?" said the stranger, hunkering down. "Do you know it?"

"No. You?" The man shook his head as he prepared to give Breathnach mouth-to-mouth resuscitation. He removed the pillow and tilted the head so the chin was up and the mouth open. He pinched the nostrils and breathed into Breathnach's mouth, pausing to listen for the return of air, and then repeating the process. He worked for some minutes, but it was to no avail. He stood up and asked the assembly if anyone knew heart massage, but with one accord they drew back a step, shaking their heads.

"God, this is terrible," gasped Kevin.

Mrs. O'Neil stood up stiffly from her kneeling position. "Sure and he's gone, poor soul," she said aloud, and she blessed herself. "Caitlin, be a good child and run and ring up Father Byrne."

"Is he Catholic?" asked James Fleming, the stranger.

"In Ireland there's a good chance, isn't there?" said Mrs. O. as she began to finger the rosary that she'd drawn from her apron. "Mr. Conlon, go on and see to the guests. Somethin' will have to be done. Go on," she urged. "You'll find the words."

Kevin moved away and left Mrs. O'Neil with the body. Then at a loss for something more to do, James Fleming walked to the front door. The afternoon had grown absolutely pitch-black with a powerful wind. Not a glimmer of light showed from the sky or the deep countryside that surrounded the old house. He shivered as he stepped out onto the front step. Below in the distance he could see the lights of the town, moving lights as of cars, and he longed to see the ambulance pulling into the drive. Perspiration stood out on his forehead as he reacted to the shock of the scene that had greeted him.

"Christ, what a way to start a weekend," he murmured.

Inside Kevin Conlon was helping his customers on with their coats. He had thought it best to urge the visitors to leave before he addressed the anxieties of his lodgers. As he passed through the foyer with the various afternoon revellers, he threw the switch that lit up the floodlights fixed on all four corners of the house. The sighs of relief and the babble of curiosity were carried on the wind as the visitors hurried to their cars. Girlish giggles of excitement from the younger crowd, more sober speculation from their elders. But all with one accord had found a fruitful subject for gossip that would fill the weekend, if not the week ahead. James stepped aside and let them pass, thinking fleetingly that perhaps letting everyone go was not a good idea. But then, what could he have said to detain them? Irresolute, he turned to speak to Kevin Conlon but found he'd gone inside to his guests. James followed him, and listened to his appeal that they perhaps retire to their rooms.

Oh, God, Conlon, definitely not a good idea, thought James, realizing that all these people would need to step over the enormous corpse to get upstairs. He hurried to Kevin's side, whispering this observation.

"Ah, yes, indeed," said Kevin. "Please, if you will just follow me. I can lead you upstairs by another staircase."

This group was more sober. They had known the man

in a sense. Most of them had seen him at dinner; some had even attempted to open conversation with him, with no result.

They walked in ones and twos behind Kevin, who led the way through a door off the foyer. Together they passed through a maze of interconnecting halls to the rear staircase that led from the basement level all the way to the attics, a door opening onto each floor.

James returned to his post at the front door, studying Mrs. O'Neil, who prayed with her eyes closed, not glancing at the mound at her feet.

The first car to arrive was a black sedan. A young priest leapt from it without shutting the door and ran to the steps.

"In there, Father," said James as the red-faced young man nodded and sped on, his bag in his hand.

At long last came the faint donkey-cry of a siren. James could see a red light flashing, showing between the swaying branches of the hedgerows. The ambulance at last appeared, the driver gingerly sizing up the Lodge's ancient twin wrought-iron gates, before proceeding. James motioned the medics into the house, but he did not follow. He'd seen enough for one day.

He paced a bit and then walked, unheeding of the wind, to the car park. He opened the boot of his red Citroen and took out his briefcase and a pair of riding boots.

Pretty tough on Conlon, he mused, but perhaps by tomorrow things would resume their normal course. Still, he may not feel up to writing a will. On the other hand, the shock of sudden death might make it seem more imperative. James returned slowly to the house, his eyes adjusting to the wild night. Now he could see patches of less inky black moving against the sky—low scudding clouds carrying away the rain and leaving a raw chill in the air.

He turned the corner of the house in time to see the

stretcher being heaved into the back of the ambulance. Kevin Conlon stood silently as it slowly reversed and then turned out towards the gates. His shoulders sagged noticeably as James came up to his side.

"Pretty bad," said James.

"Indeed, indeed," said Kevin sadly, looking at James for the first time, and sticking out his hand. "Kevin Conlon, proprietor." He managed a small smile.

"James Fleming, guest." And the two men shook hands warmly.

"So it's you? Come in, come in. We don't often have such a dramatic greeting for our new guests. Drink?"

They passed through the foyer together where neither blanket nor any sign remained of the events of the previous hour.

Kevin led the way to the small snug bar to be found off one of the corridors and poured two large Hennessy brandies. They carried their drinks into the lounge to gain the warmth of the now dwindling fire. Kevin drank in silence, finally glancing over to the source of the drip.

"Ah!" he said, relieved. "At least that's stopped. Don't think I could have dealt with a plumbing problem just now. Listen, Fleming, have your drink here by the fire. I've got to see to the dinner and return things to some semblance of order. I'll send someone in by and by, to show you to your room." Kevin shook himself into action and suddenly looked younger than his forty years.

James smiled and waved him off. "Take your time," he said.

Stretching in front of the fire, he found his mood of shock and sadness passing off quickly. He leaned back and surveyed the room. It was even better than he'd imagined it. The brochure Conlon had enclosed with his letter failed to do justice to the rich, warm ambience of the Lodge. James slipped his notebook out of his briefcase and glanced over it. Now that he was here, Conlon's letter had taken on more meaning.

Yes, it would be a simple matter of a couple of hours to write out Kevin's will, he decided. A free weekend here would cover the cost of his time and more. He seldom did work in kind for clients, but he'd happily make an exception in this case. He sipped his brandy and let his mind contemplate the pleasures of the weekend ahead.

"Mr. Conlon? You asked me to give you a wake-up call . . ." Mrs. O'Neil called through the door.

"What's the hour?" Kevin ran his hand through his thick black curly hair and yawned silently.

"It's just gone six."

"Thanks, Mrs. O. I'll be down directly."

As he dressed for the day he reviewed with a mild sense of accomplishment the events of the previous night. Somehow he had found the right words to soothe his guests. He'd gone to each bedroom in turn, chatting and explaining. All of his lodgers had come down for the only slightly delayed dinner. He was pleased Sean had carried on—nothing had burned or overflowed. Caitlin's elder sister had come in her place to serve, a lovely steady girl who shooed her little sister off home.

As he locked his bedroom on the third floor he remembered the curiosity seekers he'd turned away, telling them the evening meal was completely booked out. It had been better that way. The lodgers had drawn together, sharing in the event like some distant relatives meeting at a wake. There'd been no sorrow after the shock. After all, no one had known the man. It was sad, but there it was.

He had been perhaps the most affected. He shrugged. One life. Gone. Somewhere, someone would be bereft, grieving when they received the news. He looked at his watch for the tenth time. The local garda who'd arrived shortly after the ambulance had departed had said to expect someone very early the next morning. Kevin was relieved. He'd like to hand over the responsibility as soon as possible.

He ran lightly down the narrow back stairs to the kitchen. First he opened the grillwork door that dated from the house's asylum days and then opened the more recent wooden door. The kitchen was warm and welcoming and he drank a steaming cup of fresh coffee and wolfed down two slabs of wheaten bread with strawberry jam. It was reassuring to see Mrs. O. laying out the trays for the dumbwaiter, to hear Sean humming as he stirred the oatmeal and then began to prepare the egg mixture.

"Busy day ahead, Mr. Conlon," said Mrs. O'Neil.

"Very. And it's time I got going to Mrs. McGrory's for the bracks, right?"

"Yes, surely. She said they'd be ready after seven."

"I'm off then. You're all set for the breakfast?"

She nodded. "You won't forget?"

"The tinkers? Of course not." He smiled as he ran back up the stairs to the ground floor, and out to his Range Rover parked in the courtyard at the back of the Lodge. The sky was still October dark but with a thin slice of the dawn showing on the horizon. Isolated cold drops of rain hit the windscreen as he pulled out of the gates and stopped for a second to see the morning break behind the humped backs of the Ox Mountains. He opened the window and took a deep breath of crystalline air. Then he engaged the Range Rover and hurtled down the narrow road. At ease at the wheel again.

He'd only had to stay for one cup of boiling hot tea with the tiny Mrs. McGrory. Of indeterminate age, she was as small as what the tourists might picture a leprechaun to be. But she'd strong arms and large hands with prominent knuckles. She lifted the trays of dense fruity barmbrack into the back of the Range Rover as easily as Kevin. He began to peel off some notes from the wad in his pocket.

Time for a bit of dickering.

"Fifty punts," he said, offering ten fives.

"Well, now, let me see. This time the flour, well now, I'd a bit of flour left from another batch for the hotel in the town, so I'll not be charging for that . . ."

"Indeed, charge me. . . ."

"Not a'tall. On the other hand, the rings cost me more than I'd thought. Let me see. Twenty rings and there were the extra. Twenty coins. Twenty little black shrivelled peas. No, they cost me nothing. And then I got twenty little twigs and wrapped them. But you know, Mr. Conlon, the fruit now, it was dear. Dearest I've seen it in years. I'll take forty pound of your hard-earned money."

"Fifty, please."

"God bless you, I'll take forty-five, if you'll take the extra dozen with you."

The deal was done and Kevin drove off in good form. At the beginning he'd found all of these dealings so very difficult. Mary hadn't been much better. She'd been shy of talking money. And he'd been next to useless, knowing little of the value of what was involved—goodwill included. But over the twenty years they'd been at it, he'd improved. Or so he thought. The local suppliers might not have agreed.

Kevin cruised along the ring road of the town, passing on and out to the fields that fringed the bay. He saw the caravans with their roofs gleaming in the slanting rays of a now bright morning sun. He hoped he wasn't too early. But this day of all days he didn't want to be too late either. He pulled the Range Rover over and stepped out into the absolute stillness. A very few tractors were plying the fields and milk lorries were to be seen on the roads. Otherwise, there was no one, in particular not the police. He strolled over to the van of the itinerant he'd spoken with earlier in the month and knocked on the door.

"Brendan?"

Muffled sounds came from the van and then the door opened, letting out the stale powerful aroma of cigarettes and frying bacon.

"Mr. Conlon, you're right early. Good thing too," said the young man with the straw-coloured hair. He leapt down, tucking his shirt into his trousers. "There'll be hordes here in no time."

Kevin surveyed the quiescent countryside and smiled. "Hordes."

He followed the man to the car parked behind a hedgerow on a precarious slant. It was jammed with boxes.

"How many was you wantin' again? Hundred sticks, wasn't it now?"

"Not for me . . ." started Kevin. "Twenty and you know it."

"Ah now, I can't be lettin' these go in lots under twenty-five. It's how they come, you understand." The tinker ripped open a box to reveal the loose sticks, not bundled in any way. "Sure, they only go in lots of twenty-five. Or more." The man's eyes twinkled.

"We agreed twenty."

"It's to be a clear night, you know. They'll be hordes here in moments snapping these up. I know for a fact there's a big party planned that'll be sendin' these up to the stars of the night, this night on Finner Strand. Give the soldiers a bit of a scare, I'd say. No, you'll be wantin' a deal of these, to keep the spirits away."

"Go on with you. Spirits. You don't believe in any spirits." Kevin laughed, but stopped when the young man blessed himself.

"Well, the ones in the bottle now, they'd be powerful enough, you'll agree?" Kevin attempted to redeem himself.

But the young man smiled with his mouth only.

There was a longish silence.

"Twenty-five it is," said Kevin, "I need twenty-five for the . . . lads."

"The lads, is it? Is that what you do be calling the guests at that fancy motel o' yers?"

Kevin gave him a quick look. He'd thought he'd been anonymous all along, with his stories of the lads he was planning a party for. Either the man was a chancer or he knew Kevin owned Cromlech Lodge.

The tinker laughed. "Ah sure, I knew you to see, and yer wife and her father before her. Used to come every year to buy them off me old lady. Missed ye all, these last few year." He looked away, his small blue eyes cold and blank. He looked back.

"Sixty pound."

"Fifty and no more."

"Done."

Kevin loaded the sticks of illegal fireworks into the cartons he'd brought for the purpose and secured them tightly to the interior wall of the Rover so nothing could jostle or move them. An early display of fireworks on the main Donegal-Sligo Road was not part of his day's planned activities!

"God keep ye, Mr. Conlon," called the tinker, "and you're wrong. It's the spirits I believe in, more than the ground beneath my feet or the money in me hand."

Kevin shivered. The man's words had quickly recalled to him the events of the previous night and he pondered, as he drove, on Breathnach's sudden death. Death—so close at hand again. He shrugged off his mood of depression, valiantly keeping to his resolution to be cheerful for Miriam. The sight of her standing at the end of the long driveway that led to the boarding school succeeded in lifting his mood. She ran gaily towards the Rover as she saw it approach.

It was so good to have her slim strong arms hugging him, hanging onto his neck as she chattered about her classes and about the exciting weekend ahead. Halloween! Like her mother, it was one of her favourite days, October her favourite month.

She took the news of Breathnach's death with the curiously impersonal wisdom of any twelve-year-old and her attitude determined his own as he met with the local inspector who was waiting at his ease in the lounge.

After some brief remarks the graying grizzled man came to the point.

"We're after identifyin' the man—to a degree, Mr. Conlon."

"That's marvelous, but how, if you don't mind my asking?"

"Ah, sure, dogged detective work," said the man, laughing. "We telephoned the number of the only David Breathnach in the Dublin directory. His car had a Dublin registration, you see. 'Twas simple then. One of them taped messages answered. Breathnach was an auctioneer, you know, dealing in real estate. I rang up a few of the local lads and they said they knew the name well. Very big in Dublin it seems. The Dublin police are lookin' up his next of kin."

"You know, Inspector, I learned virtually nothing about Breathnach while he was here, as I told the garda last night. I confess that I'm very curious as to why he *was* here, at least at this hotel."

"How so?"

"Because in the short time he was here, God rest his soul, he didn't seem to be on a holiday. He seemed to have a purpose . . ."

"Perhaps we'll know more when we speak to the next of kin. But the autopsy will be going ahead . . ."

"What?"

"It's usual in cases such as these."

"Such as what?"

"When a person dies, not in his county of permanent residence. Don't you see, the medical examiner can't sign the death certificate until the cause of death is established. After that, the body can be released for burial." He sighed. "I best be goin', Mr. Conlon. Work to do today, more like tonight. Halloween seems to give some people license for mischief."

Kevin turned his head quickly, to cover both a smile and a rising red flush of guilt.

"You'll be having a party here then?"

"Yes, but how did . . ."

"Ah, we hear things you know. It's nice that you're keeping up the old ways. A bonfire, I imagine?"

Kevin smiled again. The pile of wood and sticks and even logs was evident in the back field, so high it was to be seen from the road from the west.

"Yes, I've been collecting wood from the fields, and even from the shore. It'll be massive, if the rain holds off."

The two men stood on the front granite step like two seasoned farmers, glancing up at the sky. And, like seasoned farmers, they acknowledged that there was no way of knowing, given the wild unpredictable nature of the weather on the rugged coast and mottled mountains of Sligo, what the weather would be like for five minutes together.

Chapter Three

James Fleming's eyes lit up as he entered the dining
room for luncheon and saw before him three long side-
boards laden with food. He'd had a strenuous exhilarat-
ing ride on one of the local stable's best mounts and his
appetite was whetted. It seemed a long time since his
massive country breakfast and although he should have
changed out of his riding boots his hunger could not be
denied.

He loaded his plate with thinly sliced roast beef, pick-
les, beetroot, hunks of fresh baguettes, and wedges of
Irish cheddar cheese. Choosing to sit alone at one of the
white linen clad tables that were arranged around the
large wooden-floored room, he was too busy eating to
notice his fellow diners. But once his immediate hunger
was satisfied he couldn't resist sampling the Limerick
ham, the Dublin Bay prawns, or indeed the lobster claws
from the Galway coast with a smooth mayonnaise
d'hôte. Now he ate at a leisurely pace and allowed himself the luxury of sizing up his companions. They were
few in number.

At the table nearest him sat an older couple, not elderly, but faded and spare. It struck him that they were rather deeply engaged in conversation. The woman—an American, from her accent—was occasionally laughing and blushing as she very delicately sipped her consommé and tore her bread into small pieces; the man was attentive to her every word and nuance. At another table were a couple in their thirties, he guessed. He thought he detected fatigue, even strain, in their pale faces, and yet their hands touched often as they talked over the meal. James watched as additional lodgers arrived. Only guests of the hotel were served at midday, so he now had a clear picture of his fellow guests. And he happily passed the time in an attempt to determine who or what they were and why they were here.

A frail elderly woman was the next to take her place. She had a small sweet powdery face and beautifully kept silvery hair. Moving slowly, carefully, she took but a little meat and a bit of salad. She brightened noticeably as a man and woman approached her, the elegant wife, he assumed, arming her to their table. All three were well dressed in the county style. The women in their twin sets and pearls and good tweed skirts, the man in his heavy tweed three-piece suit. They were smoothly affluent, at ease with themselves and their prosperity.

The threesome were quickly followed by a smooth-faced portly man in his sixties, with a full head of steel gray hair, an erect stance, and twinkling blue eyes. He was immediately joined by a lanky youth in his teens. James was interested in the relationship: son? grandson? The youth was pimply but pleasant, surprisingly unselfconscious. James mentally totted up numbers. No, a few yet to be accounted for. He made ten, so three were missing since Mrs. O. had informed him there were, or rather had been, fourteen guests—with Breathnach's death the number stood at thirteen. She had shivered then and blessed herself.

James's mental arithmetic was satisfied by the entrance of a second couple in their thirties. The man was tall and dark, dressed casually in a loose-fitting but well-cut black silk suit and open-necked custom-made white silk shirt. His companion was a languid, striking, red-haired woman with the pale complexion of her colouring, dressed in a similarly Continental style.

His curiosity was distracted when he noticed the slender serious-faced young woman who had just come into the now noisy dining room. Without glancing around she went directly to the sideboard and spent some time hesitating over the delicious array. James leaned back in his chair, replete with food and anxious for a cup of tea. He strolled over to the side table where the urns of tea and coffee stood, straightening his brown-flecked Norfolk jacket and the tweed tie that he kept for country weekends. He poured out his cup and turned in time to cross the woman's path as she also turned, as he guessed, to seek out an empty table.

"Hello," he said softly, smiling.

She looked up startled and smiled briefly.

"James Fleming. Would you like to join me at my table?" he said in his most gallant manner. "I've just arrived, you see," he finished lamely when she didn't respond.

"Thank you, but I'd rather not," she said without looking at him again. James felt a flush rise to his face as she nearly pushed past him and found a seat at a table at the side window. Self-consciously he returned to his own seat balancing his cup of tea that now was not so welcome.

He was embarrassed. He hadn't meant to seem as though he were picking her up, but at her rebuff he realized that that was all it had seemed to her. He glanced in her direction as she ate, sitting stiffly, her eyes constantly averted from the dining room and seemingly drawn to some nonexistent scene. She was expensively yet casually dressed in a dove gray cashmere sweater and French-cut, baggy style, dark gray trousers. Her skin was pale, almost translucent, and her eyes were shadowed beneath high arching brows.

On an impulse he returned to the sideboard and filled a plate with strawberries in a glaze. He put a small pitcher of cream on the side with a spoon and brought it to her table. Setting it down, he said again, softly, "Sorry if . . ."

She glanced up and merely nodded.

His conscience relieved if not his pride, he left the room to wander upstairs to change and keep his appointment with Kevin.

"Fleming!" Kevin shifted the heavy carton he was carrying as he came slowly down the main staircase to the lobby. "I'm running way behind my own schedule. Perhaps we could talk a bit, while I ferry these things down from the attics."

It took James and Kevin, together with the help of Caitlin's two brothers, upwards of an hour to carry down the various trunks from the upper rooms that nestled under the slanting roof of the old house. James was astonished at the width of the three interconnecting rooms and by the enormous amount of goods stored there. As he maneuvered a trunk with Kevin, down first one narrow staircase and then another, he had the opportunity to question Kevin about the attic and its contents.

Kevin laughed. "Mary and I were interested in collecting all kinds of odds and ends from sales-of-work and jumbles, but not even we could have accumulated the raft of things up there. God, all that stuff dates back generations. Mary loved to poke around up there when she had a free moment. There are quite a few remnants still there, from when the house was an asylum for the bewildered."

"An asylum for what?"

"For the bewildered, believe it or not."

"You're not serious," panted James, intrigued but breathless with the weight of the iron bound trunk.

"Indeed and I am." Kevin's eyes twinkled. "Great story, isn't it? This house left the O'Donnell family— my wife's family—towards the end of the last century. A complicated story really, but what Irish story isn't?" He laughed again as they shifted the weight on the last landing. "The O'Donnells got it back eventually, but it was home, for a while at least, for a lot of bewildered souls. I tell you, this house could tell some great tales. And then there's the ghost . . . You know, there's been a cottage or a hovel or a farm or a house on these grounds for nearly three hundred years. But I forget, Fleming, you really don't know anything about me or this house."

"Not much," rejoined James. "Madigan told me a bit about Cromlech Lodge—the hotel that is. And about you wanting to write a will. He said you were in school with him at Blackrock, and that you were a good friend. I admit that was enough for me."

"You know him well then?"

"Professionally only. But he's been . . . a help." James looked for the right word.

"A good barrister then?"

"The best."

"He was a right little bastard when we were in school together. Forever in trouble. A rebel really."

"Consequently attracted to the law then." James laughed as they eased a second trunk onto the carpet in the lounge. He wiped his brow. "What the hell are we doing here anyway?"

"Sorry, I forgot to tell you in all the excitement last night. I'm throwing a bit of a party for the guests. It's Halloween weekend as you know, and I thought it might be fun if we all dressed in costume. I didn't advertise. It's for the hotel guests and staff actually. You'll join us?"

"Surely. And the trunks?"

"Oh, these are clothes, hats, bits of cloth, old eye-glasses, swords, ribbons, loads of things. I've been sorting out up in the attic and I put together a good array of materiel—I hope." The hesitancy was there, which James had noted before.

"From the weight of these, I'd say you did."

"I brought in some new things too. I don't know. I hope they're a creative bunch." They returned up the staircase.

"Any reaction from the events of last night?" asked James.

"Not as much as I'd feared. No one has chosen to leave and that's significant. I couldn't decide if the party was in poor taste, so I just went ahead. Mary loved Halloween."

"Mary?"

"My wife. She died, was killed in a bad crash a year ago. She . . . she used to dress up on Halloween as a witch," he said as he smiled inwardly, "and greet the hotel guests. She'd make her own barmbracks too, for the afternoon tea."

He glanced at his watch. "Christ! I've got to put on some speed. The guests can use the lounge from two to four for examining the goods and putting together the costumes, but tea starts at four as usual."

James and Kevin and the lads ferried the remaining trunks and boxes down, and Kevin arranged an interesting display around the comfortable room.

In time James found himself with his fellow guests enthusiastically pawing over the open trunks and boxes while Mrs. O'Neil and Caitlin helped out with pins and thread and needles, and with advice and running commentary.

Kevin was off in the town and James finally withdrew, happy with his choice of a large black Galway cape with a crimson lined hood, a swatch of black cloth he thought

29

he'd use as a sort of cummerbund, and a black felt slouch hat. He wasn't sure of his chosen persona yet, but awaited a flash of inspiration on the night. He had lingered long enough, exchanging pleasantries with his fellow lodgers and waiting in vain for the quiet girl to arrive. But in the hour he was there she failed to show.

At last he showered and changed and threw himself into the chintz-covered chair, but the room was cold and he was restless.

His ride of the morning seemed a long time ago now and his lack of activity, professional and otherwise, annoyed him. He grabbed his jacket and headed for the fields, pondering on Kevin Conlon's life and wishing he could fill in the holes. He saw that the day was slipping away with no chance to meet Kevin in his study as agreed. He'd planned to leave immediately after the mid-day meal on Sunday, but now he wondered if the morning allowed them enough time for the writing of the will. But all such thoughts were banished by the fresh wind that drove across the undulating fields, broken only by low loose stone walls and brittle hedges, and the magnificently preserved cromlech after which the Lodge was named.

James drew closer to inspect it, running his hands over one of the three lichen-covered standing stones and then sheltering beneath the massive capstone that lay across them, forming a giant's table or pagan altar as some would have it. He marvelled at the age of this stone arrangement, dating back to Celtic times at the very least, perhaps coincident with the monuments at Newgrange and Knowth and the hundreds of other cromlechs that dotted Ireland. Sligo County, for whatever reason, was particularly abundant in cromlechs. James looked to the low mountain called Knock-na-Rea and at Queen Maeve's cairn on top of it, clearly visible for miles, and he wondered if a connection existed. What a frustration not to be able to know more of those peoples—Celtic and pre-Celtic, and how they had lived. A slight sense of uneasiness filled him, not unfamiliar. He had experienced it before, on his rambles over the years when he'd found that he walked into a faery ring, a circle of stones half buried in the earth, left untouched by centuries of superstitious—or reverent—farmers.

He moved on, walking briskly to get the blood stirring. His booted feet tread easily on the spongy earth, crushing the sage-coloured sedge and matted grasses. All growth had seemingly ceased and the landscape had taken on a monochrome hue—a muted blend of brown and green and gray.

His eyes were drawn ineluctably to the encircling horizon. Ben Bulben, the Ox Mountains, Knock-na-Rea ahead, and behind him in the distance, the thin line of shimmering silver sea. He gulped in the clear crisp air and exhaled it, again and again. And he strode vigorously, bounding over low fieldstone dry walls and startling the thick-coated woolly sheep that grazed comatosely on grass that still grew in sheltered nooks and crannies. Dusk was falling rapidly as he retraced his steps, his head clear, his spirits soaring after such a walk, his eyes stinging with tears that the now sharp wind drew as it smacked his face. He bent nearly double into the wind, almost missing, off on the horizon of the cromlech field he was in, a fellow hiker seeking similar exhilaration. She was passing away to the left, the wind wrapping her long green coat around her legs, her hair blown flat back against her head. But he knew the profile from their brief meeting in the dining room. He smiled to think that they shared a love of the fields and the wilds, of the ancient Irish past, and perhaps a love of solitude too. And he hoped that the solitary woman would join their festivities that night when he could remedy his bumbling approach of a few hours earlier.

The lounge was jammed with people upon James's return. The crowd spilt into the lobby as he pushed in to retrieve a large cup of tea and some thickly buttered barmbrack. The girls standing near him squealed as one of them drew a thin gold-coloured ring from her mouth.

"Oh, my God! She'll be married this year and no doubt," they chorused as the girl blushed.

"Not me," shrieked another as she took a bit of twig from the slice of brack on her plate.

James examined his own slice in the spirit of fun around him. Nothing. But his next held a shrivelled pea. He held it aloft. The guests around him groaned. "Poverty," one called out.

"Lord, I hope not." James smiled.

Three older women near him roared as they all withdrew rings from their brack. "And we've enough of marriage here," they laughingly announced.

"Jaysus," exclaimed the portly man, "I've a branch in me mouth!" And he extracted a sizable twig, holding it aloft.

"Get yerself a pint then, and be drownin' yer sorrows," rejoined one of the locals, and everyone laughed.

More people joined the throng, but the room filled and refilled in an orderly fashion. No one had come this day for a quiet afternoon tea. The spirit of the day was on them with their simple delight in the traditional bread and its concealed tokens of prophecy. James entered into the fun and soon struck up conversations with a number of men. They moved across the foyer to the snug bar James had visited briefly the day before. The ubiquitous Mrs. O. was pulling pints and lining them up on the drip tray, with her sleeves rolled up over strong muscular forearms.

"You've many talents, Mrs. O," said James as he thirstily reached for his designated pint of Guinness, its ivory foam running down the straight pint glass.

"Indeed and I do, Mr. Fleming."

The bar too was crowded and James listened to the men from the town speculating on the weather for the night ahead. Among them he'd found a fellow train enthusiast, albeit one who didn't travel the rails but who had an extensive collection of models. The man proudly and in loving detail described to James the intricacies of setting up his model of the train station of Montreux in Switzerland. James had passed through Montreux on a train trek and was able to reminisce about the wonderful steam engines he'd been fortunate enough to have a chance to observe. As six o'clock drew closer and most of the visitors left to return to their homes, James bid farewell to his new friends and joined his fellow lodgers as they lingered in the bar, to pass the time before dinner.

The Halloween party began in earnest at 11 P.M., after the bar was closed to the public and the residents of the hotel and the small staff gathered in the now decorated snug. Lit only by the light of the candles placed in the many carved turnips that were arranged around the room, on the bar and on the low tables, it seemed now more eerie than cozy. An enormous pumpkin held pride of place in the cold hearth, its evil grin leering at the guests who had arrived—all with goodwill, and all dressed in costume.

Kevin in the character of a banshee, with white wig and shawl, greeted his guests. Miriam drew applause as she entered the bar, dressed in diaphanous white and looking very much like a girl by Gainsborough.

But it was Mrs. O'Neil, dressed completely in black from her head to her toes, who startled everyone as she came from behind the mahogany bar bearing a steaming caldron of mulled cider. Although complimented by the lodgers she maintained a stubborn, almost sullen, silence. James wondered if her mood was part of her persona or not.

The guests, fully rigged out, warmed their hands on the Russian tea glasses that held their cider and cinnamon sticks. James was impressed in particular by the portly man and the youth who arrived late, dressed as Old Father William and his son, from *Alice in Wonderderland*. With great vigour the older man, whose name was Dunmor, entered into his part. James satisfied his curiosity as they chatted and he learned that the young man was in fact a grandson, a favourite grandson, whom Dunmor took off periodically to travel with him both at home and abroad. Dunmor seemed a jolly man and his rouged cheeks only added to the impression as his blue eyes twinkled under bushy brows. Money was obviously not a problem and James mildly envied the cossetted youth. More so because the boy was so unaffected. Within moments they had the attention of the small party and launched with good singing voices into a rendition of Lewis Carroll's witty poem.

James clapped heartily with the others and Kevin, almost surprised by the success of his idea, called out for more party pieces.

Shyly the three older women guests gathered together in impromptu harmony to sing "The Last Rose of Summer." The earnestness of their tremulous singing gave the song itself an added pathos. James himself was feeling pressured to perform and he wildly racked his brain for the faintly recollected words of poems and songs from what now seemed his remote childhood. But he was preempted, much to his relief, by the lanky dark man who removed a penny whistle from his pocket as simply as another would remove a handkerchief. The melancholy magic of the ancient Irish tunes that poured forth from the pipe combined with his shabby appearance and unkempt hair to transform him into a figure of the wandering storyteller, the seanachie, who roamed the country before the turn of the century.

His wife, whose name was Edna, was similarly dressed, with a torn shawl and a heavy shabby skirt reaching to her bare feet. She lounged languidly near her husband, her red hair falling over his knees: the two of them like characters from a Jack Yeats sketch. The performance was inspired and at its conclusion was quickly explained by the fact that the man, Hugh, was a well-known rock and traditional musician who, unable to resist the temptation, had blown his cover. The crowd clapped long and loud and demanded an encore. At this the chef, Sean, dressed unimaginatively as a chef, joined him with his fiddle, and the room pounded with traditional jigs and reels.

As the crowd handed round more drinks and refreshed themselves following their exertions, the young woman who had caught his interest twice that day stepped forward. Pale and drawn, and dressed, or rather swathed, in white sheets, her demeanor was so striking that the group fell silent immediately. Without preamble she began to sing in a clear, strong voice, the last three verses of "The Croppy Boy":

At the siege of Ross did my father fall,
And at Gorey my loving brothers all,
I alone am left of my name and race,
I will go to Wexford and take their place.
I cursed three times last Easter Day
At Mass time once I went to play;
I passed the churchyard one day in haste,
And forgot to pray for my mother's rest.

I bear no hate against living thing
But I love my country above the king.
Now, Father! bless me, and let me go
To die if God had ordained it so.
The priest said nought but a rustling noise
Made the youth look up in wild surprise;
The robes were off, and in scarlet there
Sat a yeoman Captain with fiery glare.

With fiery glare and with fury hoarse
Instead of blessing, he breathed a curse:
'Twas a good thought, boy, to come here and
  shrive,
For one short hour is your time to live.
Upon yon river three tenders float
The Priest's on one if he isn't shot—
We hold this house for our lord the king
And amen, say I, may all traitors swing.

Silence met the last lingering words. The choice of
song was so surprising that only courtesy seemed to
rouse the applause initiated by an intrigued James. The
girl, still alone, merely withdrew into her costume and
stepped back against the wall, refusing to catch anyone's eye.

Kevin quickly gathered the little crowd, with his call
that the midnight hour was approaching. The lights having been doused, they followed him through the rear
passageway and into the back gardens by the glimmer
of hurricane lamps just barely illuminating their steps.
Sean and Hugh followed them up at the rear, playing
their instruments, the music urging them on.

James found himself falling in line between the tall
English professor, Gorman, and Mrs. Trask from New
York. And he felt embarrassed to be coming between
what he perceived to be a blossoming romance. He'd
much rather have been taking the hand of the "ghost,"
as he'd deemed her, but she was far ahead of him in the
line, being led by the gangly young Dunmor.

As they all emerged into the dark garden, the wind
whipped their clothes, their cloaks, their hair, as they
tripped and felt their way. But Kevin led them onward
into the field. The cromlech loomed ominously in the
dark and near it the towering pile of wood. The two
musicians had moved to the front of the straggling line
and the air around them was full of snatches of evoca-

tive traditional tunes. James felt for a moment a part of Yeats's strange poem about the Fiddler of Dooney, felt too that he'd stepped back into a painting by Jack Yeats himself, as he joined the strangely dressed crowd as it gathered near the cromlech.

Clouds like torn wisps of gray chiffon blew across the moon, whose light lent a magnificence to the already wild scene. The bare branches of the slender trees on their immediate horizon were bending and twisting with a life of their own. And the large hedges were suddenly unrecognizable, taking on the shapes of gigantic sleeping beasts.

If Kevin had been able to have a Halloween setting made to order, he couldn't have asked for better. Waving at his guests to stay back, he jogged quickly to a line of what seemed to be sticks, barely discernible as they protruded from the ground. The little crowd was mystified until Jack and Anna, the couple from Dublin, screeched with delight into the wind. "Fireworks" was their cry and it was quickly conveyed to all of them.

The small rockets fused and rose wavering into the sky perhaps fifty feet and burned there, spinning out their multicoloured sparks before being carried away in the wind. Kevin lit them in sequence, and of the twenty-five he'd bought from the tinker, twenty-two were sound. The bright coloured lights lit the crowd's upturned faces as they gazed skyward in awe, as any child would have done. And James wondered, not for the first time, at the child that lived on in people when chronological age blotted out all other traces. The group applauded loudly and joked at their daring and Kevin's, looking over their shoulders for signs of the local police.

Their enthusiasm and levity remained as they then watched Kevin light a homemade torch, the smell of the kerosene catching them all sharply in the nostrils. Quickly he touched the torch to the base of the tinder-dry pyramid and the branches and wood caught instantly and began to blaze, fanned as it was by the wind. The howling flames roared up into the night and sparks blew and burned in the air. Murmurs of appreciation drowned out the earlier cries of concern that the fire would spread. As the flames ate through the tangled pile, Kevin and the guests called out "Happy New Year" and greeted one another, laughing in the wind. It was, as most of them knew, the last day of the old Celtic year, the eve of Samhain, when the souls of the dead were loosed among the living.

James glanced around him, suddenly aware of other distant bonfires, whose size he could not judge, burning here and there in the night on the sloping hills and fields that surrounded them. The lights in the turnips and the pumpkins that lit up the windows of rural Ireland recalled the ancient feast. And, he wondered, were those lights to lead the souls back home, or were the leering faces of their shells meant to scare them off? Perhaps a little of both. The Christian feast had dovetailed with the pagan feast, and James questioned, in his heart, if the strange atmosphere surrounding him were not more supernatural than natural in origin.

They stood in silence, riven by strange and primitive feelings. The cromlech seemed to grow in size as the huge fire cast it into shadow, burning as it did with great initial ferocity. They stepped back farther as the heat rolled towards them. James felt it on his cheeks but he stood mesmerized by the leaping crackling flames. His eyes followed the embers as they rose high in the air, burned bright and then fell into ash. The crowd remained until the final branches collapsed into the flame, until the ashes and embers dwindled, until at last Kevin appeared with buckets of water to sluice down the embers. Still silent, their ebullient mood deflated, they walked back to the hotel, led by Miriam with her lantern. And somberly, they bid each other good night and retired to their rooms.

*　　*　　*

James had been asleep, he believed, for only a matter of minutes when he heard the footsteps, loud and sharp, walk across the unrugged floor of his bedroom. His eyes opened wide, straining against the immediate darkness. A terror gripped his body and with difficulty he forced his head, on a rigid neck, to turn towards the source of the sound. Nothing. Neither sight nor sound greeted him. Sweating and suddenly cold, he eased himself slowly up against his pillow as though being observed by someone and hoping not to be noticed. His eyes adjusted to the dark. But the room held nothing strange or startling. He reached to switch on the lamp and when sudden confident electric light did not illuminate the room, he froze again. Could it be that Kevin had forgotten to turn on the electricity from the main switch after the party had ended? He turned the lamp on and off until he lost track of which way the small button should be, in the on position.

He lay back on the pillow having convinced himself that he had woken from a vivid dream. As he let his eyes fall shut he heard the steps again, but this time, he believed they came from directly above his head. In a sense he was relieved. No bodiless spirit was pacing his room. And why believe it was a spirit now walking across the floor above him? He tried the lamp again. Nothing. The steps had stopped again. Wildly he felt that each time he moved the steps stopped. He shook his head, trying to shake the fanciful notion away. But nonetheless he lay perfectly still. And the steps began again. Sharp, clear, above his head. This time James leapt from his bed, grabbing his heavy Foxford dressing gown and tying it around him. He rushed to his door and stepped out into the short dark corridor. No light gleamed from any source. He tried to orient himself.

He realized that at his end of the house there were no guest rooms above his own. He tried to recall the layout of the attic he had visited only that morning. Surely it was an attic room that sat above his own. He felt his way down the corridor to the door of the attic stairway and turned the knob. It responded easily, but he paused, cursing the fact that he had no light, suddenly fearful of what might greet him.

But if he were to sleep again this night, he wanted to verify that Kevin or one of the lads was merely putting away the costume trunks. The fact they were doing this in the middle of the night in the dark was irrational, he observed. But it was easier to believe in that kind of irrationality than one of a supernatural kind.

He felt his way up the dusty stairs, catching splinters in his fingertips. The stairs, he recalled, led straight into the attic, with two wooden railings rising up on either side of the open stairwell into the centre of the room. His hands felt the cross struts. He had reached the top. He remained perfectly still. A bit silly, he observed, since he'd made enough noise coming up the stairs to warn anyone of his approach. He waited. It was silence that greeted him and he didn't know if he were grateful or not. Some minutes passed.

"Who's there?" he called at last, surprised by the tremor in his voice. But silence answered. He continued to wait. Minutes had passed when he heard a tiny rustling sound. Suddenly breathless, he thought he felt something brush past his face and he involuntarily shut his eyes.

Then he heard a footstep, a shuffling perhaps. He opened his eyes staring to his left, sensing the source of the sound, but seeing, he thought, merely a patch of gray against the darker gray of the room. And then it was gone before he could verify that he'd ever seen it.

Something had changed in the atmosphere of the attic room. He realized with a sense of relief and a returning sense of foolishness that the room was now empty. But as anyone who has entered a room and become aware through whatever sixth sense he possesses that someone else is also there—although no sound or sight gives the proof—he was aware that someone besides himself had been in that attic. And that now that someone—or thing—was gone. Down another staircase, he rationalized, although he hadn't seen one earlier that day with Kevin. He backed down the stairs and shut the door quietly. And he returned to his room, to sleep at last, but only fitfully on this, the eve of Samhain, when the souls of the dead walked the night at their will.

───── *Chapter Four* ─────

In the cheery breakfast room early the next morning, with the sun streaming through the blue gingham-curtained windows, James Fleming felt renewed. And as he observed the hearty warm faces of Caitlin and Mrs. O., and the slightly more fatigued but pleasant faces of the other few guests who joined him, he began to feel foolish. Only the pricking of a festering splinter in his right index finger served to prove to him that he hadn't dreamed the events of the night before.

Fleming, as any of his friends would tell, was not given to imagination. No more, no less, that is, than any Irish person. But in his youth he'd prided himself on his logic. His pragmatic turn of mind, as well as his father's profession before him, had led him into the field of law. Content with his own company, confident but unassuming, his personality had not inclined him to the primary role of a barrister. He much preferred, at least until recent years, his quiet work behind the scenes in what was now his own firm of solicitors specializing in wills and estates. And even his recent involvements with cases which were of both a criminal and at times sensational nature had not led him far from his chosen path. Affairs of the heart were another matter. And so too were his twin passions of train-riding and travel.

All that Dublin represented for him, professionally and personally, seemed very far away this morning as he sat over his bowl of porridge and chatted with the amiable youth, Danny Dunmor, scion of grandfather Dunmor who was taking advantage of a lie-in this morning after the Halloween festivities.

"Last night was a bit of fun, then, wasn't it?" said James for want of starting up the conversation.

Danny smiled wryly. "A bit tame, as well." He shrugged. "I'd say there was more drinking at a Mother's Union outing."

James laughed loudly, glad to see the boy had a bit of spirit and a clear sense of himself. "Indeed, but don't tell me you've been to many bonfires such as that?"

"No, and never at one that was a hen's spit away from a cromlech either. That made it for me, I admit. A story to tell the lads at College, if I get the chance." He was rueful.

"How so . . . you're hardly failing your first year at University College? Lord, term just began . . ."

"Oh, I shouldn't have spoken of it, but just let me say, no I'm not failing out. I've just got started. I dunno. P'raps I'll just leave and take a job for a couple of years."

"I see." But James didn't.

Mrs. O. approached with the silver coffeepot and strainer and filled their French coffee bowls to the brim. After this she lingered, to James's surprise, placing a motherly hand on Danny's shoulder.

"Eat up there, me boy. And you'll grow another three inches. You wouldn't believe it, Mr. Fleming," she added in a kindly voice, "this boy changed beyond knowin' since he was last here."

"You come here regularly, then?" said James.

She answered for him. "On and off, with his grandfather—him that's upstairs now, sleeping it off I'm afraid."

Danny laughed. "Right you are, Mrs. O., but don't worry. We're going for a good healthy walk later today, before lunch."

"Don't you be missing Mass now." She looked pointedly at James. "Mass is in half an hour's time at St. Paul's, that's the nearest Catholic church."

"Thanks, Mrs. O. Perhaps you could tell me the times for the C. of I. church too?"

Mrs. O. lifted her eyebrows but dutifully informed him that he had already missed Morning Prayer.

"We seem to be the last down for breakfast," he added as Mrs. O. turned to leave.

"You are the last." She smiled as she began to remove the leftover sausages, eggs, and bacon from the sideboard to the kitchen.

James was chagrined. He'd thought he'd risen early, hoping to see Kevin, and here he was among the last. He felt irrationally disappointed. Had the interesting young woman risen early too?

He decided, after seeking Kevin and not finding him, to go for another ride and he set off from the Lodge to walk to the stables. The soft breeze rustled the hedgerows and the pungent scents released by the lingering warmth of the autumnal sun wafted around him. Abstracted by the beauty and softness of the view, its hues of gold and orange, under a panoply of blue, he failed to see the approaching couple until they were virtually in front of him.

"Fleming." Kevin's voice startled him. "Who's the sleepy-head today then? The ghosts keep you awake last night?" he asked laughingly. James shivered and looked closely at Kevin to see if he was serious but his smile belied it.

James turned his attention to Kevin's companion, the nameless girl whom he'd wanted to meet on a better footing.

"Good morning to you," he said softly.

She merely nodded. He glanced at Kevin, willing him to make the obvious introductions. But Kevin, placidly teasing him, overlooked this point of etiquette. He slapped James on the back, urging him on to his ride.

James protested and moved to turn back.

"But, James, it's your holiday . . ." Kevin walked on with his companion.

"Kevin, look, let me walk back with you, I'm rather anxious to get down to our business. You do know I'm leaving today?"

"Not to worry, Fleming, you're in Sligo now. Just slow yourself down to our pace. There's time enough. Give me a shout in the kitchen when you get back." And they were gone, leaving James more irritated in not having a chance to get to know the young woman than at failing to write up Kevin's will.

But last wills and testaments faded from his mind as he began his ride. His mount, a big broad-backed bay, responded well to James's expert handling but with no heart in him. James walked him for some long distance along the quiet road before he turned into a boreen to which the stable-hands had directed him. The rutted dirt track ran between two enormous fields, well-defined by dry stone walls. For once the prevailing wind had died down and the fields were stiller than ever. The horse's mood suited his own and he let him walk, trotting occasionally upward as the field imperceptibly rose to what, in the end, was a plateau with a breathtaking view of the countryside. James sat on his mount, resting his eyes on the rugged scene. From this height he was surprised to realize that he was looking down on the buildings that comprised Cromlech Lodge. Like an architect's aerial view, the relationship of all the buildings was laid out before him, abutted by the sprawling grounds. The cromlech stood out dark and brooding, hardly diminished in its power by the distance between James and itself.

James's attention was caught by a neighbouring field on the far side of the house. Within it he could now discern what would seem to be the foundations of a house perhaps, certainly a building. And near to that he could see an arrangement of mounds, barely apparent under their brown shrivelled grass covering. The mounds were serried and something—James could not tell what—surrounded the ranks of mounds, something black he thought. James urged the horse down the field and at last the beast seemed to come out of his morning doze. James gave him his head, feeling the power and joy of the horse as he began to gallop. He took the low stone wall and narrow ditch behind it with ease and was resentful when James slowed him to a trot.

Together they nosed around the area that James had determined held the curious rectangle. Suddenly he spied the remnants of what had been a painted iron railing, now rusting into disintegration in the low matted grass. And just beyond that he saw the pathetic mounds. Perhaps they had once been level with the surface of this rough field, but years of rain and wind had eroded that comforting blanket of earth from around these sad resting places and they rose up now to remind the stray passerby that here lay someone buried—lonely, isolated, and unmarked.

James shivered as he looked down on the graves, for graves they were. He tethered the horse to a low-growing leafless shrub and walked around and between the mounds. There was nothing, no markers, no indicators of who had lived and who had died, or when or where.

He was intrigued. Looking back from his vantage point to the main house at some distance, he saw the foundations that he'd seen from above. They were the support of what would have been a quite sizable building. He knew the Lodge had once been the manor house of a wealthy man during the early nineteenth century. If this were the family plot, then surely the family stone would be present, or some memorial, James thought. He had had occasion to observe a number of such plots on estates in counties all over Ireland. They all shared the conventions of the period in which they'd grown popular. There was usually a chapel of stone or marble that would have been used for funeral services. There was generally a substantial monument enshrining the family name. And there would be markers on some if not all of the graves. But here James hunted for evidence of what might have been, and found nothing. His curiosity entirely aroused, he remounted the bay and turned back for the stables. He was as anxious now to question Kevin about his discovery as he was to complete the task for which he'd come.

James found Kevin below stairs in the kitchen. The whole staff was busy laying out the numerous foodstuffs which promised a substantial country Sunday dinner. The smell of the joints roasting was tantalizing and James felt the sudden sharp pangs of hunger. Reluctantly he followed Kevin to his minute study off the main lobby where, as compensation, he was offered a delicious nut brown amontillado which Kevin poured into two Waterford crystal sherry glasses of the Powerscourt pattern. They sat crowded at Kevin's cluttered rolltop desk and went quickly to work.

James took voluminous notes as Kevin succinctly and with barely repressed sighs of sadness took him through the recent history of his family and the Lodge.

The sum of the story was that the Lodge, then a small hotel, had been inherited by Mr. John O'Donnell when he was in his early twenties—that would have been 1930 approximately. He and his wife had Mary in 1950. On the deaths of her parents, Mary inherited when she herself was only twenty. Mary previously had spent a brief two years at a hotel and catering college in Galway, a county where she'd some distant cousins. It was there where Kevin had met his beautiful black-haired Mary. She'd returned to run the hotel and Kevin had stayed on in Galway to finish his course. He'd worked abroad but the love they'd found in Galway always drew him back and they were married in 1976. Miriam was born a year later and they'd lived and worked and prospered together until a year ago when Mary died in the car crash on the way home from the local Grange meeting hall.

It was immediately apparent to James that Kevin had not yet recovered from the loss of his wife and that it was only his concern for Miriam, their daughter, that kept him going. That he could continue Mary's dream and build something for Miriam had been his mainstay. Kevin, however, didn't speak of this directly. James was moved by his pain to consider that despite his own losses he'd never known the quality of this pain. He moved on quickly to more practical matters.

"Mary left a will, I take it?"

"Yes, it was very simple. She left everything to Miriam."

"I'm a little surprised." James hesitated.

"I know, there was some confusion at the time. But it had been a tradition in the O'Donnell family that the property go to the eldest child, as opposed to the spouse. Mary was an O'Donnell and kept to the tradition. I could have disputed it I suppose, but I had no reason to."

"But as spouse you had rights of inheritance which still stand."

"Yes, I know. That's why Madigan mentioned it when we met at the school reunion at Blackrock. He suggested I write a will clarifying the entire issue so that, God forbid"—he paused—"Miriam's position would be perfectly clear if I . . . you know."

"Yes, and you are very wise. It should be straight-forward."

"Indeed. I merely wish to leave everything to Miriam."

"No bequests?"

Kevin looked blank.

"You know, perhaps to your own parents, brothers, sisters, any of the staff here?"

"Oh, I see. I never thought. Well, my own parents are dead, God rest their souls. I was, like Mary, an only child. Extraordinary, isn't it? We used to say that our experience as only children brought us close. And now poor Miriam. She too is an only child."

James wanted to say that that might not always be the case, that Kevin might find love and marriage and children again. It was something he'd wanted for a long time for himself; and now suddenly he wanted it for this man he barely knew but whom he had grown to like. But he did not speak. He had all the evidence he needed that Mary was still very much alive in Kevin's heart.

So instead he commented truthfully, "Miriam is a very lovely child, Kevin."

"Yes, she is," beamed Kevin. "Now, I have two dozen famished people to feed. Are we done?"

"Only in a very broad sense. I need time, of course, to do this properly, but it worries me that you have no will at all, Kevin. I'm not being morbid. It's my business and . . ."

"I know, James, not to worry. It's the same problem insurance agents have . . . you don't have to persuade me. Just tell me what you want me to do." He stood up restlessly, contradicting his own words.

"I want to draw up a simple will, a standard form, and have you sign it today, before I leave. It could stand as a temporary document until I can draw up more de-tailed papers. I need to look at the copies of the deeds to all of your properties, here in Sligo and elsewhere, liens, bank loans, statements, so on.''

"Right." Kevin was abrupt. "We'll talk later or whenever." James found himself pursuing Kevin.

"This is not on the point, Kevin, but my curiosity is killing me." He briefly described his find of the morning.

"Fascinating, isn't it? I felt the same when I first stumbled on it with Mary in our courting days. I spent three summers here, working with her and her parents, and later with her on her own—before we were wed. Mrs. O. was able to tell us."

"Mrs. O'Neil?"

"The same. She's worked in this house since she was a girl. She knew the O'Donnells and through them learned much of the history of the house and lands. It was herself who told us about the graves."

"Are they O'Donnell graves then?"

"No, no. Remember when I mentioned that the house had been an asylum for some years . . . ?"

James nodded. They were in the dining room now and Kevin proceeded to lay out the cutlery, expertly and quickly.

"The house was a home for the bewildered, as they used to say. Great word! So much more descriptive and accurate than *insane*, don't you think?"

James agreed.

"It was operated by a French order of nuns. Their special vocation apparently. The house, Cromlech House, as it was then, was let—for a pound sterling—by an O'Donnell. That's another story I have to tell you! But about the graves. You see, in the Catholic Church, at least in those days, a person who committed suicide was considered to have committed a mortal sin." He looked at James's blank expression.

"If a person dies in the state of mortal sin, that person cannot be buried in consecrated ground."

"But how can anyone know the state of another person's soul?" James was skeptical.

"The Church would make an assumption—on the very obvious evidence," murmured Kevin.

"Such people were sick, mentally sick."

"No, the Church might make the assumption that they were in despair. Perhaps it did not look closely enough at the cause of that despair . . ." His voice deepened. "Despair and pride are the two great sins against the Holy Spirit. It's always easier to see pride demonstrated in action. It's the obvious sin. But despair happens in the heart, in the soul. The evidence of the suicide was the evidence of the despair."

"But how can that despair possibly be culpable?" retorted James.

"It was seen to be because it meant the person had abandoned hope. To give up hope is to challenge the infinite mercy and power of God, in His person of the Holy Spirit."

"So in a sense," James said, then paused as he made the connections, "despair was an inverted pride. It's as though the person says, I am so sick, so sad, so evil, so bereft, that no one, not even God, can help me?"

"I think that's a fair translation. To despair to the point of taking your own life was a mortal sin. By taking your own life you took from God what was rightfully His. Yes, to do so was a form of pride."

"But what are the graves then?" James dreaded the answer.

"Just what I said at the start. They are the graves of the poor souls who committed suicide during their stay here, when Cromlech was an asylum."

"So many?" James was horrified.

"I know," Kevin said softly. "But not all are suicides."

"What do you mean? You just said . . ."

51

"Did you see the small mounds, the little ones along the far right side?"

"I did, but . . ."

"They were the babies."

"Oh, God."

"Mrs. O. explained that they were either babies that were stillborn, or died soon after birth, or were victims of infanticide."

"This is horrific," exclaimed James. "They, surely, were innocents. Why were they not buried in a proper grave and churchyard?"

Kevin continued quietly around the room, filling the water glasses with iced water from the pitchers.

"Well, first, they'd be babies who died before they were baptized. If the mother were deemed mad they couldn't say she'd formed the intention of having the child baptized. Then the ones that were, well, killed by their mothers—it sounds so harsh—but again if the child hadn't been baptized quickly enough . . . oh, don't you see! The Church could not say the child was in a state of grace and therefore could not be put into holy ground. And remember, James, any number of the children born into that house would have been illegitimate. In those days even that was sufficient reason to refuse baptism and then as a consequence to deny a Christian burial."

"But, Kevin, this is madness. There were over ten of those little mounds! God knows how many more that aren't apparent. How could there be so many babies?"

"James, James, it's easy to see you're a city boy." But it was said kindly.

"Enlighten me then, please," said James.

"Do you think everyone who passed through those old gates was a certifiably insane man or woman, young or old. Senile old maiden aunts, whom no one wanted. Young people who had physical illnesses that seemed like spiritual or mental afflictions to the outside world. Epileptics, whatever. And there would have been the young women who had to be got out of the way. In other words, good Catholic girls who got pregnant and weren't married. They too could be seen to have taken leave of their senses. And those girls who had their babies here sometimes were deranged. We know a lot more now than they did then. What did you do with a girl, a victim of incest perhaps, who was carrying a child?''

Kevin paused as he saw James wrestling with this piece of social history. It was old news to him but he well remembered his own reaction and Mary's when first they learned the background of the neglected graves.

"Are there records?" James said at last, ever the solicitor.

"I believe so. The whole issue repelled me, I admit, but I know Mary pursued these matters when she used to poke around up in the attic. The whole history of the place intrigued her. She toyed with the idea of writing up a pamphlet, you know the kind, a little paper-covered thing that we could have kept at reception, for visitors and tourists. But with the hotel and caring for Miriam in those early years, she never got beyond keeping notes. . . ." Kevin heaved an unconscious sigh, and busied himself with placing the white damask serviettes in the wineglasses set at each place.

Filling the silence, James offered the idea that some day Miriam might like to take up the project.

"We'll see," said Kevin as they turned apart, Kevin through the rear door that led to yet another stairway to the kitchen.

The house was a virtual rabbit's warren of narrow stairs and halls, thought James, as he himself hastened toward the small snug, intent on a sherry aperitif and a glance at his notebook. He was comfortably absorbed in both tasks as he sat in the old choir stall—highlight of the higgledy-piggledy seating in the small cozy room.

Guests and visitors alike chatted animatedly, but James was deaf to all as he drafted the wording of Kevin's proposed will. His work whetted his appetite and he followed, sheeplike and hungry, the small crowd into the dining room.

Fate smiled upon him at last. One of the only vacant seats was at a small table for two by the farthest window and as Caitlin shyly walked him towards it, embarrassment and anticipation mingled on his face.

The mysterious girl he'd been longing to get to know looked up to greet him.

"We meet again," she said with no particular tone to her voice.

"I'm glad," said James as he carefully sat down, anxious not to catch the long white tablecloth with his angular knees. "I wanted to compliment you on your singing last night," he said.

"Thank you," was her only reply as she studied the elegantly handwritten menu. A traditional Sunday dinner was in store. Potato and leek soup, bread rolls, roast beef, gravy, served in a boat James was pleased to see. Roast potatoes, mashed potatoes, onions in a bechamel sauce, marrowfat peas—without which no Irish dinner was complete—there was even an individual portion of kedgeree that brought back James's childhood memories.

While the meal was quickly served by Caitlin and Kevin, and the wine was expertly poured—a house burgundy—by Mrs. O., conversation was impossible. But at last the meal was before them, and James tried again.

"Yes, your signing *a capella* was impressive. I just wondered at your choice."

"Why?" She cut her meat precisely and raised it to her lips, never glancing up.

"Well, um, for a start it wasn't terribly Halloweenish," he stumbled.

"I see." She took up a tiny portion of potato, eschewing the peas altogether.

"But then I suppose the Lewis Carroll wasn't either." He smiled through his food. "May I know your name . . . ?"

She seemed about to answer, her sombre brown eyes just starting to soften, when James was startled by Kevin's sudden appearance at their table.

"Excuse the interruption." Kevin was clearly agitated. "Fleming . . . James . . . Can I ask you to come with me for a couple of minutes?"

James stood up, bewildered at the panic he saw in Kevin's manner. He nodded to his companion and walked quickly through the dining room.

Kevin grabbed his arm as soon as they were in the reception area, whispering, rushing over his words.

"I can't believe it, James. I refuse to believe it—that's why I want you here. Here, come on, come on. In here."

They turned into the now deserted bar and James recognized the inspector he'd met before. He nodded cordially, as introductions were made.

"Now," said Kevin, "Inspector Cronin, if you would please repeat what you said for my friend, because I just cannot accept this." He shook his head in disbelief.

"Right then. Our medical man did an autopsy on Breathnach. It seems he certainly had a very damaged heart. All kinds of medical terms to describe it. Not a good heart to sustain someone of his size. In a sense the medical examiner was looking for something of that nature as cause of death. But it wasn't. As he continued to look for the cause, he found that Breathnach had lost all his, what they call, electrolytes—that's sodium and potassium basically. This happens, but 'tis rare, you see, or so he said. The condition causes mental confusion and eventually death if the electrolytes are not replaced. Today it's as simple as putting the patient on a drip bag containing the necessary minerals in solution. Now he wondered how the poor man's body was so drained and he tested a residue he'd found all over the skin.''

"And there was a lot of that," said James dryly.

"As you say," said the inspector. "This powdery substance turned out to be your common or garden mineral salts. You know, what we liked to soak our feet in after a long day on foot patrol! Simple item, but in large amounts dissolved in a bath it acts as a sort of leach, I suppose we could say in laymen's terms. The salts in the water draw the salts from the body. And this was the real cause of Breathnach's death."

"This is fantastical!" said James.

"I'm inclined to agree, sir. Doctor Mahon is this very minute trying to locate any other case of this nature."

"You mean he's contacting other doctors and hospitals?"

"Yes. But he's convinced he's right. He wants to show me evidence of other cases, fatal or otherwise, to reassure me. *He* is quite clear about the cause of death."

"This is certainly remarkable news," said James, when Kevin said nothing. "How do you propose to act on it?" But he anticipated the answer he sought.

"Well, sir, I have to consider this initially as murder. There'll be an inquest of course. I need to physically examine the premises. I've got our one and only county forensic man outside now. Mr. Conlon here has told me about Breathnach's bath and the singing"—he smiled at that—"and that the room has been left vacant. My man will start with the bath and then the room and so on. I think what is alarming, Mr. Conlon, is that I'll need to question everyone who was here yesterday in the hours preceding Breathnach's death."

Kevin groaned and James silently agreed. It was an hotelier's nightmare: the insult, the inconvenience, the unpleasantness caused to the guests; the aspersions cast

on his staff; the hotel's reputation at stake. He saw it
all pass across Kevin's pinched gray face.

"Surely it can be seen to be accidental, Inspector,"
said James persuasively. "The man's feet were aching,
perhaps, and he tossed in the salts thinking to relieve
those aches. You said yourself his heart was weak, he
was surely overweight . . ."

". . . and unfit as hell," cried Kevin. "He'd gasp for
air just walking up those very stairs."

"Gentlemen, that's exactly the conclusion we may
draw. It may be as simple and as sad as you describe—
an accident away from home. But under the circumstances—you see, I have a group of transients involved
here—it is imperative that I question anyone who might,
and I say might, have been involved, before they leave
to return to, in some cases, very distant homes. You're
a solicitor, Mr. Fleming, and I imagine that you understand my position."

"I do, but I understand the potential damage that can
be done to Kevin and to Cromlech Lodge, which repre-
sents his livelihood. What can I do to make this easier
for everyone?"

"Thanks, James, but I'll have to handle it as best I
can. God . . ." Kevin interrupted and left the room.

James looked at Inspector Cronin.

"He's gone to inform the guests in the dining room,
and the staff. He is a bit upset . . ." said Cronin.

"Of course. Listen, if you're waiting to take statements,
Inspector, would you mind taking mine now?" He was
about to add that he had planned to leave for Dublin in
the late afternoon, but as he began to speak he realized
that perhaps that might not be the wisest move.

"Grand, grand, let me just get my man upstairs while
all is quiet."

James was impressed with the speed and precision
with which Cronin asked his questions and noted his

answers. It was a mere matter of a quarter of an hour when James was free to return to his dinner. But almost all the guests had departed, including his dinner companion. James sat and enjoyed a fresh plate of food that Mrs. O. brought out to him as soon as she saw he was back. She sat down at his table without preamble.

" 'Tis dreadful, Mr. Fleming. My heart goes out to young Kevin, it does." She shook her head sadly. "He's had nothin' but trouble, for these last two years." James was horrified as this stolid, competent woman broke into tears. "Ever since . . . Mary," she finished her sentences with effort and smothered her tears in a large cloth.

"You knew her well, I understand. Kevin mentioned you've been here at the hotel many years."

"Oh, Mr. Fleming, I knew her since she was a girleen and her parents before her. Kevin was a lovely strong black-haired lad when he arrived here that summer. Full of the joys, you know the way, all divilment and fun, but mad about Mary. And such a willing pair of hands I'd never seen. He was a wonderful help and when they married he took such a load off Mr. O'Donnell, I can't tell you. It was Kevin who put this place on the map. In the last twelve years Cromlech Lodge has become what you see now. Before that it was just an ordinary country hotel like so many others."

James had nearly finished his meal when they were both startled into silence by a young intense-looking man who opened one of the rear doors of the dining room.

"Blast it," he said, smiling, nearly as startled as themselves. "I've never seen such a house!"

"And why would you," said Mrs. O. crossly, "whoever you might be!"

"Beggin' your pardon, missus. I'm with Inspector Cronin." He stuck a bucket out in front of him as if in explanation.

"The forensic man?" said James.

"The same. And pretty pleased too. You see this?" He shook the bucket in front of him. "It's tea towels!"

"Indeed, and this makes you happy?" snapped Mrs. O. "Coming in here and disruptin' the household."

As the young man spluttered to explain, James intervened, knowing the man was ill-advised to blurt out his exciting forensic discovery, and he said as much. The young man blushed and passed on his way.

Mrs. O'Neil shrugged and cleared away James's place, leaving him free to work on Kevin's will. After a matter of an hour or so James went in search of Kevin, finding him at last in the kitchen.

Kevin read over the simple will and then he and James were able to call on Sean, the chef, who'd been dozing in his quarters off the kitchen.

"We need one more witness, Sean," said James. "Is Mrs. O. about?" Sean grunted sleepily and set off to find her but returned within seconds.

"I met Sinead here on her way in, will she do?" he said, arching his eyebrows at the pretty young woman by his side.

Kevin explained that Sinead, Caitlin's sister, came in on Sundays to help with both dinner and the increasingly popular Sunday evening high tea.

"Jaysus, you know I nearly forgot it was Sunday with all that's going on? Miriam should have been home by now. I'll have to go fetch her back from the stables. She's gone and fallen in love with the horses and spends every free minute mucking out for them. I could pay for her lessons but she insists she'd rather swap mucking out for free riding time."

He stood up, and without more ado, Sean and the blushing Sinead, being of proper age and neither mentioned in the will nor related to Kevin, signed the brief document. Kevin asked James to wait for him and took off to retrieve his horse-loving daughter. Sean and Sinead, most obviously wishing to be alone with each

59

other while they made preparations for the tea, drove James from the kitchen with their calf-love antics.

James returned to his room and collected his luggage, carrying it down to the reception area where he settled his bill with an increasingly annoyed Mrs. O.

"Contemptible, I say. Keepin' these guests confined to the hotel. Nearly half of them were set to leave hours ago. I can't tell you how good they've all been, sitting around here peacefully. A nice class of people, Mr. Fleming, and it's not right to be keeping them from their own plans."

James agreed as he checked his bill. As Kevin had promised, all but his phone calls had been "on the house." He felt a bit guilty, having had so much of a good time pressed into a mere weekend. His few hours' work had hardly earned his keep.

He sat and waited for Kevin to return, aware of the questioning going on in the study, aware too of the preparations for the tea. He pondered as he dozed in the lounge, which seemed, now when it was empty, to be the drawing room of some comfortable prosperous family.

Whatever the romance of the hotel for all of its guests, the whole fabric and rhythm of its life was daunting to consider. It seemed to James that he'd done nothing but eat since he'd arrived, eaten without a thought of how all that food was brought in and prepared and served and cleared, the atmosphere being always that of calm and peace, warmth and an indefinable sense of comfort. It all rested on one man's shoulders, on his taste, his judgments, his decisions—in every area of the hotel. From bed linens to bananas, from brandy to bathroom tissue. And now that same man had to deal with a murder investigation on the premises—one that could endanger the reputation of the Lodge which he'd worked so hard and long to cultivate. James realized yet again how much Kevin must miss Mary.

"Hoary old problems, then, James," Kevin's light voice carried from the doorway. Miriam was skittering at his side, covered with bits of straw and clots of mud.

"Not a bit of it. I was merely wool-gathering waiting for you, in fact. I've the . . . em . . . the document in question here." James glanced at Miriam and back at Kevin. "A copy for you, one for me, and one for your main bank. I'll be contacting you about the final papers in due course." He stuck out his hand to shake his host's.

"You're leaving? Now?" Kevin blurted inadvertently and then cleared his throat.

"Tomorrow's Monday, unfortunately for me," said James, smiling. "And I've a bit of a drive before me. I thank you for your hospitality." He hesitated. "And I'm sorry for your trouble."

Kevin walked him to the door. "I see, I see," he murmured. "I thank you, James. Sorry . . . it's just foolish of me, but I had such a sense you'd be around for a while. This whole affair has rattled me," he whispered out of earshot as Miriam swung herself around one of the narrow stone pillars that supported the porch's roof.

"Listen," James heard himself saying, "if for any reason you need a solicitor, perhaps in light of what's happening now, you can call on me. Dublin isn't that far."

"Not in that car of yours, I daresay." Kevin laughed, his face relaxing slightly, smile lines creasing his tanned cheeks.

James walked slowly towards the car park with a strong sense of leaving behind unfinished business. He turned his head and was not surprised to see Kevin and Miriam still standing on the wide granite front step, dwarfed by what seemed for a moment the vast and ominous presence of the house that was Cromlech Lodge.

Chapter Five

The following week passed quickly for James, immersed as he was in settling a large estate, but the disturbing events of the previous weekend were never far from his thoughts. He repeatedly found Cromlech Lodge haunting his dreams and straying into his conversation. Kevin's story of the asylum and its unhappy inmates was as vivid to him as the corpse of Breathnach. He found himself wanting to ring Kevin, wondering how the police investigation was progressing, but he hesitated to intrude.

And so he was relieved on that rainy November Friday afternoon when Madigan dropped by his offices. Impeccably dressed, the famous barrister lounged on James's leather couch. After a brandy and very limited chitchat he came to the point.

"I've had a call from Kevin Conlon," he said, his rich voice sombre. "I'm afraid that he's about to be charged relative to the incident that occurred during your weekend there." He stared at James. "I'm surprised you didn't let me know what had happened."

"Look, Madigan, when I left, it seemed to me that the whole thing would be resolved as a natural death. The police theory seemed fantastical to me."

"Well, it's not to them. Conlon rang me today and he seemed rather worried. I'd like you to work with me on this one, James. It seems your kind of case."

"Madigan, despite my involvement in a couple of things with you, you cannot characterize me as having a 'kind of case.'"

"Nonsense," said the urbane Madigan as he stood up to pace, reminiscent of his courtroom stance. "You are deliberately misunderstanding me. I can hire detectives or investigators if I wish. I don't wish to. I don't think this case needs that approach. It needs what you can offer. The family solicitor with time on his hands, a bachelor free to move about, free I might add to make connections of a certain kind." He laughed at James's chagrin.

"Primarily this case needs you, with your ability to ferret out old stories, buried secrets. Or perhaps it's your ability, so like Keats's, to hold contrary beliefs simultaneously. I've never known anyone who can believe and not believe in a person's innocence the way you can."

"What are you saying? That your friend Conlon had something to do with Breathnach's death?"

Madigan laughed again. "No, not in the way you think. But I suspect he's connected."

"So you accept it was murder?"

"You will too, when you get there."

"Whoa!"

"You got on well with Kevin Conlon?"

"Yes."

"He's going to need help if he's charged. I, of course, will handle it if it ever gets to court. But as you know well, I have what they like to call a high profile. How

63

can I snoop around Sligo? But you can. Look at your calendar.''

His tone was commanding and James did as he was bid.

"Well, there's nothing actually requiring my physical presence in Dublin. Apart from the fact that I should be soliciting new business to keep this practice afloat." James's tone was wry. He waved his hand as if to illustrate the fact. "You know I have a lot of people on the payroll, whose livelihoods depend on me. And for that I need work, and not of this kind, I might add."

"Conlon has money."

"You know what I mean."

"Well, perhaps I haven't been steering clients your way, Fleming. There's always that potential."

"Bribery, now, is it? This must be important to you, Madigan."

"It is. Take it on, won't you? If, as you say, the case is weak, you'll be back in Dublin shortly." But Madigan sounded doubtful.

"Is there something you're not telling me?" James was sharp.

"No, just a sense born of experience. When there's substantial property involved I always smell the proverbial rat. Breathnach was in real estate. I'm looking for a connection that mayn't be there. That'll be your job, Fleming."

"Okay, okay. I'll delegate things here and head on to Sligo in a few days' time." He walked Madigan to the door and they shook on it, James still mildly reluctant. But as he shut the door behind Madigan he let out a soft low whoop. The thought of solving this case challenged him, exhilarated him—but he was loath to admit this to Madigan.

James laughed and rang for Maggie, his invaluable, redheaded, levelheaded assistant. Yes, indeed, as his predecessor had said before him, "The game was afoot"!

Kevin ran his hands through his hair for the hundredth time as he passed up and down the empty lobby. The last few days had been a nightmare to him and he waited as a drowning man for James Fleming to arrive.

"You're late, Fleming," he said ungraciously as James ran lightly up the front steps and thrust open the door. If James was surprised at the man's tone he didn't show it.

"Come on," said Kevin, "let's walk. I feel I can't breathe in this place." He set off abruptly towards the fields at the rear.

"Can you bring me up-to-date?" said James as he strode to catch Kevin.

"What can I say?" Kevin was almost shouting. "I'm sorry, it's just that I cannot, cannot believe this is happening to me."

"What is your status, then?"

Kevin slowed his pace. "The police consider me the primary suspect. They found a huge residue of salts in the tea towels that had soaked up the leak when Breathnach's bathtub overflowed. Because they found some boxes of mineral salts, open and unopened, they have made the assumption that someone—me—put the salts in his bath. They have assumed it couldn't have been Breathnach himself—as you suggested—because they didn't find any sachets or packets in his room or in the bathroom or in his luggage. God, it's so bizarre."

"Indeed," murmured James. This version of the story jibed with Madigan's outline of recent events. "Anything else?"

"Just that they close-questioned all of the guests, the staff, and any number of the people who had come in that day for tea. Apparently no one loomed large as having any connection with Breathnach."

"If no one of them had any connection, then why single you out, why suggest that you had a connection?" James was alarmed, wary that the police had indeed found something incriminating.

"The police have established that Breathnach was a real estate broker. And they've learned that he'd told a few local realtors here in Sligo Town that he was attempting to purchase Cromlech Lodge—can you imagine?—for a cartel I'd suppose you'd call it, of European hoteliers. The police conclude that he and I must have had some disagreement. That I was threatened by this attempt to take over the hotel!" His laugh was sarcastic now.

"Did you? Did you have any discussion or as they say 'disagreement'?" James asked carefully.

"James, as God is my witness, that man and I barely spoke. He never identified himself as a real estate broker. He did ask me if I'd ever considered selling this hotel. I think I brushed him off. He wasn't a pleasant character and I thought it pushy that he was questioning me at all. I do remember clearly that he broached it twice, though . . ." He paused, obviously thinking back.

"Any witnesses?"

"Possibly. Both times we were in company. Once, I remember, it was at the evening meal. I was helping serve and he put his hand on my arm. Very aggressive. I think that was why I was so brusque. The second time we were in the snug."

"What did he say then?"

"He pretty much wanted to know if I'd consider selling out. I think he started to talk about profit margins or God knows what. I remember I just laughed. For God's sake, it was the farthest thing from my mind. And to tell you the truth, Fleming, I didn't take to the man, at all."

That's all too obvious now, my friend, thought James,

but aloud he asked, "But did you ever mention the subject?"

"Subject?" said Kevin, pausing at last in his tramp over the uneven ground.

"The subject of selling—to anyone else?"

"Of course not."

"Are you in any financial difficulties?"

"No, no more than anyone running a business. The hotel is in the black. God, if I needed money of that kind—to keep the hotel afloat—I could sell off some of the land." He waved his hand at the expanse that surrounded them. "The land is our money in the bank." Despite the chill wind, he was sweating and he wiped his brow with the back of his hand.

James was quiet, mulling over the weakness of the police's case but alarmed at the level of Kevin's anxiety.

"The thing to remember, Kevin, is that you've not been charged with any crime. Breathnach died in your hotel. It's natural I suppose that they consider you first and foremost. They are seeking a motive to explain their faulty premise. How about means and opportunity?"

"I told them I greeted Breathnach when he arrived that day—the day of his death. He was as usual ungracious. He went upstairs and I rang for Caitlin and asked her to go up to his room and run the bath as he requested. I was alone then in the foyer. Yes, I suppose they think I could have dashed upstairs, put the stuff in the bath, and returned to the foyer."

"Let's hear about this leak then."

"Caitlin told me about a leak she'd spotted in the lounge. It was during the afternoon tea. Sure, I didn't want the guests to see that sort of thing. Give the place a bad name . . . hah! Not as bad as it's got, now they think I murdered one of my own guests in his bath."

Kevin indicated that they'd turn back towards the hotel. "I got a bucket and towels and put them under the leak. Wait, before that I was setting up with Mrs.

O. in the lounge. We were amused because Breathnach was singing in the bath. We were just under his room, and we could hear his singing—it was funny at first and then a bit annoying really—the same song. You know the one that goes, em, 'I did it my wày.' Typical of the man, I'd say."

"Did you hear anything else?"

"No, steps don't carry through the ceiling. It was just the singing. He was loud and the house was very quiet. You know, James, that very afternoon I'd been looking out at the rain and the view and thinking that things were just beginning to get better."

James let the silence linger as they walked more slowly. "How so?" he asked.

"It was so awful after Mary died. I didn't think I could go on. But one does, one does go on in some horribly automatic way. I had Miriam to think of. I'd do anything for that child. And I saw how she needed me when Mary was gone. They had always been so close." Kevin's voice grew hoarse and he stopped speaking.

"Has this affair affected business?" James changed the subject.

"Ach! A couple of reservations cancelled out, over the weekend, some people in the immediate vicinity who've heard the rumours. Thank God, the news hasn't travelled any farther . . . yet! But I'll tell you, despite those two cancellations, our locals have increased! Late November is not a big season in any hotel, but our weekend dinners and teas are still busy."

James grimaced. "I see. So people want to visit the scene of the crime, even eat at the scene of the crime, but you imagine they'll draw the line at sleeping at the scene of the crime."

"Yes, charming, isn't it?—human nature. I wanted a modicum of fame for the Lodge, but not notoriety. Can you imagine how I feel—that people are coming here out of morbid curiosity?''

"It'll die away . . .''

"Oh, wonderful!''

"Sorry, no pun intended.''

"You know, James, I grew up in a small village in County Dublin. And I live in a village situation now. The memory of a village is as long as time itself. Where did you grow up?''

"Rathfarnham—a real suburban experience." James laughed.

"Yes, I can imagine. There's no comparison, James, to a village where generations of families have lived, lands abutting, fields abutting. Histories and stories intertwined for hundreds of years . . .''

"Of course, of course, I've had some experience in that regard.''

Kevin looked up quickly.

"Another case, some time ago . . .'' was all that James would say, because any mention of that particular story always brought with it the painful reminder of his parting with Sarah Gallagher.

The two men walked back towards the rear of the Lodge. As they approached from the side James could see the ominous cromlech rising up in the crystalline air. He recalled his previous visit, just three short weeks ago, when he and his fellow guests had stood around that very cromlech. And as they'd shared in a festival of the Celtic spirit, one among them had been working evil. He shivered.

"Listen, Kevin, I want to get started straightaway. It's nearly three weeks now and the trail is getting bloody cold. The first thing I intend to do is speak with Cronin and have a look at the transcripts of the statements he took. After that, it may be that I'll have to interview some of the guests myself—''

"Oh, Lord, not again." Kevin interrupted as he

Ann C. Fallon

pulled open the door of one of the outbuildings and dragged forth a tall stepladder.

"I'll be discreet, Kevin. If anything, those guests would be on your side. They shared your board and lodging after all. You were their host."

"Who makes such fine distinctions these days?" Kevin shrugged. "If they did, then one of those guests committed the great crime of killing someone under my roof. So much for niceties. Here, give me a hand." Kevin, with a focus for his energy, was briskly assembling his tools.

James carried the paint pots and brushes while Kevin, lumbered with the ladder, moved awkwardly through the back of the house to a rear staircase. James went on ahead.

He easily found the room which Kevin intended to redecorate and he laid down his burden. The room, stripped of furniture, was the farthest in the right wing of the house, tucked into a corner beneath one of the gables. The house's architecture had undergone so many permutations that James couldn't even guess what the room's original function had been.

The paper was ancient and its flowered surface was clean but very faded. The carpet was up and James could gauge the age of the room by the wide and sagging floorboards. It was an oddly shaped room and somehow unappealing. He jumped as Kevin charged into the room.

"Here's the list I kept of all the guests that weekend. All but two claimed they were returning to their permanent home addresses."

Scanning the names James recognized his fellow lodgers; most of them, he was relieved to note, were living in the greater Dublin area. However, Mrs. Trask, the American woman, and the Englishman, Gorman, were both listed as staying at the same hotel in Ballyhaunis,

70

County Mayo, a matter of a few hours' drive from Sligo Town.

He tapped the paper and arched his eyebrows. "Trask and Gorman?" He left the question hanging.

"I know, I know!" Kevin laughed heartily for the first time that day. "A winter romance, I think. They stayed on a week or so beyond their original reservations. A common interest in Yeats, you see."

Kevin worked quickly as he talked. His bottled-up energy poured itself out as he sponged down the walls, readying them to be stripped. "They spent hours visiting Yeats's grave over in Drumcliffe, and then tramping up Ben Bulben. They're both quite fit. That's not an easy climb at this time of the year." He paused, glancing out the small paned window towards the looming mountain, its smooth, sloping sides mirroring the shadows of the low scudding clouds. "You know, its face changes almost constantly. A magic mountain, surely." He sighed and turned back to his work. "Mary and I used to climb it in those good old days. She'd been pleased to see I'm attacking this little room. It was her least favourite in the house and we seldom used it for guests. . . . Jaysus!" A strip of paper adhering to many much older strips came away from the wall, bringing with it chunks of plaster and revealing dark, damp patches beneath.

"Bloody hell! It's even worse than I expected."

James fell in with Kevin's work and began stripping the paper on the far side. "It's a small room, Kevin. It won't take us long."

"No, but I'll have to treat the walls and that'll take some days to dry out thoroughly. No, she never liked this room. Said it gave her an odd feeling. She used to get odd feelings in lots of places though. At the cromlech, at the cemetery. Obvious places, I suppose. But there were other places in this house and some of the outbuildings that used to make Mary go cold. I've never felt anything of the sort myself. How about you?"

71

James didn't answer, reluctant to mention that he didn't like the small room either, reluctant still to mention the episode in the attic.

"James? Don't tell me you have a feeling about this room too?" Kevin turned to look at him.

"No, nothing like that. It just seems removed from the rest of the house."

"That's it exactly." Kevin pulled another strip off the wall and began on the lining paper beneath it. "Mary used to say that too. You see, you've got the gift, James." Kevin laughed and James went along with it, feeling bad that he wasn't being completely honest.

As James worked he wondered at his own hesitancy in speaking. Was it that he thought Kevin would laugh at him? Obviously not, since he spoke so seriously about his wife's sensibilities. What Irish person didn't have that sense of always being in contact with something other than what was commonly perceived to be real? Very few people dared scoff. And it had not been so long ago when James himself had visited a fortune-teller. Of course it had been during an investigation. In the line of duty, so to speak. He'd never have sought her out otherwise. She too had said he had the "gift." He remembered her reading of the tarot cards. Her intimations that words and money, and women and wheels, were in his future. And a crying child. A calling woman. He shook his head. It could mean anything, be interpreted any number of ways. And yet it had shaken him. He stopped working, musing that he'd never had the nerve to ask his mother about the one point the gypsy had insisted upon. That he had had a sister. His mood deepened and he suddenly decided to quit the room. He was wasting time.

"Well, speak of the devil." James heard Kevin's words as though from a distance.

"Come, come here." Kevin was on his knees at a rough hole in the skirting board that had been obscured beneath the paper. He reached into the small space. "Mighty strange, I'd say . . ."

"A child's hidey-hole," offered James. "This room is so small it might have been a child's once."

"Wait, this . . . there is something!"

He withdrew his forearm, covered in a filthy black dust. In his hand he held what seemed a small package or parcel. Carefully he unwrapped layers of cloth, the outer layers falling to pieces in his hands. The cloth beneath was cleaner, the fabric intact. Within the wrappings he found revealed a small bound book, crumbling but only slightly. James hunkered down, intrigued despite himself.

"A novel, a book of poetry?" he asked as he watched Kevin gently lay the book on some clean floor cloths. He slowly opened the cover and turned over a few blank pages. A faint script, in faded ink, appeared on the third or fourth page, like a frontispiece.

"To my darling babe, so that he might know, one day." The script was round and full, an educated hand certainly. James was filled suddenly with an inexpressible sadness. He stood up, eager to breathe but unwilling to open the window and disturb the room. Kevin reverently turned the next few pages.

He read silently for a few minutes.

"Well?" said James.

"It's a diary of some sort. The ink has faded and it's difficult to read quickly, but it seems to be a diary of a woman and how she spent her days. The language is rather flowery, you know the way. Detailed description of what seems to be springtime. Flowers, birds identified. She's commented on the weather for each of the days."

He turned to the middle. "She says she's been very sick here, oh dear . . ." He sighed and closed the book. "It's too dreary."

He took a clean plastic bag from his back pocket and gently wrapped it. "I'll just put it downstairs in the office."

"Look," said James, "I want to get started with my investigation." He picked up the guest list. "I'll bring the book down for you." He felt its slight weight as Kevin handed it to him. "Do you mind if I take a look at it?" His curiosity had got the better of him.

"Not at all," said Kevin. "I'll work on here. If you wouldn't mind, just put your bags in the room you had before. I presume you'll be in for the evening meal?"

James nodded.

"I'm counting on you, you know." He shook hands with James and turned away abruptly.

James, annoyed with himself that he'd left it too late in the day to speak with Inspector Cronin at the station, decided to take advantage of this quiet time in the hotel by questioning the staff.

The snug was empty and as he ordered a small sherry from Sean he asked him casually about his background. Sean's life, apparently, was an open book. A local lad, he'd studied cooking in Galway and had come highly recommended from a small inn in London. He was a straightforward man, with the black curly hair and blue eyes of his county. It was clear to James that he was very fond of Kevin, and loyal too. When he began to tell James enthusiastically about Sinead, he managed to head him off, having learned, he believed, quite enough already.

"Sean, if Caitlin is not busy at the moment I'd like a word with her too?"

"I can get her for you, but mind, she's been shattered by all this. She's a jumpy little thing. And the police have questioned her more than once. Go easy?"

"Of course I will." And as he waited for Caitlin he opened the small book by his side. The smell of its musty pages, the feel of the heavy paper wafted him back, if not to a different place, then to a very different time in the history of Cromlech Lodge.

Chapter Six

Dear Daniel,
You are now two weeks old and I know that you are
feeling better, though still so delicate and so frail. You
become more precious to me with each passing hour
and if I had but time and ink enough, I would record
in this journal every moment of your being. Alas, your
little demands on me, so sweet and precious every one,
will not allow of that. So I will keep this book whenever
I am able, and write herein of your first hours and days
with me. They are calling lights out now and I must
extinguish my lamp. But I shall lie beside you in your
white baby cot and wait for you to stir for your milk.
Good night, my angel, and may the angels of Him
above guard your sleep and your rest.

Dear Daniel,
The feast of Christmas is approaching and your birth
binds me closer to the birth of the Christ child. When
I look into your deep clear eyes I see in them His image

and I tremble with my love for you and with my love for Him who has granted this great gift to me in this terrible place. One day we will both be free of this place, I know that He will not be deaf to my prayers. But for now your coming has made this small cramped room a palace and my own small window a vista, a panorama of all that is most wonderful and beautiful in this corporeal world. It is in your eyes, that vista, and your breath on my cheek as you sleep against my bosom is like the wind, the Holy Ghost Himself who fills my heart and my mind with such gladness and rejoicing.

James realized with a start of insight that the room in this narrative was the room in which he and Kevin had found this journal. He read on slowly, turning the stiff, thick, brown-edged pages carefully.

Dear Daniel,
It has been a bitter winter, the worst I have known. From what little converse I have with the staff, I shall call them, they say it is the worst in Sligo in living memory. The house is cold, my darling, and it is not helping you. No doctor has come. I've begged but only today was I permitted to speak a few words with Mother Superior. She heard my words but would not let me show you to her. I know if she only glanced at your beautiful holy face her hard heart would soften. She said she would pray for your recovery. Would God listen to her prayers more closely than to your mother's? I have cried out to Him in my prayers daily, nightly, and my prayers will storm the gates of Heaven. His love and mine own will bring you through this fever in safety. I've bathed you in cool water although the warden says I'm mad. But isn't that why I am here, my darling, because the wardens of my life make claim that I am mad. Not then, perhaps, when I first came here. But now, child, I am mad with a love for you that gives me strength where I thought all strength, all sanity had been sapped from

my bones, my sinew, my very heart. You, my darling, are my heart now. Live. Live. And I know that I will triumph over my weaknesses.

James read on a few more pages, to assure himself that the child had lived, at least through that bad winter, but he closed the book as Caitlin entered the small bar. The girl's face was pale and thin beneath a cloud of orange-red hair. She twisted her fingers in her lap.

"Caitlin," he said gently, "my name is Fleming and I am a solicitor. I'm a friend of Mr. Conlon's and I'm going to help him clear up some of the questions concerning Mr. Breathnach's death. I need you to tell me, well, pretty much what you've told the police. Only this will be easier, am I right?"

She nodded wordlessly, her small eyes peering at him intently.

"Tell me about that day . . ."

"I was in the kitchen with Mrs. O.," she began simply, and then continued her clear narrative. "The bell rang for the lobby and we guessed it was Mr. Conlon and she said, 'Go on, girl.' So I hopped up to the lobby and Mr. Conlon said for me to go up to number one, that's the big bedroom on the first floor, and run a bath for Mr. Breathnach. So I hopped up there and tapped on the door. He called out to come in. I went straight through to the bathroom and put the plug in the bath and turned the taps on. I ran the hot and cold together with more hot than cold. The room began to steam up a bit. Then I checked the shelf to see if there were enough big fresh towels, and there was. Mr. Breathnach came to the door in a dressing gown and said, 'Slow the water down there, girl, or it will fill too fast.' So I did as I was bid and I slipped out straightaway."

"Did he ask you to add anything to the bath?"

"Oh, sorry. Yes, there was a bottle of bath salts on

the bath. They're in all the bathrooms. I hadn't done it you see, him being a man. Now, me Da doesn't—"

James interrupted, "Tell me about the bath salts."

"I opened the jar, shook in about half, put on the stopper, and put it back on the bath. Then I left."

"You're sure that's all."

"Yes, sir."

"But you had forgotten to tell me about the bath salts?"

"Yes." A slow blush crept up her face.

"I'm sorry, Caitlin. I know you're doing your best. Then what?"

"I think I went to the kitchen. I know at some point, p'rhaps when we made the tea, I told Mrs. O. what I'd done."

"Why was that?"

"Because she's training me you see, as chambermaid. She'll always check I've done what I'm supposed to do."

"Did you return to his room?"

"Ah no, sir, it was teatime. I was run off my feet, up and down them stairs. There was a crowd and then it was I saw the drip."

"Go on."

"I told Mr. Conlon and he seemed fierce upset."

James masked his surprise. "Yes?"

"He got all white and stern, like he does. He made me show him—"

"Made?" James was considering the impression her words would have made on the police.

"Mmm, made me take him in there. Later I saw him coming back with the pot, he was upset and was trying to pretend the drip wasn't there. You know, chatting and smiling with the customers."

Oh, Lord, thought James, Caitlin's description of Kevin's effort to maintain the Lodge's reputation for food and good service came out all wrong in this young girl's version of events.

"So you told all this to the police?"

"Yes, sir, wasn't that right?" she asked suddenly alarmed.

"Of course, it was right. Is there anything else?"

"Only that Mr. Breathnach was a big pig of a man in a dressing gown. Me Da says I shouldn't even be drawin' baths for grown men. I don't mind meself since it's the way here at the Lodge. But I didn't like that Breathnach fella and I don't blame Mr. Conlon one bit for not liking him a'tall, a'tall."

James sighed as Caitlin left the room. "Out of the mouths of babes," he murmured, as he finished his sherry and gathered up the old journal.

Passing through to Kevin's study he placed it carefully on a small bookcase and, heading upstairs, at last settled himself in his room. relishing—despite the serious circumstances—the thought that he'd be staying at the comfortable Lodge indefinitely. Having changed into an old Aran sweater and rugged cords he went in search of Mrs. O'Neil, the primary member of Kevin's staff.

He found her in the kitchen, up to her elbows in potato parings and turnip peelings, scraping the vegetables for the evening meal. She was, as always, pragmatic and forthright.

"Yes, sir, Mr. Fleming, indeed I checked on Breathnach's room, after Caitlin came down to me here. She's young, as you can see. And we, Mr. Conlon, always wants to ensure that the guests are very comfortable. I just had a quick peek in . . ."

"And from that you could tell that she'd done all her duties?" James's voice held an edge to it.

"The man was in his bath, sir, and I wasn't about to go all the way into the room. And he was roarin' out that Sinatra song. Sure, he wasn't dying at that point."

She slammed the vegetables down on the cutting board and took up the knife.

James glanced around the almost sterile kitchen, the copper-bottomed pots giving out a soft gleam to the whole setting. He waited for her to add something, anything, but she was silent. And her silences, as he'd noticed before, were forbidding.

"Well, just a few more questions then," he said at last. "Tell me about the bath salts. There seems to be some confusion in Caitlin's mind."

"We leave a variety of bath salts, sometimes sachets, never the oils because it clogs up the drains, on all the baths. They look lovely—all the colours and the lovely shaped bottles and jars. It's a little 'extra touch' as they say in the brochures. And we do it too because as you know yourself there's no showers in the Lodge. We all say it's to keep that old-fashioned feel about the place. But I'll tell you"—she waved the knife in James's direction—"it would have cost the earth to put in good showers and the sliding glass doors and the fixtures. Maybe some day. But there's another thing too. We save on the water. There's people stand in showers for upwards of half an hour, if you credit that! And the water pressure up here on the hill is none too good as it is."

James took note of her proprietal air and wondered if it ever had annoyed Kevin as it now annoyed him. "And you're absolutely sure then, there were bath salts in Breathnach's room?"

"As I said, they're in every room."

"But there was no evidence of that in his room."

"I know. The police have told us that. They can't explain it, we can't explain it. There it is."

"Could Caitlin have made a mistake?"

"Ah sure, it's a simple thing to remember if she put it in. She told me when she came in here that she'd done it. That's enough for me. The rest I can't account for."

"What did you think of Breathnach, Mrs. O.?" asked James, swiftly changing tack.

"Ach, we don't get many like him here, thank the Lord. A real jackeen, throwing his weight around, which was considerable—but you know that." She glanced up half-smiling.

James ignored her look. "Did you speak with him?"

"No, just the civilities when I was serving. But I heard him speak to Mr. Conlon about selling this place. It was in the dining room . . ."

"And you told all this to the police?"

"O' course. I told them and I tell you, Breathnach was like a little shopkeeper who decided he can open a department store and make his fortune. All hot air. I haven't an idea why he thought Mr. Conlon would be wanting to sell this place. It's not only his livelihood, it's his home." She cut the vegetables with anger and accuracy.

"You didn't like him. . . ." James said mildly, but to himself he questioned whether her concern was for Kevin's livelihood only.

"It's not for me to like or not like the guests, Mr. Fleming." She looked at him pointedly. "But he was a brute and coarse and loud with it. And so, I can say— I didn't like the man."

James felt it wise to take his leave on a more pleasant note, and he told Mrs. O'Neil how he looked forward to the evening meal. Equanimity was restored. At least in the kitchen. But as James mentally prepared for his work ahead he assessed that both Caitlin's and Mrs. O'Neil's testimony could appear damaging to Kevin's case.

The next day broke clear and fresh. As James wound his way from the Lodge towards Sligo Town he studied for a moment the low Ox Mountains with their faded blue humps standing like guardians of the route to the true west of Ireland. The West that he found as inscrutable as its mythology and as unyielding as its people, and he considered the interview ahead of him.

He wondered if Inspector Cronin would be as gracious as he'd appeared when they first met that hectic Sunday at the Lodge.

As he feared, Cronin's manner had changed considerably. It was clear that he now suspected Conlon and he readily turned aside James's comments that Cronin had known Kevin for years, if only slightly, and had known Mary and the O'Donnell family a lot better.

"The fact that there's never been a bit of trouble at the Lodge in my memory"—Cronin paused to light up an ancient briar pipe—"has little, or should I say nothing, to do with this matter at hand. There does not have to be a history of trouble in a place or person's life to justify some current trouble."

James was irritated with the man's smugness. And disappointed. He'd thought he'd detected a certain intelligence at their first meeting. "Look, I think you hit the nail on the head," he said concealing his own feelings. "What's at issue here is Kevin Conlon's past and present history. The man's character is irreproachable. Surely you'd admit that?"

"You're an old friend?" Cronin had the country trait of answering a question with a question.

"I don't have to be. I can judge a man's character without knowing him all his life."

"A good judge then, are you? Never make mistakes?"

"And you don't make mistakes either?" James countered.

"Why exactly are you here, Mr. Fleming?"

"I'm here to talk to you. I'd like to suggest that you concentrate your efforts in another direction. I would stake my life on the fact that Conlon did not kill Breathnach. I thought perhaps if we . . . we worked together we might . . ."

"Your suggestion is inappropriate, Fleming, and your advice is unwelcome certainly. In fact"—he paused—"it's just as well you are here, but not for the reason you mention. I am going to charge Mr. Conlon. Since you've identified yourself as his solicitor, then I advise you to ask your client to turn himself in to me early tomorrow morning, or I will be paying a visit to the Lodge."

James sat back in the hard wooden chair, more stunned than he cared to admit. Had his visit catapulted Cronin into action? He reached for the right words.

"Listen, Inspector, I apologize if I've been precipitous. I assure you I have only Conlon's life at the heart of my concern."

Cronin waved him away. "I was on my way to the Lodge when you arrived. Nothing you've said has influenced me either way. Three weeks have passed and the attorney general has asked for some action. I've reviewed the evidence. We have motive, means, and opportunity. Apart from the method, this was not a clever crime."

"Just my point, Cronin. Kevin Conlon is a bright man—" James spoke rapidly.

"But not a bright criminal," interrupted Cronin. "Look, Fleming, as you well know I can hold a suspect for up to seventy-two hours, without bringing charges. This is what I plan to do. Unless there is a significant change or new evidence, I will charge Mr. Conlon at the end of that time. I think I can say that I'm being more than fair, Mr. Fleming, in giving you such advance notice of my intentions. I doubt they do this for you in Dublin." The little man puffed out his chest with a superior air and James wanted to push him over.

"No, you're right on that," said James in a seemingly chastened voice, hating to always have to play the game. But his anger would only harm Kevin's cause. "And I know you will keep an open mind. Inspector, since you've been this generous, can I impose on you further?"

Cronin looked up, smiling at the thought of having bested a Dublin lawyer. "Go on . . ."

"While Conlon is here . . . with you . . . I won't be able to assist his case."

Cronin's eyebrows shot up.

"I mean to say, without being able to talk with Kevin I could be wasting my time here in Sligo. I was wondering if you would allow me to read the transcripts of your interviews with the guests and staff. I could verify the evidence you spoke of. . . ." James's manner was palliative. He waited breathlessly, knowing that once Kevin was charged, these transcripts would be unavailable to him. Had he appealed sufficiently to Cronin's small vanity?

"I don't see why not. They just prove my point. Since you're here you can read them now. There's an empty office down the hall. I'll have them sent over."

Wasting no time, James settled to work at the long scarred table, pushing from his mind how many unhappy suspects had been questioned at it over the years.

As he had noted at their first meeting, James found Inspector Cronin's work, and that of his men, to be thorough, more than competent. This competence worried him. How could this man, seemingly good at the fundamentals of his job, be led astray by what was the mere obvious? Yes, Kevin Conlon had means, the slightest of motives, and opportunity. But surely Cronin could see there was no underlying drive to kill, to murder. James wondered how the inspector could misread his man so badly.

As he flipped through the files, putting them in random groups of three, James recalled the murder cases he'd been involved in over recent years. In each there had been, at the moment of the murder, a lusting to kill in the heart of the murderer. It was that lust he must seek for now; somehow, he hoped to find in the files a clue, an insight that would direct him to the one person who had desired Breathnach's death more than life itself.

James's immediate goal was to eliminate the least obvious suspects using a set of assumptions he most probably couldn't have articulated if asked.

Firstly, he felt that he had the huge advantage of having met the group of suspects *in situ,* at the scene of the crime. Someone, either among the staff—and he had virtually eliminated them—or among his fellow guests had committed murder. That murderer had remained, had eaten and drunk, had partied and laughed, with such self-control as not to draw attention to himself or herself.

That guest, with whom James himself might have passed the time of day, had travelled to Sligo, had needed to be present when Breathnach was at the Lodge. Therefore that person had to be fairly independent in his plans, had to be free to travel at her whim. James paused.

Surely this indicated a man rather than a woman. Someone able to plan and not merely be part of the plan. Yes, a man. Or a woman on her own.

James smiled down at the first transcript that came to hand: Miss Nell Garvey, spinster, age 77. Well-established financially and socially. No. James made the leap of faith, as he doubted she had lusted for Breathnach's death. What of her nephew and his wife, who'd arranged the short holiday for the three of them? The nephew, O'Dwyer, with a solid job and obvious expectations of inheritance could—if so inclined—be contemplating the murder of his elderly aunt! James cringed as he found himself prying into entirely innocent people's private lives. Why should he or anyone have to know Miss Garvey's age and state of health, or O'Dwyer's income and how he spent his time: fly-fishing as it happened? Mrs. O'Dwyer's simple domestic life with her teenage children was even more of an open book. James set these three files aside.

He was energized to have eliminated three suspects in a matter of a quarter of an hour. Not so happy that Cronin had obviously been able to do the same.

As he set about the next group he was startled in his perusal by Cronin's sudden, almost silent, appearance at the door.

"I wasn't intending you make a meal of it, Fleming." The man's voice was sullen as his eyes roved possessively over the sheets of paper.

"I'll be out of your hair in two hours," James said amiably but the ploy didn't work.

"By noon. My man will come for the documents. See you in court, Mr. Fleming." He didn't wait for James's answer.

Working more rapidly than he'd intended, James began to scan the interviews. Of the remaining guests he highlighted three as worthy of a personal visit. On the grounds of fame and success, artistic and financial, he'd eliminated Hugh and his wife, Enda, the musicians. On the grounds that the younger married couple had won their weekend in a holiday promotion, the weekend dates having been chosen for them, he eliminated Jack and Anna Duggan, parents of three toddlers.

Keeping to his fundamental theory that guests on their own were apt to be free agents, he quickly took note of the grandfather and grandson Dunmor's address, and the address of the single woman whose name he found to be Rosemary Morris, unemployed. Curious, thought James. She was listed as a spinster, late twenties, and her address he knew to be a substantial one. How did she afford her excellent clothes, or the Lodge's steep rates? A kept woman, perhaps? He laughed—if so, where was her keeper? More likely she was independently wealthy. He briefly imagined her life, picturing it as full of romantic incident, travel, and serendipity, as his own currently was not. He would look forward to this interview!

Who was left? Mrs. Trask, the genteel New Yorker. And Professor Gorman, of a spotless academic and social background. As the only people living outside of Ireland they might have been of interest. James took note of their addresses, but as he read their statements there was not the slightest reason for him to think they could have any reasonable connection to a real estate broker from the heart of Dublin.

Doubt suddenly assailed him. On the face of it the transcripts had revealed little, even to his suspicious and intuitive eye. And obviously Cronin had felt the same. It seemed that the only person in the Lodge that weekend who'd had any conversation, however slight, with Breathnach had been Kevin Conlon. And with a witness to it to boot.

James glanced at his scanty list. Breathnach was from Dublin. The odds were someone from Dublin, or who'd known him in Dublin, had murdered him. At least that was one thing the guests he'd singled out had in common.

Dunmor's name rang a bell. He glanced at the transcript again. Cronin had asked very few questions beyond his name and age and address. A sign of some protocol perhaps? Or was Dunmor known to Cronin personally? It was a question he couldn't ask of Cronin. His thoughts were interrupted by a young garda, barely out of his teens, bursting with pride in his uniform, and idly officious with it. James's attempt to chat was met with a serious silence. And so he relinquished the documents.

Seventy-two hours, thought James ruefully, as he headed back to the Lodge, letting the Citroen fly on the ring road out of the town. He would have to accomplish a lot in that given time, to prevent Kevin being charged as Cronin so arrogantly predicted. Yes, indeed, he'd like to serve up the guilty party on a platter to that insufferable but competent little man.

Kevin's reaction to Cronin's intention to hold him for questioning had been worse than James had foreseen. A certain fatalism seemed to grip Conlon, worse than any pessimism James had encountered in his career. Kevin's first thought had been Miriam, and after some long hesitation he decided not to inform her, although he did call her headmaster with the news of his temporary incarceration in the Sligo jail. He then spent two hours addressing the running of the hotel in his absence; Sean and Mrs. O., grim-faced and anxious, religiously followed his every word. James saw at a glance that the hotel would not function for long without Kevin managing the financial aspect of the operation. But as he assured Kevin the staff could rally for seventy-two hours.

Kevin's eyes were hollow as he agreed. Overnight guests weren't expected until Friday night. If he wasn't back by then, there would indeed be problems.

James mused that Kevin had asked nothing of him. Despite that, he outlined his plan to make a quick trip to Dublin to question his short list of guests in the hopes of finding some connection with Breathnach. They both retired wearily to bed, both hoping to rise early the next day.

But sleep did not come easily to James and he was glad that he'd retrieved the old journal from Kevin's study. Ensconced in a chair by the small warming fire, he set to his reading, careful not to let fall, on the old paper, any stray drops from his glass of Bushmills.

Dear Daniel,
On this New Year's Eve, my heart is lighter and happier than it has been in past years on this portentous night. A new year begins tomorrow for you and for me. I thank God above and His Holy Mother that you survived your

illness. I could not write during that time, fearful as I was for your frail life. But your terrible fever broke on Christmas day, a true Christmas gift. And now you sleep here beside me, peaceful and calm. Your downy hair is growing and fits like a close cap to your beautiful head, soft and golden. Your lips are open now in sleep, pale like pink pearls, perfectly formed. Your little hands are open. They've been so tightly clenched these last weeks. You are opening like a flower to the sun—my love is the warmth and light of the sun in this dreary place. I have just laid my finger on your palm, even in sleep your small hand has closed around it, holding tight. It is as though you are holding my very heart in your hand, I feel such a constriction in my chest when you hold my finger. As though you were holding on to my very life. You are my very life. My darling, you are sleeping in the little gown I made you for your very first Christmas gift. In the dayroom the vice warden let me have some blue cotton and I fashioned little blue rosebuds across the front. My skill is not as it was. I have not enough practice, for often the vice wardens won't allow us needles in the dayroom. Enough. It is done and you sleep in the gown now—I would clothe you in garments of lawn and linen, of silk and satin. As I was myself as a child and girleen. No one from the family came on Christmas. I wasn't sad or forlorn, because I held you all the day. I even had a bit of fruity rich Christmas cake a kind local person sent in for the patients (this word had a line drawn through) for all of us. Perhaps next year your little tongue will taste some cake or better still the lovely marzipan icing. My candle must be extinguished now, my darling. When you awake it will be a new year, one that will bring me the happiness of a free life I have no doubt, but it can never bring me more happiness than this year of your birth.

James sighed. He suspected from the vantage point of what he knew about the history of Cromlech Lodge that

the unidentified diarist was in fact a patient in the home
for the bewildered. He wondered about that term, *bewildered*. This writer was obviously educated, hardly bewildered in her ability to express herself. He wondered if
the baby of which, or rather, to whom, she addressed
her journal was a reality. Perhaps this was her illness,
a phantom pregnancy, a phantom child. He shook his
head. The details were too real, and consequently very
moving. He read on.

Dear Daniel,
'Tis the great feast of St. Patrick, and although we are
deep in the Lenten season, we were allowed a bit of a
party today. I wish you could have been there. There
was a good plain cake, and currant buns I've not tasted
before, and even quite a good cup of tea. I felt well and
only regretted I couldn't bring you to the dayroom. The
warden says that the other women would be distressed
to see you. I must believe her. I can't always live with
such doubts about my fellow beings. Nor would I want
you to be touched or held by anyone who might harbour ill feelings. There is so much pain here. So much
I do not understand. You've been doing well taking your
bottle, flourishing in fact. I was sorry that you had to
leave the breast. I told the vice warden our Lenten diet
might not agree with you, you would cry so pitifully but
they would not alter it. Cod, cod, and more cod! The
milk they allow me is now allowed for you. I don't mind,
my darling, the cold water in the frozen jug in the morning is like nectar to me. All that is mine is yours and
more. If only you could understand what one day will
be mine. Riches beyond your baby dreams. That day
will come, I know, when you will walk with me in our
gardens at home and gaze at the blue hills beyond and
the valley at our feet. And you shall have fine things to
eat, and soft clothes to wear, and a pony of your own.
And I hope you will love the animals as I do. We shall
have a little calf, you and I, and we will rear it together,

as I did as a young girl. I imagine the animals miss me. They knew me better than the family ever did. Still no word from them, even on this great feast. The new Sister recently come from France has ordered, asked rather, that we all cut our hair. I have no glass to see myself but I'm sure it is dreadful. When they come the family won't know me. Now I'm as slim as a boy and with hair as short. Your own hair grows apace. And your wide blue eyes are watching me now as I write. But they grow heavy with sleep. Ah, my darling babe, they are closing in sleep, a smile trembling on those baby lips. It is time to take you from your pillows and place you in your downy bed. Sweet dreams, my darling.

James delayed reading further and closed the small book, his heart heavy. Each page brought him closer—he assumed—to knowing the outcome of this little story. And he hoped against reason that the fact that the diary was found where it was did not portend an unhappy ending. He fell at last into an uneasy sleep, filled with images of an insubstantial shadowy cromlech draped in a swirling fog.

Chapter Seven

"How exciting, James dear!" exclaimed Mrs. Fleming as she adjusted the floral silk scarf over the ample bosom of her dark flecked wool suit. She settled herself comfortably into the plush velvet banquette and surveyed the scene, catching the eye, as she hoped, of a number of her well-heeled neighbours. She and James were ensconced in the spacious lounge of a public house not far from James's childhood home. It was a regular occurrence, that James would take his widowed mother for a drink. This night out was long overdue, and he'd phoned her only on his return from Sligo.

"How your father loved Sligo." His mother was animated, as usual. "Of course, we never had need to stay in a hotel, not with knowing the Kegans as we do. Such a lovely home. Full staff, a little maid to bring me my morning tea. It reminded me of my girlhood . . ." James rolled his eyes to heaven, but his mother was, again as usual, too quick for him.

"You needn't roll your eyes, James. You know Mummy had servants."

"I know that you never got over it," he murmured, but she chose to ignore this.

"As I was saying, we simply loved our visits in Sligo. Can't seem to remember you and your brother Donald there. Mummy must have tolerated you at those times, she was such a dear." Mrs. Fleming shrugged off recalling her son's childhood days and brusquely addressed the present, in which she lived almost entirely. "Now, James, who are these suspects you are commissioned to question? After all, when we put you to the law, we never expected you to be doing this ridiculous detective work."

James bristled. "May I remind you, you did not 'put me to the law'! I chose it freely and after a lot of thought."

His mother patted his hand with fingers burdened with a diamond cluster engagement ring, a diamond wedding band, a diamond anniversary ring, as well as a ruby finger ring. "There there," she spoke as to a high-strung child, "you haven't ordered a drink for your little mother yet. You must watch this stingy streak."

As they waited for their drinks to arrive, James explained again that no one he was interviewing was a suspect. After some consideration he mentioned the names of a few of the guests. His mother had a wide social acquaintance and her connections had helped him more than once in the past to make useful contacts. But this time only one name held any association for her.

"You met Ciaran Dunmor?" she exclaimed as she sipped her Campari and soda. "How delightful. I'm relieved, James, that you're beginning, although rather late in the day, to mix with the right kind of people. I always said politics would suit you."

"Mother"—exasperation punched every syllable—"you've never said such a thing. I have no political ambitions and I'm not sure who these 'right' people are that you—"

"There, you prove my point! You admit you don't even know the right people." Mrs. Fleming brushed a wisp of hair back into place on her carefully coiffed head.

"I give up," said James, leaning back against the seat.

"Good, so I'll just tell you. The Dunmors are the right people. A great political family. Certainly they are the right kind—almost. It's a pity really, that they are not one of us. They seem so Protestant, if you take my meaning. Despite their wealth they've always had the middle class at heart, they've always worked hard for our class."

"Yet surely they'd be more commendable if they'd worked hard for the common man?" James said through clenched teeth.

"Nonsense, dear. Who said it now, that the poor will always be with us."

James groaned.

"Yes, the poor have to muddle on. It's the middle class, our kind, that carries this country on its back."

"And the Dunmors and their kind . . ."

"Their kind is born to lead. Haven't you seen their home? See what you miss when you don't take me up on my invitations. It was only last spring I was at a fund-raising concert there. They threw open the house and grounds. A glorious day and afternoon tea laid on . . . James, call over that boy and get me some peanuts . . . yes, a lovely tea. We had a bit of a look at the ground floor. Absolutely magnificent furnishings and artwork. And the grounds, James. Rolling fields as far as the eye could see!"

"And what is their money from?" asked James intrigued in spite of himself at his mother's gossip.

"I really don't know. It's very old money, you see. Who knows now—land, I imagine. The family goes back generations. Surely you know this?" Her voice was caustic at James's ignorance of the social scene.

"All I know is that Dennis Dunmor has been in politics for years and that he's in the cabinet at present. I know I didn't always see eye to eye with his policies. I certainly did not know Ciaran Dunmor is his father."

"Ah, well, they're a political family. Ciaran, whom you've now met, was in politics before him and is now his private secretary. People say he's still a huge influence . . ." She put her hand to her mouth conspiratorially. "He did a favour for your grandfather once." She smoothed her skirt over her knees and glowed with the pride of one who has benefitted from political clout.

James held his tongue, willing now to learn anything she might know about Ciaran Dunmor.

"Ciaran, lovely jolly man. And I hear that the grandson is well on the way also to a political career." Mrs. Fleming waved at the barman and three of her neighbours waved back to her.

James thought of the sallow amiable youth he'd met and wondered aloud if he'd had any choice in the matter.

"Choice? Why should he have a choice. He'll finish at Trinity and follow in his forebears' footsteps."

"Not Trinity. He's at University College."

"Oh, well, I suppose Trinity does not want Catholics, even of their standing."

"Mother—those days are long gone!"

"Too bad but, well, the point is, you've made a good connection there, James. Stay well in with the Dunmors and there's no knowing how far you could go, if they take a liking to you."

James was about to remonstrate with her but as she beamed at her friends and nodded with pride towards James, he decided against it.

She chose to see his life from her own particular point of view, and as he'd grown older he'd grown wearier of trying to get her to see it from his. What he'd learned tonight about the Dunmor family was very interesting, possibly even helpful to him in his interview in the morning, and so, despite all, he was grateful to her.

It had been a productive day, thought James, as he stretched out on the leather sofa in his flat in Leeson Gardens. The ride from Sligo to Dublin had been swift, and a quick visit with Maggie and the staff at the office had assured him all was in hand there. He'd succeeded in making a firm appointment with Dunmor, and had even managed to fulfill his filial duty and take his mother out on the town.

With luck he could leave for Sligo tomorrow he thought, and with even more luck get Kevin away from Inspector Cronin inside the seventy-two hours. But how? He stood up again, restless at the thought that he needed something substantive, something that would prevent Cronin from charging Kevin, or at the very least postpone such an action, even in the face of pressure from the attorney general. If only Rosemary Morris or Dunmor and his grandson could be legitimate suspects. He recalled his brief and conclusive interview with Morris that very afternoon.

She had agreed to see him at her home in Ballsbridge. And he'd gone there with mixed feelings of anticipation. The detached house in its own grounds was impressive, and when she answered his ring, she was dressed as simply and expensively as she had been in Sligo.

Her manner was remote and cool and she briefly described her degree in languages from Trinity, her volunteer work with charities, her social life.

As she talked he became irrationally disappointed. He'd needed a break in this case, which Morris would not provide. And he was disappointed in himself. Rosemary Morris had implied multitudes in Sligo—or so he'd thought. Yet now he saw it had been once again an instance of his habitual romanticizing of the women who came into his life. He looked at her clear gray eyes and saw no pain behind them, no knowledge. He felt eons older, world-weary. She had nothing to say to him, nor he to her.

He thought of Sarah. Serene, talented, inaccessible. And at the same time more substantial than he had had the sense to realize. He knew now he could and should have been honest with her at the time of the Moore case. But when he had deemed the time to be right—it had been too late. She was gone from his life, into her own.

Rosemary's mother had wanted to bring in tea, eyeing him no doubt as a suitable potential son-in-law. But James had had the sense to flee. Perhaps Morris had had all the romantic qualities with which he'd endowed her that Hallowed Eve weekend, but he would not find out. Idle, flip, vain, perhaps she might have the potential to murder a lover, but she hadn't murdered Breathnach! Give me the likes of Maggie any day he said aloud, and jumped. Well, maybe not.

He poured himself a shot of Bushmills whiskey from the drinks cabinet in the corner of his sitting room, and with renewed vigour sat down to study the report which had just been delivered from Madigan's office.

The bulk of it was background provided by one of Madigan's own free-lance investigators. The inquest in Sligo on Breathnach, it stated, had been suspended, and the body had been released for burial after only medical testimony had been taken. Madigan's man had duly attended the funeral in Dublin and had noted that the attendance had been sparse: a few neighbours from where he'd lived, a few colleagues from the real estate field, and a part-time secretary and bookkeeper who seemed to be present only to see if she could get her back wages. The investigator had commented that Breathnach seemed to be a man with no family and few friends.

"Then why? Why?" James's brain repeated. Why was such a seeming nonentity murdered in such a subtle way? A sour or shady business deal would not require his elimination. And even if it did—why this manner of death? Murder by bath salts! He poured another whiskey and turned to the folder that Maggie had handed him as he'd left his office some hours before.

Wonderfully efficient as always she'd clipped Breathnach's death notices from the various papers, and the items from the Sligo papers that had mentioned Kevin Conlon's "involvement."

"Pig-ignorant, the lot of them!" he said aloud again. And then looked around self-consciously as though someone might hear him talking to himself.

"Hah! I need a cat. Then it would be acceptable for me to address the air," he mumbled, returning to the folder's contents.

He took up the long form of the Irish birth certificate and glanced at it as one would at a routine document. Stapled to it was a second form which James perused perfunctorily but then he froze—his eyes locked on this new information.

Breathnach had been married.

James couldn't believe it. Had no one thought to make this simple inquiry? Not Madigan's man? Not himself, he admitted ruefully? Apparently not. No one that is—except for the redoubtable Maggie. He heaved a sigh of relief. Here perhaps was a true lead, a line of inquiry that would bear fruit.

He studied the information in his hand. Breathnach's wife's name had been Sandra Murphy, the marriage certificate stated. Murphy, for God's sake! One of the most common names in Ireland. Age 21 years. Well then, she'd not be very old today, younger than Breathnach anyway. Spinster—of course. County of birth: Sligo.

The word leapt off the paper. This was it! He kicked off his fine Irish leather brogues and wriggled his toes with satisfaction. Yes, this was definitely it. Not only was Breathnach married, a fact that Cronin seemed to be totally unaware of, but his wife sprang from the very place where the man had been murdered. Here surely was a link to be pursued: a link even Cronin could not ignore. The woman had to be found. True, this might take a little time, but with that stated need he could buy time for Kevin.

With genuine relief James packed his briefcase with a view to leaving for Sligo immediately after his interview with Dunmor in the morning. That too would be fruitful he mused, if only to eliminate him as a suspect. No, no. The focus now was on the missing Mrs. Breathnach. James fell into bed, to sleep the sleep of the virtuous and hardworking man.

It was with pleasant anticipation that he ran lightly up the stairs of the granite clad Georgian building on Merrion Square, just steps from the Dail. He'd liked Ciaran Dunmor, and his mother's description of him had not coloured that first impression. Now he half expected to see the rosy red cheeks of the Lewis Carroll character and to hear Dunmor suddenly burst into song.

Instead, he was kept in a waiting room, cooling his heels and his enthusiasm, as he watched the time of his appointment slip back behind the dozen or so people waiting ahead of him.

From what he gathered during his long wait was that everyone was there with his hand out. One man needed a variance of the zoning law to erect a garage, or so he said. Another sought a pension for a father who'd returned after forty years abroad. Yet another was adamant that her daughter attend a prestigious local convent school to which she'd been outrageously denied admission. One and all had requests—which they felt free to share—since one and all believed in the power of Ciaran Dunmor. James's professional pride came to the fore. Having waited too long, hat in hand as he felt, he approached Dunmor's secretary, a fatuous dark-haired young man only too anxious to please. He waved James out of earshot of the others.

"Terribly sorry, Mr. Fleming. You're hardly here to . . ." He nodded his head toward the full waiting room. "I'm aware of your appointment and of how valuable your own time is. A solicitor shouldn't be allowed to wait. Mr. Dunmor fully expects to meet with you. You see, it's always like this. And he's so accommodating. 'Don't turn anyone from this door.' His instructions exactly. Let me see if I can get you in after that farmer. He's only a small problem with a right-of-way."

"But . . ." said James.

"Please, please, now, if you just tell me what it concerns, I can even speed things up. Yes?" He looked at James expectantly.

"I simply want to know—it concerns a criminal proceeding." At this the secretary's eyebrows shot up and concern flickered across his smooth face.

"Yes?"

"I was with Dunmor in Sligo . . ."

"Ah, now, that makes a bit of a difference." He rubbed his hands, keeping his eye constantly on the inner door.

"I simply want to know if Mr. Dunmor had ever met a man called David Breathnach."

"Breathnach, is it?" The man's voice was natural. "David, you said?"

James nodded.

"Well, now, sir, I can save us all time. Yes, Breathnach occasionally was in this office over many years now, many, many years. Before my time even. He was in business in a small way, real estate, flats, cheap housing, and so on. He'd do the odd job now—for this office."

"I don't understand." James strove to conceal the fact that he was actually startled by this information. "For Mr. Dunmor?"

"Not at all. No, for the constituents. Well, for example, there was a problem lately, with an eviction. An old lady, sir, all very sad. Mr. Dunmor had Mr. Breathnach find a nice clean little flat for this lady. He's a good man."

"Breathnach?" said James but the man only glanced at him.

"Dunmor, sir. He'd help anyone."

"Anyone else? I mean, anything else you can tell me of Breathnach?"

"Ah . . . before that he was in here the odd time. Not an easy man to deal with, mind you, but salt of the earth. Mr. Dunmor does know the salt of the earth. There was another case—a house owner wanted to sell a fine piece of property but the sitting tenant couldn't be budged and it was ruining the sale. I remember Mr. Breathnach was most successful there."

James paused, debating whether to ask this man if he knew that Breathnach had been murdered. After all, it had made the papers at the time. He decided against it, and wanting now to clarify the issue with Dunmor himself, he took a different tack.

"Right! I thank you for your help. I really do have to get back to my office," he said in his most pompous manner, yet smiling to himself. "I'd ask that you reschedule my appointment with Mr. Dunmor . . ."

"But I've . . ."

"Indeed you've been most helpful, but there's another matter—a bit more personal." James hoped he'd struck just the right tone of secrecy and supplication. The young man's eyes widened.

"But of course. Enough said, Mr. Fleming. I'll phone your secretary with a new date. Again, a thousand apologies for your inconvenience."

With that Dunmor himself appeared at the office door, heartily slapping the back of the farmer whose red face was beaming with gratitude and respect. Dunmor glanced across the man's shoulder and caught James's eye. Slow recognition spread across his face as he tried to place him. With the dawn of knowledge he called out to James.

"Sligo, am I right?"

James, aware of all the eyes turned on him, merely nodded.

Dunmor signalled his secretary to bring James in and he found himself at last in the inner sanctum.

"Your name was familiar when I saw it on the appointment list. It was only when I saw your face that the old memory clicked." The hearty manner never left him and James again felt the warmth he'd sensed in Sligo.

"Terrible business, isn't it?" said Dunmor before James could speak.

"Which?"

"Aha! you must have many pressing cases." The man smiled benevolently. "I was referring to the business with Kevin Conlon."

"You've heard then?"

"Indeed, I hear a lot of things, as you can imagine. How can I help you in particular?"

"I'll get to the point. I've been interviewing the various guests from that weekend in an effort to help Conlon clear his name and reputation. When I was waiting just now your secretary indicated that Breathnach did some work for you in the past?" He watched Dunmor's face carefully but the man just nodded.

"I understand from the police that no one . . . admitted, let's say . . . to knowing Breathnach?"

"Ah, now that's your problem, is it, Fleming? I'll be frank. You're in the legal profession, and I believe you've had your brush with notoriety here and there . . . yes?"

James nodded, realizing that in the inner circle of old families and old money, his role in a number of recent cases might have been discussed.

"It was unwelcome," James agreed.

"Then you'll understand how unwelcome—as you say—the slightest bit of notoriety would be to me, to my son."

"I don't quite understand."

"Sit down, Fleming, and I'll explain. I am my son's secretary. I deal with a variety of things for him, and on his behalf. I have influence. He gives me a free hand. What I do therefore reflects or rebounds on him. We are a public family, or rather I should say, a family of public servants. I think you met my grandson. Yet another incipient public figure!" Dunmor leaned back in the well-worn wing chair and lowered his voice.

"I did not admit to having knowledge of Breathnach because I did not want the situation in Sligo connected in any way with my son, or that poor man's death in any way connected with the fact that my grandson—an innocent youth spending a few days' holiday with his old grandfather—was present in that hotel. What purpose would it serve? I knew I had nothing to do with that man's death! As God is my witness. I would take this oath on the altar of the pro-Cathedral. But if I had mentioned that I had dealings with Breathnach to the police there would inevitably be questions, leaks. What had my son or my grandson to do with this man? Nothing! And yet there would be talk. Isn't there always bloody 'talk'?

"James, may I call you James? I love that hideaway— just because it is a hideaway. Been there before. Grandson too. And I refuse to allow mere coincidence to play itself out and turn something simple into a complicated mess that the news hounds would lap up."

James nodded. His heart agreed with Dunmor, but his head still hesitated. "But what if your connection with Breathnach, no matter how innocent, came out anyway?"

"Through you?" The man's voice was soft and sad.

"Not necessarily. What if the police find the connection that you've already denied? Isn't that worse?"

"Perhaps, but they may not. If they were actively seeking alternatives to Kevin Conlon as the guilty party then I doubt that you would even be here. Listen, James, Breathnach was in and out of here maybe once in a year, or once in every two years. Took care of minor issues relating to real estate. Usually I never even saw him. One or another of my assistants would speak with him. How more tenuous can the connection be, I ask you, and yet the papers would blow it all out of proportion."

"Perhaps."

"I hold this job a sacred duty to my son. He is a great man, James, and has a long political future ahead of him."

"Higher office?"

"I hope one day. I hope I live long enough. And there's his son after him. Look, it would not help the police's case to prosper if I told them I knew Breathnach in a small way."

"Would it help mine?" said James quietly.

Dunmor looked at him seriously for some moments. "What are you asking?"

"Will your knowing Breathnach help me in any way to clear Conlon's name?"

"Oh, James, I don't for a moment believe Conlon killed Breathnach. He's a fine, young, hardworking man and runs one of the best hotels in the country. To my mind the police case is bunk. Why would Conlon want him dead, a minor broker from Dublin? It's ridiculous. But what is also without real meaning is that I met Breathnach maybe five times in ten years. So I have to say no to your question. My knowing Breathnach will not help or hinder your cause in any way."

James nodded. He was satisfied with Dunmor's frankness, his analysis, his acknowledgment of the realities of political and public life. Yes, he'd concealed information from the police. But it was, as he stated, not useful. James would have preferred the matter to be clarified but that, he considered, was his fastidious nature and had no bearing on the matter at hand. He'd accomplished what he'd come for. He knew in his heart that Dunmor had no part in Breathnach's murder. He stood up to go, conscious of the many people in the waiting room.

"I thank you for seeing me," said James. "Tell your grandson I said hello. Despite all the trouble since, I have a vivid memory of you and your grandson performing at the Halloween party."

Dunmor walked him to the door, throwing his arm around him in grandfatherly fashion. "James, if I can be of help, just let me know. You're well thought of in certain circles—a good lawyer is hard to find." He pressed a card into his hand. "This is my direct line. I'd appreciate it if you kept this conversation *sub rosa*."

James shook hands on it. And as he passed through the office full of petitioners, he silently agreed with them that the man's charm was irresistible.

Chapter Eight

The flaming red Citroen ate up the flat midland highway and the mountainy winding roads that formed the bulk of James's journey between the two county capitals of Dublin and Sligo. As he drove farther west, and the roads became less populated, he let the car have its head, like a stallion scenting the fresh country air. Only forty-eight hours in Dublin and he'd found a lead. Well, Maggie had found it, but only he—at this point—knew its significance.

He glanced at the digital car clock and was encouraged. He'd be well able to reach the Sligo police station before the end of the official day. With some luck, he could convince Inspector Cronin that he had substantial new evidence in Kevin's favour.

As it turned out, Cronin's mood was both irritable and irritating. As he sat in Cronin's spartan office, it was apparent to James that the inspector had learned nothing from Kevin. For there was nothing to learn, but James refrained from voicing this, choosing instead to present Cronin with the startling news of Breathnach's "missing" wife. James knew, that if Cronin saw its significance, it also gave Cronin a bit of a breather with the powers that be. But none of this was stated directly.

"Your client seems recalcitrant, Fleming," said Cronin, biting just a little too hard on his pipe and snapping the stem. James repressed a smile. Cronin fired it in the basket. "It doesn't suit me at this juncture to charge Mr. Conlon. He's free to go—for now. But believe me, Fleming, we'll be watching him. And as you know I can bring him in at any time."

"Of course. But with luck this new lead will prove . . . helpful?"

"I doubt it, Fleming. My men are tied up on a terrorist . . ." He paused, having said too much already. James looked away as though he'd not heard.

"This Sandra Murphy Breathnach . . ." Cronin resumed. "I warn you, Fleming, you'd be better served helping your client to confess than chasing ephemera." He turned on his heel and James wanted to hoot. He'd played it exactly right—he'd bought time for Kevin! Cronin's men wouldn't be following this lead, but then he had hardly thought his news would be greeted with enthusiasm by the inspector. No matter. Cronin was releasing Kevin and that was the main thing.

"James!" called Kevin as he raced down the station's narrow corridor moments later.

"Kevin!" They were like old friends, thought James as he grasped his hand warmly.

"Good to see you—at last. Let's get out of this bloody place!" He threw on his anorak against the cold.

Within a mere twenty minutes they burst in the door of Cromlech Lodge bringing with them the cold crisp air of a November night. Pungent turf smoke drifted out from the fireplace in the lounge. The lamps were already lit against the seasonal darkness and cast an amber glow on the reception desk and the gleaming wooden floor, and on the rich carved Belgian rug in its centre.

"Welcome home," said Kevin, laughing.

"Thanks, Kevin, and you too! It is starting to feel a bit like home here," he said, and suddenly realized that what he'd said lightly he meant in earnest.

"You seemed so excited on the drive here. You must tell me what convinced Cronin to release me. Wait, wait. Let me tell Sean and Mrs. O. we're here." He was back in seconds, with a bottle of whiskey by the neck. "All is well," he said, his face beaming, relaxed. "Dinner is in full swing. We've got the lounge to ourselves." He uncorked the bottle, poured out two generous measures and raised his glass to James. "Right, begin."

James warmed his backside at the fire and his soul with the whiskey as he recounted his work of the past two days.

"In a nutshell, I've hit on a piece of information that the police had overlooked, and I believe it's definitely to our advantage. You see, Breathnach was married. His wife's name is Sandra Murphy"—he paused dramatically—"and she came originally from Sligo!"

Kevin waited.

"That's it," James said at last.

"That's it?"

"Don't you see, Kevin?" James exclaimed. "There may be no need to look far afield for a suspect with a motive to murder Breathnach. I admit at first I believed that the murderer must have been one of the guests that weekend, someone from Dublin, someone who had somehow arranged to be here when Breathnach was. It followed that Breathnach did not know that person—at least to see. And from that I concluded that there had to be some hidden motive of which I could have no idea. At least initially. That's why I scoured Cronin's transcripts—to see if there was some more subtle connection. I narrowed the field to three of the guests. . . ."

"Yes?" Kevin looked quizzically at James.

"I'm pretty satisfied none of them was involved."

"Go on, go on . . ."

"When I learned that Breathnach was married and that I had in my hand the name of his wife, I did some further checking. Today, just before I left Dublin to come here, I checked the death certificates for a listing under the name of Sandra Breathnach. No one of that name is registered as deceased. This may well mean that she's alive. It gives us, Kevin, the Sligo connection, if I can coin a phrase."

Kevin mulled this over. "She may not be dead, but she could be abroad, James. She might have come from Sligo but that doesn't mean she's still here. Where were they married?"

"Ah, according to the marriage registry they were married in Dublin forty odd years ago."

"It seems pretty thin to me. I'm sorry, James. I guess I was just hoping that you'd had it all wrapped up somehow."

"Unfortunately, no. At this point, this information, thin as it is, raised enough of a question to get you temporarily off the hook with Inspector Cronin."

"I have to accept that. Obviously. He let me go. And I'm grateful. I just hoped for something more substantial . . ." Kevin sighed and poured another whiskey, his earlier ebullient mood rapidly abating.

"Look, Kevin, truly this is a break. I believe the whole connection is here, here in Sligo. The wife was from Sligo. There's no *other* connection between Sligo and Breathnach!" James threw himself into a chintz-covered fireside chair, the long day and the long drive suddenly catching up with him.

"But there is a simpler explanation, James. Breathnach was here in his capacity as a real estate broker. Okay, he didn't tell me whom he represented. But doesn't that show his shrewdness in his approach to me? He had told brokers here and in Dublin that he was fronting a consortium of investors that wished to purchase this entire property. Right now, it seems a little crazy that some crowd of rich Europeans want this isolated place, but not if you look ahead. All trade barriers, all customs barriers will be done away with before we know it. Then the Europeans can walk in here and buy property as if it were in their own backyard. It is feasible that some groups want to get in here to Ireland ahead of time. Buy up prime property now before prices rocket because of demand. But *he* didn't tell me any of this. All he said was, would I think about selling. He was sounding me out. Shrewd bloody bastard . . ."

"Whoa! You're making a great case against yourself."

"How so? Because I'm saying that what Breathnach told everyone might in fact be true?" He stood up restlessly and threw a full shovel of coal on the fire, then idly stirred it with the poker.

After a pause of some minutes, James reopened the subject. "You seem to be saying that Breathnach was here on a mission, to buy this property. Accepting that, you would seem a likely suspect of sorts. He could have been here, I suppose, doing that, and his wife . . ." He faltered.

"And his wife discovered he was here? Followed him here. Look at the assumptions you're making. We, all of us, have assumed they were estranged. Was she following him from afar?"

James paused. "Okay. I know there are problems—of logistics. Nonetheless, I think that the fact there is a wife in the picture . . ."

"Assuming she is still alive!"

"Yes, assuming that, then I think I must pursue it. Cronin himself saw it as enough of a threat to his case. I would like to go with my gut reaction on this. However, you are the client and you can direct me as you wish. I merely repeat that there *is* an important connection here—between Breathnach and Sligo, in the person of his wife—and I'd like to run it to earth. Remember, no one yet has turned up evidence of this conglomerate you spoke of. Yes, Breathnach bragged around town but Madigan's man has gone through Breathnach's papers at his office. There's no correspondence with Germans or any other group . . ."

Kevin shrugged. "He could have done such dealings over the phone, James. The whole project could have been at the very initial stages and there'd been no written work. And that's *my* gut feeling." His voice showed his irritation, signs of the disappointment he tried to conceal. He stood up, corking the bottle. "Well, James, no doubt I've work to do—after my two days' hiatus, courtesy of the Sligo police. And I imagine you've some sleuthing to do here in the town. Do what you think best . . ." He waved his hand vaguely.

"Right . . ." James tried to keep the conversation going as Kevin withdrew into himself. "Did you ever finish the little room upstairs?"

"Ach, indeed I did." Kevin's usual courtesy reasserted itself and he smiled. "Looks rather cozy now. Have a look yourself. By the way, I read a bit of that diary. Pretty sad—didn't finish it. Perhaps you'd like to have a look at it while you're here. I'll leave it in your room." James nodded as he watched Kevin wander dispiritedly from the room.

The following evening, James was glad to retire to his room after a long and strenuous day.

That morning, so many hours ago it seemed, he'd begun with enthusiasm, simply going through the telephone directory—looking for a Sandra Murphy in the hopes the woman had resumed her maiden name. There were no Sandras but there were very many Murphys and he methodically approached his task, taking them in alphabetical order. By teatime he'd visited or spoken to twelve separate families of Murphys just in Sligo

Town alone. From them he heard numerous stories of women who'd left Sligo for Dublin possibly forty years before. There was a Mary, and an Ann, a Teresa called Tess, a Margaret only known as Maggie and another who was called Peg. He'd learned that people commonly used a nickname or a second given name, so that one story of a Bridget revealed that her baptismal name was Assumpta. James's head was reeling from too much irrelevant information. There'd been no one who'd known of a Sandra Murphy. And yet after he'd spoken to these families he realized that Sandra could have been known by another and perhaps totally unrelated name.

As he bathed and changed he reflected on his initial excitement. He'd been so convinced that he'd strike gold in Sligo that he'd undertaken what he now perceived as a burdensome task himself. He looked again at the seemingly endless list of names in the phone directory, and grimaced at the thought of the fruitless interviews behind him and the dozens ahead of him. Lord, there'd been three sets of Murphys on one crooked Sligo street alone! His jaw ached and he flexed it, reflecting that he seemed to have done nothing but chat and drink strong tea for hours—and to what end? Discouraged, he tossed his notes aside. One more day of this tedium and he'd call on Madigan's offer to send a man to do any time-consuming footwork that might arise in the course of the investigation.

He went downstairs in a better frame of mind and enjoyed sharing a late supper with Sean and Kevin. They regaled him with amusing anecdotes of their disasters in the catering and hotel trade. It had been a welcome sight to see what a relaxed Kevin was like.

James at last rolled into bed, his mind relieved that he'd phoned for Madigan's man to come in on the case. And while that man pursued the elusive Sandra Murphy, he would accede to his client's wishes. This way, no more valuable time would be lost.

As he dozed he considered. Maybe Kevin's theory *was* right—the key might lie in Breathnach's stories about fronting a consortium. But were the stories lies or truth? If truth, then who else was involved? If lies, then why fabricate such an elaborate story, if not to shield another purpose or another party? Either way, there had to be a reason for Breathnach's visit to Sligo that particular weekend. It was this reason he must discover and then perhaps all else would fall into place.

He reached to put out the bedside lamp and was reminded suddenly of the first time he'd stayed in this very room. The hair on the back of his neck lifted—the house seemed unusually still and he found himself waiting for the sound of steps above his head. None came. Only the sound of a high wind rising, shaking the shutters and whistling down the chimney of the small fireplace. Sleep was retreating and he propped himself up in the comfortable down-filled comforter and reached for the little journal Kevin had left on his bedside table. No better night, he decided, to finish this tale of seeming woe.

Dear Daniel,

At last, my darling, I write of good news from home. The family has written to Sister Jeanne. They are coming. She didn't let me have the letter but as she held it in her hand I knew Father's script. This must mean we are going home—at last, my darling, you will see a different, softer beauty than Sligo can provide, with its barren mountains and wild fields. Gentle rolling fields await you. And the flat plains where horses frolic and gallop. It is early spring and I know the lambs will be gambolling on the new growth of grass. And the cows too will be out of their housing now, grazing, moving their large bodies like young calves. And then there'll be the calving time and you will have a little calf for yourself.

I tremble that we will see the man who has not been honourable enough to name himself your father. Perhaps he spoke the truth that day when he said he was ignorant as I. Perhaps. But marriage cannot sanctify the act we committed, for he is my cousin and it is not allowed by church or state. I do not rail against him, sweet babe, for without that one day your father and I spent in the fields of Kildare, you would not be here beside me as I write. I know that God has forgiven me my sin, for that day represented a great sin. But when I look into your innocent face I know He and His Holy Mother have forgiven me. I know, because all their love shines at me through your clear eyes. I write this now but when the day comes I will tell you myself and you will understand.

The nuns come here from France and they are terribly strict. Because of this you were not baptized in the church. But, dear boy, your mother has taken care of that as I have taken care of all things. I baptized you the day I held you in my arms alone at last in this little room. I took the pure water that comes from God's own streams and poured it over your dear little head. I said the great prayer that we all say and baptized you in the name of the Father and the Son and the Holy Ghost. This small book is my testament to that truth. But why do I fuss, when I have so much to prepare? I know that my father will love you as he loves me, he will protect us both. And all that he has will one day come to me and thence to you, his grandson. I know he will take care of all this for me and for you. The man who is your father has many good qualities that I know will also come to you. His coldness, his ruthlessness, are perhaps learned in the hard realities of the world in which he moves. I think that I will finish this little journal the day I leave here. When we return to the big house I will buy a leather bound diary to record our new life together—in that book will be none of the sadness that this little book tells of, but neither will it hold the quality of joy I felt in being entirely alone with you, dear son.

The next few pages held lists, James was puzzled to see, but he determined they were lists of the author's few belongings, a list of the child's clothes and simple handmade toys. He smiled at the little inventory. The author had jotted down a list of things to do, repairs to be made in her linen and the baby's, a plan or sketch of a little suit, with the word *blue* written beside it and the word *cambric* underneath. His heart lifted as the author's must have—as she readied herself and the baby and her few worldly possessions to return to the bosom of her father and home.

Dear Babe,
How I wish mother was alive to see you. I admit I never missed her, her memory having faded years ago. But now somehow, I see her kind face before me. The circumstances of your birth might have saddened her, but she would love you and she would be proud to see how well I care for you, I who knew so little I could hardly take care of myself. The warden told me to prepare for an interview with Sister Jeanne tomorrow and I am too excited to write. Sleep, little one, the happy day draws near.

Relieved that the story was to have a happy outcome, James was nearly tempted to put down the book, but he had to be sure.

Dearest Child,
I can barely hold the pen as I write this. Sister Jeanne told me today that consumption has entered our walls. Many of the women here have fallen gravely ill. I knew nothing of this. We are to be confined to our rooms, entirely, no more meeting in the common room or for meals. This is a precaution she says that may only last a few days. But, darling, she says you are at risk. That you are too tiny and frail ever to survive, and so they are removing you to a kind woman in the village whose

house is free of contamination. She will care for you and keep you robust until this danger is past. I begged her to let me go with you, begged that both you and I might stay with the kind woman in the village. But she says the risk is too great: that I, a grown woman, may already carry the contagion in my lungs. So then I begged her to let us, you and I together, leave early, since father is expected in a few days. I thought we both might flee to health and safety together. But she says she cannot wait for letters to pass back and forth through the post. I asked her to send a telegram, but she said most firmly she could not bother a man of my father's wealth and position. She was doing as she had been instructed. I can only think the doctor has advised this. I must trust this doctor whom I've never met, and Sister Jeanne, and God and His Holy Mother. My tears are wetting this paper and I cannot see for weeping. Sweetheart and centre of my life and being, we've never been apart. How shall I live through these next few days until father comes and we are reunited. You leave to-morrow morning. The kind woman is to come for you and I must have you and your few little possessions ready. I'm in an agony greater than any pain I've ever known and fear surrounds me. But I know I am well. And you are well, robust and healthy. Just a few days, my darling. I will keep this journal to ease my pain until I rest my eyes on your wondrous baby face. Good night, darling. Oh, how will you sleep without me near you? How will you eat from another's hand? Dear God, I don't think I can let you go. But your safety must come first. Again good night, God give us strength to survive this new and terrible ordeal.

James abruptly stood up from the bed and threw on his Foxford dressing gown. He poured himself a whiskey from the bottle on the dresser and drank it down. For warmth—he said aloud to the glass. He knew now he'd have to finish the story—there were only a few pages of script left in the bound book.

He sat in the chair, reluctant to be ensconced in a comfortable bed, more aware than ever that these were the living words of a young woman who—he believed—had passed these fateful, painful hours only yards from him, down the hall, in a small and cheerless little room.

Dear Son,
You are gone from me and the emptiness overwhelms me. The warden took you from my arms at the door of this very room. I could not meet the kind woman as I expected to. I am confined to this room and they bring me meals, and water to drink, water to wash myself. Never before did this room seem like the prison it really is.

It's as though I have been in a stupour since the day I was conveyed here in the carriage from the train. Have I been so blind all these months! Now as I look back, I realize that I was brought here just when my figure would have shown your presence. I know I was very ill in those early days at home, when I first realized what was happening to me, to my body. Perhaps if mother had been alive I could have stayed at home, calmer, more secure, in my thoughts of the future. But it was all so black then, when I was told that the man who is your father could not be allowed to marry me.

I hadn't seen him since that day in the fields of Kildare, but I heard of him. I believed he loved me. But the stories of his engagement to the woman in Dublin seemed to unhinge me. Dear child, I should not write this, but it weighs so heavily now on my heart. Yes, I should have been stronger. Those black moods and the weeping, my fruitless begging to see him, the foolish hope that we could marry still. Yes, I see father had no choice. I was mad then. A madhouse was my rightful home.

But as my body burgeoned, somehow trust returned to my heart, trust in God and the future. And with your birth, I welcomed the pain of labour. It was like a great wrenching, a wrenching away from that unhappy past. Your birth, child, you yourself, gave me the strength to return to my senses.

I am seventeen years of age, I have my life and my strength, and I will keep them. Yes, my mood is lifting. Gone are those old days of blackness and madness. Much as I hate this home where no one has spoken kindly to me, where we are not allowed even to speak our surnames, where the friendless cannot even befriend each other, it is still the place of your birth and will be sacred to me always. What are a few more days to wait, although every hour I am apart from you brings pain.

The next few pages carefully noted the dates and days of the week, as though the author truly was marking the passage of time—as prisoners scratched the days off on the walls of their cells. James saw there were only two more prose entries—and he dreaded to read on.

Dear Son:
You are gone.
I write these words for there is no one, no one at all to speak with.
My heart and my soul do not believe what my mind tells me over and over eternally. I cannot get the words out of my head or the sound of Sister Jeanne's voice. You took a fever on the second day and despite all good and great efforts the fever burned and wasted your tiny body. You fell into a troubled sleep, and thence to a profound untroubled sleep, and then ... I would say I pray to God that you did not know I was not there, that you did not miss my arms, my lips, my love, the beating of my heart against your own. But I cannot pray, nor will I ever pray again to the God who took

you from me, the God who took the very soul out of my body. . . .

James closed his eyes against the pain of her words. Wishing to put an end to it he read the last brief entry.

They tell me father is coming tomorrow. Too late for you, too late for me. Sister says the answer to her telegram revealed a broken man. I don't care. He comes to take a dead woman home. This is my good-bye, dear child. I couldn't even say good-bye because of the contagion. They tell me you were buried but not where. They said father will tell me. But I shall never speak to him. Let them call me mad. Too late he is coming for me. Too late for you, too late for me. They tell me I am to take nothing from here, not even clothes. That it is better to leave the past behind. So I will leave this little book here in this room where it all began, and where it all ended. This room will be its tomb, this little book the body of my dreams. I will bury it as I could not bury you. Oh, my son, how did you go into the darkness alone? I would have died with you just so you would not have had to go into that darkness, into that cold, cold ground alone, without my arms around you to warm and protect you. How will I live, how will I live?
                        Signed, Aileen Bandon Dunmor
                        This twelfth day of May, 1915

Chapter Nine

Aileen Dunmor. Ciaran Dunmor. The coincidence of the names, James and Kevin both agreed, was too intriguing to be ingored.

While Madigan's local man tracked the whereabouts of Sandra Murphy of Sligo, James postponed his pursuit of Breathnach's business dealings and concentrated on the mysterious Aileen Dunmor.

Reminded by Kevin of the centuries' worth of accumulation in the attics, James spent the morning rifling boxes and trunks.

He'd methodically worked his way through half a dozen trunks, starting with those tucked under the eaves, examining the contents of each. But he had little to show for his effort as he finally sat back on his heels and brushed the dust from his hands.

One trunk had contained faded daguerreotypes of stiff men and women and sombre children. Another held bolts of cloth which disintegrated as soon as he'd lifted them. Then there were the trunks of belongings from every period. These he could only assume to be a sort of lost and found: wallets, shoes, hats, books of every description, old-style flannel nightwear and nightcaps, hair combs made of ivory, brushes of all kinds with bristles falling out, small black prayer books, and dozens of rosary beads, handbags, and notebooks—the detritus of generations of visitors to the hotel.

"No luck then?" said Kevin as he joined James.

"This last trunk was a bastard. It's taken me ages to go through these papers and now I realize I am looking at receipts and records from the first five years of the house after the O'Donnell family got it back from the nuns. Much too late for our purposes. This may be hopeless, Kevin."

"Perhaps. I know Mary spent many hours up here. She used to repeat some of the stories she'd pieced together from the papers and documents she'd find. I'm so bloody sorry now that I didn't pay closer heed to what she was telling me. What I do remember is that many of her tales were about the period when the house was the asylum."

"Speaking of which, you know I wanted to ascertain that there was no question about this house and property and the line of inheritance. To eliminate any possibility that Breathnach might have come upon some information in his line as a real estate agent."

"Yes, yes. I thought it was a long shot and I was right. Mary's solicitor here in Sligo checked into it for me. The history of the house since the turn of the century is very clear and very legal. The O'Donnell family leased this house and grounds to a French order of nuns, *Les Soeurs des Malades*. The O'Donnells apparently had run into severe financial difficulties and could not maintain the farm. Times were hard for Catholic farmers, for farmers of all kinds. What the records show is that the O'Donnells were determined to hold on to the house, cognizant it had been in the family for hundreds of years. So instead of selling up, they leased it. After

Ireland established its independence, Mary's father succeeded in obtaining a workable mortgage, and some grants from the government available at the time. He approached the nuns who had only two years left of the lease. They had become aware themselves of the changing climate—political and social—and apparently they saw their work was done here. They were willing to let the lease go and it was quickly and legally done.

"O'Brien said the paperwork is all in order. They'd paid something like forty pounds a year, a nominal sum, but the house had survived and that had been the O'Donnells' goal. O'Donnell senior, that's Mary's grandfather, lived long enough to see it return to the family and then promptly died!"

"Hah! Like Moses and the promised land! But what happened to the patients? Did they just turn them out onto the road?"

"No, for God's sake, James, they didn't move out in the night. It took time to relocate the patients, to pack . . . I assume," he added wryly, noting the huge number of boxes that surrounded them. "Shall I give you a hand?"

Together they loosened the straps of yet another wood and iron-bound steamer trunk, the leather crumbling in their hands. The smell of must rose to their faces as they bent in the poor light to view what seemed to be stacks of correspondence. Picking up the yellowing paper James sighed; the ink had faded significantly and it would be hard going to read it. They divvied up the bundles and sat tailor fashion on the bare wooden floorboards and began their perusal.

"Aha!" exclaimed Kevin after a few moments. "James, I think I have it! These dates, they're from 1903 and onward." He waved a sheaf of papers, glancing through them as he spoke. "Yes, 1903, 1907, whoa, 1901. Well, they're not in any order . . ."

James glanced at his stack loosely bound with tape.

"Yes, I see. But . . . yes! They're from that period. Look." He held up a letter written to the local bakery asking, in poorly expressed English, for a reduction in the price of the flour if it were bought in bulk. It was signed "Sister Jeanne."

"Well, that gives some credibility to the diary then . . . the Dunmor girl clearly mentioned a Sister Jeanne who was the head of the home at that time." James read on quickly through the pile but disappointment set in. "All these are, are receipts, look, hundreds of them."

Kevin nodded. "I know. I have the equivalent here. Tradesmen's bills, workmen's bills, bills for feed for the poultry, for hay, for milk, for . . . look . . . for linens from the shop in the town! It's still there, Shea's, on the main street. God, it's like living history."

"This is a receipt for eggs they sold; they must have done some kitchen gardening in their day."

They read on; Kevin in his own way engaged in the continuity of the fabric and history of the family home, James intrigued with the self-sufficiency that the dockets, receipts, and letters indicated. Suddenly the house in which he sat seemed full of activity, of personalities, and he had a strong sense of the strange institution that had operated and survived in a remote spot in a dark and lonely period of Ireland's history.

"These documents make it all come alive," he commented to Kevin who nodded absently. They worked on in silence till at least this one trunk was thoroughly investigated and empty.

"Bloody hell! I've never seen the likes. Not one scrap of real information and yet the whole social history of the asylum is here in our hands, even down to the beeswax candles for the little chapel," said James crossly.

"I know. Another hour lost," said Kevin. "But perhaps it stands to reason. The nuns didn't bother to lug all these receipts back to France and yet they probably didn't feel very confident about destroying them either.

What in the end are you hoping to find?" Kevin asked as they stood up at last.

"I'm not sure, but I think the fact Dunmor was here that weekend, that same weekend Breathnach died, and that perhaps a relative of Dunmor was once a patient here when it was the asylum, might have some significance." James shrugged. "I was hoping to find some actual proof that would verify the journal: dates, documents, medical records perhaps, money must have been paid to keep her here. I wanted something that might indicate also that this Aileen Dunmor was in fact a relative of the present Dunmor family."

"But even if you do, are we any further along? If we prove a connection between Dunmor and this girl, what does it give us? There is still no connection between Dunmor and Breathnach. This long dead girl is hardly the connection, James. James?" Kevin looked questioningly at James who appeared preoccupied.

But James was in a dilemma. When he'd met with Dunmor in Dublin he'd agreed to keep his association with Breathnach confidential, but now with Kevin's trusting face before him he regretted that decision. He wanted to tell him that there was a connection, however slight, between Dunmor and Breathnach. He glanced at Kevin as he piled the papers back in the trunk.

"Listen, Kevin," he said at last, deflecting Kevin's question. "I just want to satisfy my own curiosity about this Dunmor girl. Let me go through all the remaining boxes while I'm here. If I find nothing, perhaps I'll give Dunmor a call and ask him directly. Depending on the outcome, I'll abandon this line of inquiry. Or not!"

Kevin agreed and they parted company.

After further unproductive hours of searching, James made good on his statement and got Dunmor's secretary on the line. He asked to speak directly to Dunmor, and Brendan, in his most fawning manner, explained the difficulties of that very thing. But James heard the fawning and thought not for the first time, how useful it was to be a solicitor.

"But, Brendan, Mr. Dunmor did say I should call him if I needed help?" He let the statement hang.

"Indeed, but you see he's actually with his son, the government minister, at this very moment and I cannot interrupt. Perhaps if you could tell me what it concerns?"

James hesitated for a moment as he fingered Dunmor's card with his private number. Was it that urgent? He considered and decided it wasn't. Brendan could take the message which was simply, could Mr. Dunmor let him know if he was aware of a female relative named Aileen who'd lived around the turn of the century?

"I will of course, but it strikes me as rather a personal question, Mr. Fleming." There was both loyalty and a rebuke in the man's tone that startled James. "Is this an urgent request?"

"No, it's merely information which I need to tie up a loose end."

"I'll have him return your call at your office."

"No, wait, please tell him to call me in Sligo. He'll know the number, I'm sure."

"I place all his calls," said Brendan frostily. James had obviously transgressed and the charming manner was wearing thin.

"Thanks, Brendan, there's no rush on this. . . ." James put the phone down with a feeling of having been bested. After all, what would Dunmor think—busy as he was with affairs of state—of this boneheaded question coming out of the blue? James shrugged. He was glad he'd not phoned Dunmor on his private line; the man would have thought him a nuisance.

After a quick call to Maggie in Dublin, to check on work in progress there, he put down the phone. The afternoon light was fading fast but he was disinclined to return just then to the attics and his bootless research.

He sat and looked out the narrow mullioned window

at the barren hoar-bound field that seem to run on forever to the horizon of blue-hazed mountains. An emptiness swept over him. Perhaps after all he wasn't cut out for country life. He'd often thought he'd prefer it but now, just now, it repelled him. He thought longingly of Dublin, of the hustle and bustle of the office, of his idiosyncratic staff led into the breach by Maggie. He thought of busy streets, of crowded pubs, of, he had to admit it, the fumes of the buses mingling with the odiferous River Liffey and the malt swill from Guinness's brewery.

He lifted the phone again. He wanted to ring someone, anyone, in Dublin. But who? He wanted to hear someone say that he was missed. By whom? He knew. He wanted to hear Sarah Gallagher on the line. He put the receiver back on the old black phone. Even if he had the courage to ring her, after all that had happened, what would he say? "Hello, I'm in Sligo, and the wind and the empty fields and the barren mountains are oppressing me"?

Fresh air, he decided, would blow these cobwebs away and he went out. Heedless of the cold, he turned for the stables and was glad to find that Rory, the big bay, was available. Horse and rider set off together, their moods oddly in tune, and they rode hard and long for upwards of an hour until both were exercised. He turned the horse for home and in so doing, crossed once again the path that led to the small sad graveyard. As before, he tethered the horse and stood contemplating the graves in the twilight.

Aileen Dunmor's baby son must be lying here, he thought grimly. And the thought disturbed him. Here, as he understood it, was the last resting place of the unbaptized babies. Would Aileen have told the nuns she'd baptized her son herself? Would they have thought that valid? He doubted it. There would have been no church ceremony, no record. The "kind" woman would

126

not have known what to do once the baby had died. No doubt the nuns had seen to it the child was buried here. He moved among the mounds, frustrated to think that no marker or stone could tell him where among these pathetic relics lay the baby, Daniel Dunmor. A longing gripped him to know where the child was, a wild longing to have the baby's grave marked. No, not merely marked, but moved. To consecrated ground. He, and only he, knew now that the child had been baptized. The evidence of intent and of action was there in the journal. Surely it was a charge upon him to resolve this unhappy situation.

When Dunmor returned his call, perhaps he could tell him of Aileen's child's fate, as well as of Aileen's—but he was again assuming Dunmor was related. Dunmor was a famous name, a name to conjure with, but it was not an entirely uncommon name. Perhaps, in the end, all of this was coincidence. Just as Breathnach's connection with Dunmor had been coincidence—easily explained and as easily dismissed.

James had wanted to say a prayer, for the people who rested at his feet, but his heart was like a stone in his chest, no feeling came there but cold and pressure. Cold. He suddenly realized how cold he was and with a sudden stab of guilt looked towards the horse he'd ridden so hard and then allowed to grow chilled and stiff. He ran quickly to the beast, rubbing its coat with his arms. Leaping lightly on his back he led the grateful horse in an easy canter back to the stable where he waited and watched as the stable girl rubbed him down and blanketted him. He lay his face against the horse's jowl and felt him nuzzle his ear. "Sorry, old boy. Won't happen again." And as he walked slowly back to the Lodge, with its warm welcoming light streaming from the windows, he wondered at his irresponsibility and the blackness of his mood.

*   *   *

James's mood was not improved by the visit of O'Brien, Madigan's man, who had less than nothing to report in his search for Sandra Murphy. James decided hesitantly to call off the inquiry. It seemed hopeless to find her in this foot-slogging way. He knew that there was the final possibility of advertising in all the national papers as well as the Sligo papers, but he was reluctant to show his hand, both to the murderer and to Inspector Cronin. The latter would instantly realize the trouble he was having in establishing Breathnach's missing wife as a viable alternative suspect.

No one had phoned while he was out and as he stood in Kevin's study he debated with himself. What had seemed like fruitful leads here in Sligo had suddenly evaporated. He longed to have a single direction in which to focus his considerable energies and yet for now the case seemed to him fragmented, spiralling out instead of in.

He snatched up the phone and dialled. Expecting to hear Brendan's voice on the line or even a tape at this late hour, he was pleasantly surprised to get Dunmor himself.

"Fleming! What can I do for you?"

James asked if Brendan had conveyed his message.

"Message?" Dunmor's voice was a blank.

Now that James had to ask him directly, he realized how strange his question might seem. "I spoke to Brendan this morning, Mr. Dunmor. I asked him to relay a question to you . . ."

"Dear me, dear me. Brendan, is it? I'm so sorry that your valuable and billable time"—here he laughed his deep rich laugh—"has been wasted in any way. You see, Brendan left today, on an errand to Brussels. The Minister"—his voice swelled with pride—"keeps a small staff there, to monitor developments at the European Community, gathering information. I'm taking my own calls—until I get a replacement for Brendan."

"I'm sorry to put you to this trouble, at this time."

"What was your question, Fleming?"

"I'm working on Kevin Conlon's case." He waited for Dunmor to get the issue into focus.

"Yes, go on."

Suddenly feeling pressured, James decided to keep his information vague. "In going over some old records here in Sligo we came across the name of an Aileen Dunmor. I was wondering if the name meant anything to you."

"I'm not sure I understand?" said Dunmor. "Is this connected with Conlon's case? Is she involved in some way?"

"No, no." James hesitated. "This person lived actually at the turn of the century and I was struck with the . . . to be frank . . . the coincidence of her name in these records and your presence at the hotel."

"How so?" The man sounded aggrieved.

"I thought there might be some connection, family connection . . ."

"I doubt it, but you've tickled my curiosity. Listen, I had arranged to have drinks with my grandson at Uncle Tom's Cabin tomorrow night . . . sorry . . ." James heard voices in the background. "He can't make it and I relish my quiet drink midweek, away from all this." James could see the amiable face and the large-handed gesture, indicating the crowded anteroom. "If you're in Dublin tomorrow, why don't you join me? We can chat about Conlon's case. I like that young man. I'd like to think I could help you sort things out for him. Who knows? I've got resources at my fingertips, and a network of people to call on . . . sorry . . ." He spoke again.

"Fleming? You there?"

"Yes, and yes. I'd be happy to meet you tomorrow night, say nine-thirty?"

"Cheers." Dunmor was gone, back into the whirlwind of his role as a minor Solomon.

The next day, after an arduous, frustrating drive through the many market towns between Sligo and Dublin, James had the luck to find a parking spot on Dame Street near Dublin Castle and the Registry of Births, Deaths, and Marriages.

Let this be it, he breathed as he wrote out all the details on the form and approached the distraught-looking clerk. People thronged around the office, impatient and irritable. Frantic fathers waved illegible bits of medical scrip at the clerk in a vain effort to register their babies' births. Sombre-looking women in widow's weeds sat more patiently, used to waiting all their lives on errant husbands, and waiting still to get the bit of paper that would perhaps lead to a pension.

An hour later James emerged a deflated man. As the clerk had patiently explained, the fact that there was no record of the birth or death of Daniel Dunmor or of Aileen Dunmor was understandable. He only told James what he already knew and had forgotten in his haste. That the bomb and fire damage which had occurred during the "troubles" in 1921 had destroyed hundreds, nay, thousands of such records where they were housed in the Four Courts along the Dublin Quays. The records for the years James was interested in all had been filed at the Four Courts. The records just didn't exist. That didn't mean the people hadn't lived, or died.

The man's speech was a practiced one, repeated hundreds of times before. He advised James to go to the parish where the parties had lived, or been baptized, or died. Many parish records could supply the information he needed.

As he ran to his car to make it in time to join Madigan for lunch, James considered what the man's words meant.

Everywhere he turned: blind alleys, dead ends. But wasn't the recurrence of so many dead ends in itself important?

Breathnach—a marginal existence, and no trace of his wife or child.

Aileen Dunmor—no record she ever existed, except the words written in her own hand.

Baby Daniel Dunmor—no record of his birth, his baptism, or his death.

Wasn't the very absence of written records of every kind, ancient and modern, significant?—that verification of such ordinarily simple things as who had lived and who had died was missing?

And as he pulled into a parking space along St. Stephen's Green, he pondered. Was there a design in all this that indicated not random chance, not mere coincidence, but a mind actively at work?

Chapter Ten

Madigan waved to James from a window table in the high-ceilinged dining room of the University Club. James hurriedly took his seat as Madigan ordered him a gin and tonic.

"Sorry, Madigan, the traffic on the road from Sligo was a mess. Every pig lorry and flock of sheep from here to Mullingar decided to take to the high road."

"Not to worry," Madigan said easily. "I haven't ordered yet." They raised their glasses of gin and tonic in a toast to their alma mater, and then perused the short menu.

When the elderly waiter approached, tottering on spindly legs as he had done for as long as either diner could remember, Madigan ordered roast beef for both of them.

"There's nothing like a traditional midday meal, a break from the usual haute cuisine. Simple, uncomplicated fare—unlike our lives, heh, Fleming?"

James observed Madigan's sombre mood. He knew from the papers he was embroiled in a very difficult attempted murder trial, and he thought it wise not to inquire how it was progressing.

The potato soup arrived and still they spoke of trivia as James let Madigan set the tone. Together they speculated on how their ancient waiter was still able to convey two brimming soup plates to their table across the crowded dining room without spilling a drop.

"He's been here since I was at College," said Madigan, "and he looks just the same, not a day older."

"Well then, he's looked ninety for the past twenty odd years." James laughed. "Can you imagine the conversations he's overheard in all that time? I'd like to pick his brains some day."

"Always the sleuth, James?"

"Not at all." James reddened.

"Oh, yes. I've noticed this trait before, as I've commented to you. You've got a bit of sleuthing ahead of you now. Firstly I apologize in getting this news to you so late. It's been on my desk for a day or two now but with this other case . . ." He waved his hand as if pushing the matter to one side. "The great thing about my investigators is that they do the obvious first."

James laughed. "That's a valuable asset. For myself, well—I admit I have not been pursuing—all the time—the most obvious line of inquiry in this case. But I do believe I'm making progress. And I want to tell you about it first."

"Go on." Madigan was clearly interested.

Quickly, James gave Madigan the salient details concerning the Lodge's history as an asylum for the "bewildered," and Kevin's recent discovery of the journal. When he mentioned the name of Aileen Dunmor, he had Madigan's complete attention.

"Dunmor himself was at the Lodge that weekend, correct?"

"Yes, but there's more," James continued, confessing that he'd been looking for confirmation of this young Aileen Dunmor's life, of the birth and death of her child, only that morning, but without result.

Madigan shook his head, noting, as James listed them, the stone walls he kept running up against.

"It certainly seems as though it was very important, then or since, to have all records of this poor girl, Aileen Dunmor, and her child, Daniel, expunged."

"Yes, exactly! It's as though she'd never lived, never had that child. . . ."

"I see your point—the lack of evidence seems contrived. And the coincidences are too striking to ignore. On the other hand, some events were beyond anyone's control—the fire at the Four Courts, for example."

"Of course, but whoever is involved would know that as we do, would know those records relevant to this time period were destroyed."

"I agree. Whoever is involved, or was involved I might say, knew that to his own advantage perhaps. Tell me, did you do the obvious? Did you contact Dunmor?" Madigan moving, as he did, in wide political, legal and social circles, which in Dublin constantly overlapped, knew both the man and his power. He waited sombrely for the answer.

"Yes, I did. I've spoken to him on the phone and . . . we are meeting later for a drink." James ended with a flourish.

Madigan was impressed, knowing what Dunmor's schedule was like.

"What did he say on the phone?"

"That he didn't recall any relative of that name. I didn't press him, hoping to get more out of him tonight."

Madigan nodded as he finished his soup.

"Listen, Madigan, there's something else. It has to do with Dunmor, but not with this question of Aileen. But before I begin, I need to explain. What I want to tell you was told to me in confidence. What I need to know is: If I were to tell you in your capacity as a senior barrister, would the seal of confidentiality be broken?"

"Does it pertain to Kevin Conlon's case and Breathnach's murder?" Madigan's courtroom demeanor asserted itself.

"Yes."

Madigan considered for some moments, sipping his gin as they waited for the main course. He lit a thin cigar and watched as the blue smoke curled slowly above his head.

Finally Madigan spoke. "Yes, I believe you can tell me, but first—did you solicit this information or did he volunteer it in general conversation? In other words did he tell you before, or after, he spoke, that he wished you to keep it confidential?"

"It was after, and on that point, I should say that I'd learned the information firstly from his secretary."

"Right then. We're safe, go on and tell me!"

"I hope this isn't anticlimactic . . ."

"Not to worry, tell me anyway."

"Right. Regardless of what Dunmor told the Sligo police in his statement, he did in fact know Breathnach, over a period of years, in Dublin." James related the details.

"Very interesting indeed. On the face of it, his explanation seems sincere, yes? Politically it might have been wise, but legally it was not. You obviously attach some significance to his having known Breathnach, even in this small way."

"Yes, as of now I'm trying to substantiate the connections between Breathnach and Dunmor, between Dunmor and Aileen Dunmor, and Aileen Dunmor and Cromlech Lodge. Either I am not seeing it or . . ."

"You are missing some vital clue?"

"Right first time." James laughed.

"Well, then, let me tell you my news—but I'm not promising it's the vital clue!" They smiled at each other like two schoolboys as the ancient mariner removed their soup plates and swapped them, with grace and aplomb, for full dinner plates, and then tottered away, negotiating the acres of white linen-covered tables.

"While you were in Sligo my man turned up a piece of information at the Registry of Births. In sum"—his voice was animated slightly—"Breathnach and the woman, Sandra Murphy, had a child!"

"I don't believe it," said James. "Or should I say, I can't believe I overlooked this."

"Indeed. It was a daughter, a girl named Mary . . ."

"For God's sake, the single most common name in the country."

"I know, I know, but I've sent the folder on to your office. Have a look at it."

"Is that it?"

"So far. But I thought it was valuable. Is it likely they're both gone out of the country? It doesn't fit the historical pattern. If anything, if the marriage broke down, then Breathnach would have left, and they would have stayed. Even if the mother, Sandra, is dead, then it is still unlikely that the daughter is also dead. Chance is in our favour that one of these women is still in Ireland."

"And neither came forward at the announcement of his death, neither came to the funeral?"

"That's where you come in. I'd like you to find some-one, anyone, who knew Breathnach forty years ago. Someone must remember him or the wife or the child. People don't just disappear without a trace. Not in Ire-land anyway!"

James hesitated. He'd been hoping to follow the Dunmor angle for just a while longer, but he also had no wish to alienate Madigan.

"Right, say no more. Tonight I'll interview Dunmor and with luck resolve this issue of Aileen, and tomorrow I'll get on Breathnach's trail." And with that they fin-ished their meal, gossiping shamelessly about the latest financial scandal to hit one of the major semistate bodies and the lawyers who were involved.

It was exactly half-past nine when James pulled the Citroen into the car park of Uncle Tom's Cabin, the curiously named pub ensconced in the heart of a southside suburb of Dublin. As he emerged from the car he saw Dunmor approaching from across the way. He was a big active man, despite his age, and James saw from his gait that he was fit and spry, with a spring to his step many younger men lost at forty.

"James," was all he said as he grasped his hand warmly. They walked in step towards the side door that led to the gentlemen's saloon bar, furnished with lacquered old barrels for tabletops and hard wooden benches for seats. A few heads turned, nodded to Dunmor and turned back to their drinks.

"This is what I like, my boy," said Dunmor confidentially. He loosened his tie and ran his finger around the collar of his pure white shirt. "People here, they know me, who I am, but over the years they've come to acknowledge that when I'm here I am incognito, so's to speak. They respect my bit of privacy. You know, I talk to people all day long. It's great to get out, get a bit of hush, a few jars. Just feel I'm meself, just plain Danny Dunmor."

James started in his seat, familiar as he was now with the name. "Daniel, is it?"

"Och, one of those stories, you know. My name is, as you all know, Ciaran. But the family, they always called me Danny, my first name, and when I'm off duty, it's the name I use. Feels like the real me." He laughed jovially as was his habitual custom. "What'll ye have?"

They drank their first deep rich pint of Guinness in silence, both in their own way grateful for the hush, as Dunmor had said.

"Now, then, James," said Dunmor as he wiped his

mouth on the back of his hand in the old country way and signalled, almost imperceptibly, for another round. "How can I help you out?"

James briefly sketched in his question, keeping to the minimum of details, sensing this man only dealt with broad outlines of issues—whatever they might be.

"My God, it's a startling coincidence, as you say, James. I had given some thought to the matter after your telephone call but what you are telling me now is most interesting. Sure, Peg, that's my wife, God rest her soul, would have loved this now. And I wish she was here for more reasons than this, I can tell you." He looked suddenly, fleetingly saddened. "Yes, she was a great one for the family tree. She would have been able to tell you straight off if there was an Aileen in our extended family."

James felt a sudden disappointment. "Do you yourself recall anyone of that name? I know it was obviously a very long time ago . . ."

"You forget, my boy, that the past isn't so distant from me as it is from you. I'm almost twice your age! But to answer your question, no, I recall no one of that name, or any mention of her. And now I want you to tell me what this is all about."

For the first time his voice was slightly less cordial and James wondered if he had transgressed too much on the man's obvious good nature. He was uncertain now how to begin but there was little alternative to the truth.

"Mr. Dunmor, I've been chasing down a lot of blind alleys in pursuit of anything that might help Kevin Conlon. In doing so I've been, let's say, reviewing a lot of paperwork pertaining to the history of Cromlech Lodge. Since Breathnach claimed—although I'm not inclined to believe the story—that he wanted to act as an agent to purchase the house and grounds, I was looking for, among other things, something in the history of the house itself, that might have made it, the house, valuable to someone or some group—the man claimed to be acting for a group.''

"A consortium—is that what you mean?"

"Yes. I assume that it was Germans, perhaps French, trying to get a foothold in Ireland a year or two early."

"That's understandable, surely."

"Yes, and believable. It's just that I wondered, why Cromlech Lodge? It is, after all, so intrinsically Irish."

"I see. You feel that wouldn't interest them. But, Fleming, look at the grounds, the extent of them, the views. Who knows, perhaps they'd have a golf course and sports amenities in mind. There are the mountains nearby for hiking and climbing—and the Continentals do love that. And there's great fishing, and no pollution! That's a big point with them, I know. You make the mistake, Fleming, of picturing some summer resort place with swimming and Jacuzzis. The Continentals already have all that on their doorstep in the Mediterranean. Instead, Ireland, Sligo, can offer something different—magnificent dramatic scenery, outdoor sports year-round. Hunting, fishing, clean air and waters, peace and quiet. And there's one more thing! The cromlech that lies on Conlon's land. The Germans especially are interested in our Celtic mysteries—the cromlech, the passage graves in nearby villages, the cairn on Knock-na-Rea."

James considered for a moment. "I take your point. It does make Breathnach's claims more valid when you describe the property as being attractive in those terms. I had even fleetingly thought there was something on the land . . ."

"Buried treasure?" Dunmor laughed amiably and ordered again.

"Well, the equivalent, perhaps some mineral deposits. It's not a field I know anything about."

Dunmor slapped James's knee.

"Listen to me now, James, I'm an old man and I've

learned some simple truths. Look at the whole situation and take the straightest line through it. Cut away the chaff and go with the simplest explanation that will answer all the points. And that will be the truth. You lawyers go in for too much obfuscation. You make things more complicated than they are. Look here: Breathnach is in real estate and says he's fronting for a group of developers. There is no real reason not to accept that at face value. Just because you can't see that developers would be interested doesn't make it less true.''

"Then why Breathnach? Maybe that's what is bothering me.''

"Then turn it around. Ask why *not* Breathnach? Because he wasn't very attractive and still had rough edges to him, hmm? Or that he was a minor player on the real estate scene?''

"Yes, exactly. Why would a European group hire Breathnach?''

"Well, I agree he was a bit player on the scene. But remember, I knew him slightly and I'll tell you, he was ambitious. And he was aggressive—pushy, you know. That's how he came to me. He offered his services. We didn't go looking for him! When you finally do locate the investors involved, they may tell you the same.''

James didn't reveal that they were having trouble doing just that, and remained silent.

"I'm telling you, James. Take the straightest line from A to B and it will be the answer you're looking for.'' He took a deep draught of his pint.

"But if you're right, Dunmor, then it may still put Conlon in a very poor light.''

"Not at all. The police are just taking the easy way out, not the straightest line. If they look at it, they will see eventually that it would be foolish for Conlon to kill Breathnach. What would it achieve? So Breathnach is gone. The investors are still interested. Breathnach was merely the messenger, not the enemy. Listen, Conlon wouldn't kill Breathnach—all he had to do was to say no, to him, to the investors. He's a businessman, for God's sake! He doesn't kill people for asking questions.''

"That's it exactly. I'm glad you state it so clearly . . ." James brightened and took a gulp of his own drink.

"Yes, of course, that is unless Breathnach threatened him. Then there'd be cause, mmm?" Dunmor studied James's face.

"Threatened him? How?"

"Perhaps Breathnach knew something and was using it to pressure Conlon? Perhaps Conlon did indeed take action?"

"Of course not . . . I suppose great pressure, great loss, a great threat can move any of us to do things we don't believe we're capable of. All right . . . But Conlon would have tried other avenues first."

"Exactly. There you go. Your logic is true. I didn't mean to make you doubt your client. I just wanted to force you to put your beliefs on logical grounds, not on grounds of affection! Come, come, drink up and we'll talk of other things."

They chatted about a wide range of subjects, ending up with Dunmor's opinion on a recent hotly contested by-election. James was impressed with the man's political experience, with his description of the machinations and the personalities at work in the famous backroom of politics. As closing time drew near, Dunmor returned to James's original question.

"You know, James, you still didn't identify this Aileen Dunmor. I am curious. What can you tell me about her? Who knows, we might yet discover she's a long-lost relation."

"It's a sad story, I'm afraid, and I think that's why it caught my attention. That and the coincidence of your name. You see this Aileen was a guest, in a sense, at the Lodge, only many, many years ago. I was struck by the coincidence that you also have an association with the Lodge."

"Oh, yes, indeed. I've stayed there a number of times. I'm very fond of Sligo and it's far enough away from Dublin for me to escape the political scene. Go on, I am curious, as I said . . . She too was a guest, perhaps?"

"In a manner of speaking. She was a patient there."

"A patient. I don't understand."

"The Lodge, for a period of years, was a home, as they used to say, for the bewildered."

"What!"

"Just for a while. The house reverted to the family eventually. But anyway, this young woman was there for a little while."

"She was a mental patient!" Dunmor's voice sounded slightly offended.

"It was a long time ago."

"I see. Well, you know, James, Dunmor could have been her married name. At any rate, I don't remember any mentally ill relation in our family." He was abrupt.

"I imagine she only suffered from nerves, you know? The old Victorian description, or the vapours."

"Right. Nerves. I imagine you're right. I seem to recall a cousin who suffered with so-called nerves. They used to send her on long sea voyages. Seemed to be the thing to do."

"Indeed, I've read of that too," James added, and as they chatted briefly about how times had changed for the better, the tension lessened. When they drained their glasses the jovial mood had returned and they walked to their cars amiably enough.

"Well, James, that was a great night. You were a good replacement for my errant grandson. Let's do it again some time?"

With the politician's ease he left that invitation entirely vague. But yet he left his listener warmed, pleased, and, in most cases, flattered.

The next morning, in an effort to trace Breathnach's movements of nearly forty years ago, James decided to start with the obvious: Breathnach's home in Ranelagh, a very old suburb of Dublin. As he searched for the narrow street a slight headache, reminder of the night before and the many pints of Guinness he and Dunmor had enjoyed, furrowed his brow. He squinted in the watery morning light.

Parking the car at last on the short street, he got out and contemplated what had been Breathnach's home for the last thirty-odd years. What was it like, he wondered, to live so long in one place? Since college James had lived in a series of bed-sits, ending finally in the purchase of his current flat. But he didn't see himself living there for the next thirty years, thank God.

This particular house was a modest redbrick three-storey building that sat directly on the pavement. The terraced houses all dated from the late nineteenth century and as a result were solidly built but had no front gardens, and only a small utility yard at the rear. The house was near the end of the row, its blue door solid, its brass knocker now dark from lack of polish.

He knocked loudly at the door to the left of Breathnach's house but there was no reply. He knocked then at the house to its right, only to be met by a very young woman with a baby in her arms. She said she never even spoke to Breathnach, having moved into the neighbourhood only in the last few months, and she couldn't shut the door fast enough in James's face.

He studied the house beside hers. Although all the houses were alike, this had lace curtains at the windows, windows that gleamed in the strengthening light of the morning sun which was burnishing the redbrick walls. He lifted the knocker, which gleamed as well, and waited. A weak voice called through the door and he identified himself. Slowly the door opened to reveal a very elderly, seemingly frail, woman who smiled up at him like a shy child. Nor was she much bigger than a child.

He stepped into the narrow hallway and Mrs. Lanigan led him to the sitting room, a tiny, perfectly square room whose window looked out onto the street he'd just left. James was startled to realize that a mere piece of glass, a single wall, separated all the life and household activity in this row house from the passersby in the street, a mere two feet away. It gave him an eerie sense of lack of privacy and, at the same time, a communion that must somehow exist between that world outside and the life inside.

"I've told the police everything I know," she said softly, when James identified himself. She watched him closely, folding her hands, again like an obedient old-fashioned child.

"I'm sure you did. What I need to know are details, or stories or, well, anything that would tell me the kind of man he was."

She blessed herself. "I knew him near forty year," she said, "and that's a heavy load of stories to tell you." She smiled and James felt ridiculous.

"Sorry. You're quite right."

She smoothed the white hair that framed her small face and pink powdered cheeks, and smiled encouragingly.

"I need to know anything about him from when he first came to live on this road, if you can . . ."

"If I can remember? Mr. Fleming, I can remember the names of the childer I went to national school with better than I can remember your name. When you're as old as I am, the past is ever present to you. These things I can tell you. The police, they only wanted to know what Mr. Breathnach had been doin' in the last few

144

months. I couldn't help them much there." She laughed softly.

"Well, then, perhaps you could just start with when he moved in next door?"

"Let me see, that would've been when my three childer, two girls and a boy, were grown—when Breathnach moved in. Geraldine got married that summer and that's how I can pinpoint the time. There he was, a young man, buying a fine house like this. He kept to himself but with the wedding and all, he would meet us, coming and going at all hours on the road, or here at the door.

"We'd chat. He was friendly . . . in his own way. I used to tease him, you know the like. About him being a single fella, and when was he going to be getting married and putting a wife and family into his fine house. I suppose I went on a bit too much, but we'd had three weddings out of this house in as many years. And I can't tell you how many up and down the road. He wasn't fat then, you see. A big man, running to flesh but not as he was later. And he'd a good job or so he was always boastin'."

"In real estate?"

"Indeed, worked for one of the big firms in town. It was years later he put up his own shingle. Where was I . . . ? Here, let's have a cup of tea. Come."

James followed her to the rear of the house to an equally tiny kitchen. A small sink and a cooker with two rings were on the back wall; a small table, neatly laid, was along another wall. Above the table were shelves, neatly arranged with foodstuffs and dry goods. James marvelled at the fact that five adults had lived here, happily apparently, for he'd taken a liking to the tiny Mrs. Lanigan.

While she boiled the kettle and rinsed the teapot with the water, she resumed her story.

"I'm embarrassed to say this now I'm so much older . . .

and wiser. But I teased Mr. Breathnach. Finally one evening, he'd a bit of drink taken, I was at the front and teasin' about him being single and all." She sighed. "He got a bit stroppy. He said to lay off, that I'd never see him married if I lived to be a thousand, that sort of thing. I was pulled up short, and thought it was the drink taken and said as much. He said he'd been married, that he knew all about it, and it was bloody well not for him. I was shocked. I didn't know where to look. Joe, my husband, God rest his soul, came out and there were words. He'd heard us squabbling. Well, after that we barely spoke. Mr. Fleming, thirty-five year living on the same road and not speaking. It bothered me, I can tell you. He'd look through me . . ."

"But why?"

"I don't know. But I guessed that he was sorry that he'd ever told me he'd been married. Except I saw him every day and knew he was a decent enough sort, I would have thought he'd murthered his own wife."

"Oh, God," James exclaimed.

"I'm not saying that he did, Mr. Fleming." She was startled at James's reaction.

"I know, it just seemed like another avenue of inquiry opening up. Listen to me now, did he ever mention a child?"

"No, nor did I ask. Wait, wait. Once, years ago, my daughter Kathy was here with her five childer. They were racketting around and Breathnach came out, looking the worse for drink and he complained over the noise. Well, Kathy now, she's a bit of a wench if I do say so meself. She goes and knocks on his door and there's a row when he opens it. She tells him to mind his own business, kids'll be kids, that kind of thing."

James closed his eyes trying to picture this road, this tiny house, crowded with children of a summer's eve. "Go on."

"She says if he'd had any himself he wouldn't be so

hard on them. She has a mouth, I can tell you! So finally he's shouting over her and says he'd had one week of a squallin' brat and that was enough for a lifetime and he hasn't to put up with someone else's bloody snot-nosed kids when he chose not to have any around himself or something like that. He slammed the door in her face and the knocker caught her off the nose. There was pandemonium and no mistake. Thank heavens Joe was passed on by then or there would have been a murder and I tell no lie.''

James marvelled at the sweet diminutive woman before him, a picture of a granny, and he reflected on the life she'd led. Unconsciously he shrugged.

She smiled. "Things they are quieter now. Not so many childer on the road. Lots of young couples who buy in here and then move on, out and up, as they say. Do you happen to know who'll be moving into his house?''

"I haven't an idea," said James.

"It's a hard thing to see a house standin' empty. Too quiet. He was quiet, you know, but still I knew he was there. He'd a woman there now and then." She glanced down. "I didn't blame him, you know. At least there was life . . .''

"Mrs. Lanigan, what you've told me has been very helpful. We had an idea of a wife and a child in his past, but you've substantiated all that for us.''

The elderly woman beamed. "You know, Mr. Fleming, I did keep his secret. Apart from Joe, you're the only livin' soul I ever told about what he'd said. I knew he'd only said it in the heat of the moment.''

"So you don't think I'll learn any more from the other neighbours?" asked James.

"I wouldn't say that, but I'll tell you, the only other people who are still here who were also here when Breathnach moved in are the O'Boyles down the corner and they rarely mixed. And Mr. Truro across the road.

He's home now. I can see him behind his curtain there. He's been watching your fine car for an hour or more!'' She laughed as she saw James to the door, and then waved to the invisible Mr. Truro.

James strolled across the tiny road and before he could knock, Mr. Truro, as old as Mrs. Lanigan, threw open the door. They chatted amiably on the step and James got straight to the point. And was rewarded with the information that Breathnach had once told him that he'd lived in Crumlin near the Submarine Pub before moving to Ranelagh.

As James waved to both elderly people, sheltering in their doorways, each preparing to eat a lonely meal and watch a bit of telly, he sighed.

Turning the car for home he realized that only their surroundings differentiated their situations. He too often ate a lonely tea and watched a bit of telly—in a flat that would hold the entire ground floor of Mrs. Lanigan's little house. And at that, there was no friendly neighbour across the road, or even across the hall, who would wave to James, who would even know whether he was at home or not, or had a woman or not, or was alive or not.

He reversed his direction and headed the car for the home of his oldest friend. At least this particular night he wouldn't be eating and drinking alone.

Chapter Eleven

When James rang Matt from his car phone he was only too glad to accept James's offer to take him out for a drink. As James pulled the Citroen up at the neat semidetached house on the north side of the Liffey, the front door flew open and Matt's four children poured out; three boys between four and eight, and a dote of girl of three, toddling on fat legs and blackened feet down the path after her faster brothers. When James emerged from the car they hugged his legs and expertly distracted him so that they achieved their goal of entering the pristine interior of "Uncle" James's flash car. Torn between defending his car from sticky fingers and runny noses, and squeezing the fat baby girl clinging to his ankle, he relented and picked her up, covering her fat rosy cheeks with kisses.

"It's all a plot, Fleming," roared Matt from the doorway, wiping his hands on a tea towel and running a broken-toothed comb through his thick brown hair.

"How so?" called James as he walked up the path, speaking through a fretwork of fat fingers that were plucking at his cheeks and attempting to check his teeth.

"See for yourself, you're here barely a minute and you've a baby in your arms. It's Dorothy's method—don't you see?—to convince you of what you're missing."

"That's right, James," laughingly agreed the black-haired Dorothy coming up behind Matt and surreptitiously handing him his wallet. "It's high time you got married."

The boys ran up in time to hear the last word and then began a chorus of "Uncle James is gettin' married," dancing around him and laughing. James extracted some pound notes and handed them freely around and they went off distracted with their wealth. But the rosy cheeked girl was not so easily dismissed.

"See, James," said Dorothy, making no effort to rescue him from the baby's fingers now entwined in his hair and moving towards his interesting tie. "She hardly knows you and she likes you. Normally she makes strange with men, but she senses you have a taking way with you."

"Well, I wish some of the women in my life thought so." He looked the baby in her deep navy blue eyes. "Tell me the secret of my charm," he whispered.

"You'd make a great father, James," said Dorothy, her sparkling blue eyes serious.

"Based on what, I'd like to know!" roared Matt yet again, as he tucked a voluminous striped shirt into his sagging waistband. "He thinks you just have to throw money or kisses at the little nose-rags and they'll keep for another day."

"Matt!" shouted Dorothy and James in unison, shocked at his characterization of the children. Silence descended and James handed the baby to Dorothy. "Where's my godson, then?" he said, looking at the three boys clearly in view.

"Forgot again, Fleming? Pick one, any one, since you never know which is yours," said Matt, but kindly. "Pat, come here to your hopeless godfather." James patted the six-year-old on the head and handed him a five-pound note. The boy's eyes widened at this additional fortune and he reached up sweetly to hug James.

"I really should come more often," said James softly.

"Right, and I know pigs might fly. Come on with ye then, I've a thirst on me tonight. Can't even remember the taste of Arthur Guinness's finest brew." He bustled to the door, escaping Dorothy's dirty look.

"You are a bad influence, James," called Dorothy. "Just be careful, won't you?" She waved anxiously and watched them as they drove off into the early evening.

"Christ, what a car, Fleming. I could pay my mortgage with this."

James laughed as he shifted gear. "I'll trade you the car for that little girl of yours," he added.

"Nope, no takers there. You'll have to have one of your own, if you're not too old, that is."

"Jaysus, Matt, don't rub it in."

"Well, then, tell me what this one evening escape-away holiday is in aid of. Not that I'm not delighted to get out for a pint in the middle of the week. Christ, that bloody school is driving me spare. See, I even talk like those bloody teenagers. I don't mind the mohawks, or the earrings, but these nose rings. I draw the line at that. But the Head is ambivalent and the kids are getting mixed messages. Of course," he said, sighing heavily, "there are more serious issues. The drugs, now. But I see the nose rings as the tip of the notorious iceberg."

James listened intently as Matt told him about his concerns and recent events at the large secondary school of which, James knew, he was a committed, creative, and vital vice head.

"Enough of me. Bring me up to speed or snuff or whatever the trendy expression is this week. Where the hell are we going anyway?" They'd been driving awhile and had yet to visit a pub.

"You will be thrilled, my friend, after all these years, to learn that I am bringing you in on a case." James's tone was mockingly serious.

"No!" exclaimed Matt. "You mean my virtue is rewarded. All these years of listening to you discuss cases about people whose names I never knew. I don't believe it. Not Mr. Stick-to-the-Rule-Book."

James reddened. "Am I really that rigid?"

"Rigid isn't the word, Fleming. I'll say this though. Since school days you've played it all according to the book. That's okay—your friends, those that are left, still like you."

James laughed. "I've bent the rules along the way. I just don't always talk about it." As they drew closer to the Submarine Pub, James explained to Matt that he was tracing the movements of Breathnach, his wife, Sandra, and their child; events that dated forty years back. And he summarized his visit with Mrs. Lanigan.

"I got this lead from her and her neighbour when I visited in Ranelagh this afternoon. I really don't know what to expect tonight. The trail might be cold . . . here we are then." They pulled along the curb and James looked over the deserted area, the road littered with glass.

"I'm dubious about the car," Matt said. "Apparently we are going sleuthing in here, yes?"

"Ah, I can't always be worrying about the car," said James, in an attempt to prove he was less than rigid, and he affected a nonchalance he did not feel. Matt was impressed.

They entered the enormous lounge-bar built on different levels and bathed in a red hue that emanated from the rugs, carpeting, indirect lighting, banquettes. Music pounded from some obscure source, blending with the vivid reds to produce a sensory experience making one feel it was already three o'clock in the morning. Two television sets were running a rugby game on videotape and, incongruous as it seemed, a jukebox blared its selections underneath the piped music. James waved Matt towards the bar as they were immediately separated by the arrival behind them of a large boisterous group of young men and women. But they found two seats at the bar and James undid his tie and put it in his pocket.

"I need to ask the barman some questions. I'm not optimistic but if I get the right guy I'll pretend that we are some relations of Breathnach. You're my brother, right?"

Matt was amused at this role-playing and only too willing. He was reminded of their college days when he and James had done quite a few wild things in the environs of numerous Dublin public houses. Somehow the dozen years since just dropped away.

In a surprising lull in the noise, James got the barman's attention. No easy task, given the number of patrons howling orders at the bar.

"Did you ever know a man named Breathnach?" asked James directly.

"Means nothin' to me," said the man. "When would it be?"

"Forty years ago, perhaps thirty-five?"

"Are you mad, man, whadda I look like? I was in nappies at me ma's knee forty years ago. You want that man there." His head nodded at an elderly man, apparently deaf to the noise and activity, who was patiently and efficiently drying pint glasses with a gleaming white linen cloth. "Bit of a character, mind you," said the barman who was off to serve an order for three pints, two glasses, a Dubonnet and red, a snowball, a vodka and white, a hot port with lemon, and a glass of milk. He remembered this order at the first go, and questioned only the glass of milk.

"Hope this old fool's memory is as good as that," whispered Matt loudly.

James waved and finally yelled until he got the man's attention.

"Can't serve ye, sir," shouted the old man. It was some time before James's agitation finally drew the man to where he was within earshot.

He leaned over the bar and listened patiently to James's question. He nodded seriously.

"Yes, sir, if you mean the fella that died up in Sligo?" James nodded enthusiastically.

"I saw the notice on the paper. The *Herald* it were. I read the death notices every day you see, at my age." His unlined face belied his age, but his trembling, veined hands revealed it. He went to speak to the barman, dutifully requesting his five-minute break from washing and drying the hundreds of glasses, and then he returned to James.

"This is my brother," shouted James, and Matt nodded kindly, stifling a smile. They no more looked like brothers, than . . . well, many brothers. He started to laugh and stopped as James glanced at him.

"I knew him many year ago. He lived local and came in every night. Who's askin, if I can be so bold?" The old man raised his eyebrows.

"We're his cousins, on our grandmother's side." The old man's small eyes scanned James's suit jacket and the quality of the white shirt and then looked at him in the face. "Guess since he's dead, nothin' I say can harm him." His voice said clearly he didn't believe James was any cousin of Breathnach's.

"Do you remember his wife too?"

The old man looked at him sharply. "So you know about her. Then you must be a relation. 'Twas strange now, was it not?"

James went along with it. "Indeed, from what the family used to say. But it's years now. Can you tell me where she is?"

"Sure I'm a barman, not the department of missing

persons. Anyway, wouldn't his own family bloody well know what the story was?"

"But they're all dead, you see," Matt blurted out, looking like a dog who had lost its master. "There's only us left. Won't you have a drink with us on your break? I can't remember now what the Ma told us." The old man relaxed and poured himself a whiskey and took Matt's money without a glance at James.

"I'm sorry to hear it. It's hard, isn't it, when there's no one left. My sympathies." The old man lifted his glass and Matt joined him. "To absent friends," said Matt, elbowing James to lift his drink.

"Ah, well. Let me see, it's a long time now but the name in the death notice reminded me. It was a strange little tale. He came in regular like. Drank stout only. Was a big man and then ran to fat; the stout helped that surely." He laughed and finally included James in his glance. "One night he brought the wife. Since he'd never mentioned her to me before I was a wee bit surprised but not much."

"Because you weren't truly friends?" Matt stated matter-of-factly.

"Yes and no. Yes, all kinds of people talk about all kinds of things. It goes in one ear and out another. I don't see them as friends but as good customers." He sipped his drink and glanced at the mounting glasses and shrugged. "I'm not as fast as I was in those days at the serving, so I do the washing now. Keeps me busy. Where was I?"

"How you weren't surprised . . ."

"Right, well, they sat at a table, not at the bar. And when he introduced the missus I realized why he'd not said much about the marriage, since it was fairly recent. You see she was expectin' a child."

Matt smirked. "Oh, I see. A shotgun wedding you're saying."

"Indeed. And like so many of those it didn't last.

Over the months he'd come in alone or with her. They didn't look very happy. And later, I asked him about the baby. He told me when it was born—at home, it turned out. A local woman helped out. They lived in a flat hereabouts. It was a warren of old flats then. He didn't like the cryin', he said. And then he didn't mention the baby and it turned out she'd left him. Took the baby and left him. He seemed bitter. And after that never mentioned either of them again, and I didn't either. Some years later he moved away. Came in once or twice after, when he was showing a property round here."

"So you can't tell us where we might find our cousin, Mrs. Breathnach, or our cousin the little . . ."

"Girl it was. No, I can't. But no doubt the family told ye she went on to Galway?" He looked curious.

James joined in at this point, saying he remembered being told by the relatives that little Mary and her mother had gone on to Galway. The old man had nothing more to add and declining James's offer of a drink, he returned in his disciplined way to the stack of glasses and the glares of the younger barman.

James and Matt withdrew to a nearby rickety table against the far wall. The noise was less here, muffled by the wall against which they leaned.

James smiled at Matt. "Well, Watson, I didn't expect you to actively participate, but I'm glad you did."

"My pleasure, Sherlock. It was clear he wasn't taking to you. You lack the common touch, James—you always did."

"Then you're mighty common." James laughed. "He took to you straightaway."

Matt waved his hand as though rubbing a blackboard clean and getting on with the next part of the lesson. "Did you learn anything useful to you?"

"Yes, firstly, it confirms what I knew—Breathnach's marriage was brief and he didn't seem involved in the child at all. It also confirms that the child was a girl. The other thing is that we have a lead to Galway. That's news to me anyway. Although Mrs. Breathnach came from Sligo, she must have had some connection with Galway. So . . .'' He sighed. "It's a new lead.''

"Leading you by the nose, I'm thinkin'.''

"Well, it will have to be followed up.''

"How about the child being born at home? Anything there?''

"Trying to find a midwife from forty years ago? Someone who probably wasn't even registered, was a good friend perhaps to the woman?''

"Hopeless, I agree. What do you make of Breathnach's whole attitude towards this woman and the baby?''

"I don't know yet. Why! Did something strike you?'' James was hopeful.

"Indeed, it did. Listen, from what you've told me here about what the neighbour said, the elderly woman . . .''

"Mrs. Lanigan, yes . . .''

"Her story jibes with this one. Not only was he bitter years later about the baby—a baby he claimed he knew for a week, but he was also bitter at the time. Don't you see a connection?''

"Not yet.''

"He wasn't just bitter years later because his wife left and took the baby. That would be understandable. He was bitter from the start.''

"I see. He doesn't mention his marriage, at least to this barman he saw frequently. She's pregnant very early in the marriage, if we can believe this old guy's memory. Perhaps we can assume he felt he had to marry her. Then the baby's born and she's gone with it . . .''

"Exactly, he married her for the duration of the pregnancy and birth. Enough to save her good name,'' added Matt.

"And the baby gets a legitimate name too," said James.

"Of course, but doesn't something strike you?"

"Just that he did his duty, albeit begrudgingly. But he did it."

"Yes, but the baby, James? We have two people inferring from Breathnach's own words at the time that the baby didn't mean a thing to him?"

"Yes . . ." said James slowly.

"Well, he was decent enough to marry her, wasn't he?"

"Yes, I'm not saying the poor man was all bad," James reflected.

"No, he wasn't. But still he has no feeling at all for the child? That's my point. I tell you, James, because I've seen it often enough over the years I've been teaching. Look, Breathnach marries to give the child a name, his name. Right? But then he loses interest at some point. No sadness the child is gone, only bitterness."

"Don't keep me in suspense, man."

"I suspect that the child wasn't his." Matt slammed his empty glass on the table for emphasis.

"Let me order and think about it," said James soberly. He was gone a good ten minutes, standing in the surge of thirsty drinkers. But on his return his face was animated. "I give you credit, Matt. Your theory explains a lot of the small puzzling details of Breathnach's early life. But if it's true, then it means that someone else was the father of Sandra Murphy Breathnach's baby. The trouble is, I don't know if this is going to be a significant detail in the whole picture, or if it is yet another dead end . . ." James's expression darkened.

"Well, perhaps a good night's sleep will help." Matt glanced at his watch. "To change the subject slightly, Fleming. If I don't ask you, Dorothy will kill me. How the blazes did you get involved with this case in Sligo?"

James told him about his Halloween weekend, the drafting of Kevin's will, and the death of Breathnach.

"My God, man, does confusion precede and follow you wherever you go? You're staying at a famous five-star lodge—you lucky bastard—compliments of the management, no less. Within moments of your arrival there's a murder . . ."

"It looked like a heart attack, Matt," said James ruefully.

Matt waved his hand. "A murder within minutes. And then you are up to your neck again . . ."

"It was pure happenstance that I was there at the time!"

"Doesn't this strike you, James? This predilection for disaster?"

"What strikes me is that Ireland is a mighty small place."

Chapter Twelve

Once again James found himself in his Citroen on the increasingly familiar road to Sligo. But this time his mood was more sombre, the excitement and exertion of the last forty-eight hours turning to fatigue and a sense of uneasiness. The day suited his mood, the sky low and leaden, with no wind to stir the dead stillness of the frozen landscape.

As the cities and towns fell behind him and the stretches between villages became longer, he let his eyes roam the lonely fields. He would have thought it all a setting straight from the pages of Thomas Hardy but for the numerous ruins that made it ineluctably Irish. Celtic crosses rose up on the barren hillsides like lichen-covered signposts pointing west. Here and there over the many miles he travelled were the remains not just of humble cottages, but of noble houses, once great manors. Moss-covered gates to what had once been a virtual castle stood as the last remaining witness to a great and storied past. Even simple crossroads seemed unnerving in the silent emptiness of the land. James tried to retrieve stories of village dances, held at such crossroads in the past, where matches were made and lives begun, but he kept recalling instead the stories of those who were hanged at crossroads, their bodies buried there as the final ignominy, the final warning to passersby. Stray threads of Celtic mythological stories came to mind, stories of phantom hounds, of ghostly warriors astride their horses, thundering across the rugged Sligo and Donegal landscapes, stories of warriors buried in the ground vertically, so as to be ready for the final call to battle. He shivered, realizing this almost surreal and mystical landscape sprang from the poetry of Yeats and he knew then he had a need of another, less laden vision.

"Perhaps," he said aloud, "things aren't as grim as they seem." He recalled his morning visit with Madigan. Robed and wigged for court, Madigan had stated peremptorily that the Aileen Dunmor lead had come to a natural close. Ciaran Dunmor, he felt, had been more than gracious to James. Madigan was more interested in the information James had gleaned from Breathnach's neighbours and the old barman. He'd liked James's version of Matt's idea that the child born to Breathnach might not have been his own. The woman whom he'd married, who had borne a child, and who had left him, was from Sligo. Madigan saw Sligo as the most fruitful lead to pursue.

James wanted to add that it was the only bloody lead they had, but instead he agreed with Madigan that indeed the trail in Dublin had grown cold.

"For Christ's sake," said James aloud as he shifted gears, approaching a long slow climb, the last before he reached Sligo, "Breathnach was killed in Sligo. The answer has got to be here. The killer must be connected to Sligo in some way, which would explain—neatly of course—why he was murdered here!"

As he parked the car in the Lodge's car park he was glad, for once, to climb out of his Citroen. This is it, he murmured. Dogged spadework had paid off before, and it would again.

"Back again, are you?" said Kevin smiling warmly as he finally joined James at his table during the evening meal. He'd been on business in the town when James arrived. "You'll be lonely, I'm afraid. There are only three guests staying at the Lodge besides yourself."

"And they are . . . ?" said James, shovelling some tender shredded cabbage in olive oil and garlic into his mouth.

"There's an Australian couple on an extended honeymoon. Young energetic pair, they're hardly ever in. Quite wealthy to judge from their clothes and conversation. And an American salesman who's over to talk with the pharmaceutical company here on the edge of the town. With his expense account he can afford our rates."

"Nice for him."

"Good for me." Kevin fiddled with the cutlery on the white linen cloth. "How did you get on in Dublin then?" His look was anxious.

As they shared a pot of tea, James briefly recounted the outcome of his interviews with the now less alluring Rosemary Morris and with Dunmor. James was relieved Kevin's mood was light, despite all, and they both enjoyed some slices of apple tart swimming in cream from the local dairy. After a pot of tea, James felt revived, ready for what lay ahead.

"Considering any of the guests from that weekend as suspects in the murder is a dead end, I'm afraid, Kevin. When I first came in on this, it seemed so perfect, so pat. The victim and the dozen suspects all closeted together for a Halloween weekend! But now I'm convinced they had no connection with the events here." James was feeling expansive as he stretched out in his chair.

162

"When I was in Dublin, on Madigan's suggestion, I did some background work on Breathnach's early life. We knew that he was married, but we've found that he had a child, and that the marriage apparently broke up after the birth of that child. What emerges is that he was bitter about these events!"

Kevin was startled. "But surely this was years ago. And you yourself gave up looking for Breathnach's wife! Are you starting in on that wild-goose chase again?" Kevin threw down the cutlery and leaned back in his chair.

"No, not necessarily. But I do want to concentrate on Sligo, on people close to the Lodge, people who would know the layout of the Lodge and the routine here, someone from this area perhaps, whom Breathnach had come to meet that weekend. I want to start with your staff . . ." He waved his hand as Kevin began to take umbrage. "Not so much your staff at present, Kevin, although I must eliminate them too as suspects. No, I want to look at everyone who's worked here. With the long history of this lodging house, a lot of staff have passed through here—perhaps one of them knew Breathnach or his wife or his child, perhaps one of them had a motive to see him dead. To get to the point, I'd like access to your employment records."

"You can have access to them, James," said Kevin shrugging, "but they're not particularly orderly. There's fifty years' worth, and they're in every sort of condition. The O'Donnells kept everything! And so have I."

"Speaking of keeping things . . . where might you have left that journal we found?"

"It's in the floor safe, in the office, under the carpet. It seemed so old and fragile I felt it was better off there, out of harm's way."

"Good. Keep it there please, and let no one look at it. Now, I'd like to get started."

Although Kevin was doubtful about James's latest approach to his case, he led the way through a small door at the rear of his office to a smaller windowless room.

"A secret room?" queried James. "No windows to the outside."

"Mmm, we thought it strange too. It dates way, way back. We thought it perhaps was a priest's hole but it's too near the original front of the house. It had to have some hidden meaning though. Who'd want a study with no view!"

"Storage—of valuables, perhaps."

"Again, too near the front. Perhaps we'll never know, like so many things about this strange house. It seems positively eerie to me of late."

"With a murder, Kevin, that's understandable."

"There's something I haven't told you."

James was struck by Kevin's tone. "What?"

"Two nights ago, we had a break-in of sorts."

"What! And you didn't let me know!" squawked James.

"I know, I know. But nothing was taken. It looked as though someone broke in at the rear door, off the yard, but when he came to the old grillwork door he was thwarted. It's iron, you see, couldn't even bend it. We checked the rest of the doors thoroughly and there was no sign of any other attempt. Perhaps he gave up or was scared off . . ." Kevin looked warily at James. "I didn't report the burglary."

"Not wise, Kevin," said James, but he left it at that, since he, like Kevin, did not wish to draw Inspector Cronin's attention to themselves at this juncture.

Kevin scrutinized the old wooden file boxes and the more modern metal cabinets, finally settling on one. "You could probably start here. The older wooden boxes are from Mary's parents' time, if not before. You'll see some of the drawers contain the guests' registration cards. The registers, by the way, are in those stacks by the wall. They date from twenty years ago when Mary and I took over. There are others as well, in those cartons. Now, in some of these same drawers are the cards for employment." He pulled one out at random. "Here we are: Pat O'Driscoll, aged sixty-seven, Sligo Town, chambermaid, nineteen-twenty-five; employment terminated, nineteen-twenty-seven. Duties: cleaning out the fireplaces and laying the fires on the ground floor. I tell you, James, I'm learning more about this place in a few weeks than I did in the last ten years. Look, here's another. Joseph Patrick Boyle, Roney Point, Wexford, summer transient, nineteen-twenty-seven, stable hand. Well, there you go, James. I'd say there's a year's work ahead of you." His tone was dry.

"There will be if I stop to read every card and speculate on the story that it tells." James smiled.

"But that's what you'll have to do?"

"I tell you, my gut feeling is that I'll know it when I see it—if it's there. Now, where are the records for the current staff?"

Kevin indicated the metal cabinet and murmuring that he'd stake his life on his staff, left James to his work.

James in fact relished the kind of patient dogged effort that lay ahead of him. Taking out his eyeglasses and polishing them on his tie, he set them on the tip of his nose, pulled a chair up to the ancient rolltop desk, and began.

The recent employment cards were at the front of the narrow metal drawer. All was in order: all the information neatly printed in a variety of inks and hands. He found Sean's card immediately; on it was the appropriate information for his social insurance, and the contributions to medical coverage, the amount of his salary, his rises in pay over the years. Caitlin, too, and her brothers, were there, listed as casual help. There were notes on work permits for the two French students who'd worked as maids in the summer just past. And there were additional cards for other seasonal help. Mrs.

O.'s card was at the rear of this stack that represented all the employees for that calendar year. Idly, he wondered, as he turned the card over, at her age. Sixty-one. He was surprised as she seemed ten years younger. Her salary was decent, he noted. Kevin obviously appreciated her years of dedication and her sundry skills.

He smiled as he replaced it, thinking how lucky each of them was, to have the other. Sandra O'Neil. He lifted the card out a second time, realizing that her name had struck him only after the fact. Sandra. As in Sandra Murphy? He sat back, considering. At no time had he ever heard anyone refer to her as Sandra. He tapped the card with his fingertips. It was a strange coincidence. Kevin had not remarked on the name at any time. But why would he? James set the card aside and moved on, examining the last five years of employee records, but preoccupied at all times by the name of Sandra.

He looked at his watch. Nearly eleven. Pocketing Mrs. O.'s card, he carefully closed everything, quenched the lights and hustled to the snug for a night cap.

"Just drawing a pint," said Kevin, "join me."

"Indeed and I will."

They sat companionably at the bar and James came to the point.

"In looking at the cards I see that Mrs. O.'s Christian name is Sandra," he said mildly.

"Mmm. I know. Well, I ought to, I fill out a dozen government forms a year on my staff. The bloody bureaucracy drives me crazy."

"Does no one call her Sandra?"

"Not to my knowledge." Kevin laughed. "She's Mrs. O. to everyone. If you asked me quick I don't think I could have told you her name." Kevin took a deep draught.

"She lives in the hotel, yes?"

"Yes, in the staff wing. Sean's there too. In the sum-

mer all the staff rooms are full. She has a nice bed-sit.
It's her home, you see. She's lived here for as long as
I can remember."

"Before your time?"

"Yes, of course, since the O'Donnells. That's how
she knows so much about the house."

"What about Mr. O'Neil?"

"I've no idea. Perhaps he died. Mary said she'd never
met him and Mary knew her since a child."

"And she's from Sligo?"

"Mmm, local like the O'Donnells. Why all the
questions?"

James paused for a moment, reflecting.

"Just curious. I know so little about the people here.
Listen, do you think it's a courtesy title, that she's really
Miss O'Neil but as she aged she adopted it?"

"Or people assumed it? No, somehow on the fringe
of my memory I do believe I was told she was married,
however long ago. It's not really something I could ask
her, you know!"

"Right," said James, satisfied for the moment, "now,
let me have another of your excellent pints!"

Early the next morning, James rang Maggie and having talked to her at some length about the McEvoy pro-
bate case that had come to the fore in recent days, he
asked that she send one of his clerks to the Registry
Office.

"Sounds like this whole Conlon case is taking place
there," cracked Maggie. "If you're not there standing
in line, then one of us is . . ."

"How perceptive," said James, realizing the truth of
her comment.

"Who are we looking for this time?"

"A marriage certificate. For one Sandra O'Neil,
O'Neil being the married name. I've no maiden name
as yet. She's from Sligo, she's sixty-one now, so that

should narrow the field. Get back to me today please," added James.

"Your wish is our command, James. Enjoy your vacation."

"Very funny, Maggie." James laughed wryly as she rang off.

The morning passed quickly as James pored over the records, year after year, yet little emerged. Nonetheless he rewarded himself with a break for a lunch of fresh brown bread, sharp Irish cheddar, Limerick ham, sweet butter, and more apple tart. After his feast he took a brisk walk, considering fleetingly that perhaps he'd take up jogging and then dismissing the notion just as quickly.

Back at the Lodge, he continued his search of the records, marvelling at how many foreign students had worked as casual labourers. By three he was surprised not to have heard from Maggie. It was routine surely that the clerk verify Mrs. O.'s marriage. Common sense told him it would be a simple matter to ask her about her husband, but courtesy at least at this stage prevented him.

A shout from Kevin broke his train of thought. There was a call for him. Maggie.

"How's she cuttin'?" said Maggie brightly, adopting a broad country accent in her use of the colloquial greeting.

"What news, Maggie?" James ignored her teasing.

"Well, the clerk spent a good portion of her day looking for your information and, in a nutshell, could not get what you wanted."

Maggie was being discreet over the phone, as always.

"Nothing? No certificate?"

"No . . . so, any further instruction?"

"On this matter, no, not at the moment." He rang off, lost in thought.

At last, putting slips of paper in the drawers he'd already examined, he crossed the room to the much older files. Just to be sure he started his search at an even fifty years earlier.

These small dog-eared cards were harder to read, the ink faded and the content much less complete. Government regulations had been vaguer then, and labour laws, and tax laws. On the other hand there were fewer cards for each year. A smaller staff, he knew, and less of a turnover of employees. The entries were simpler: names; birthdates, sometimes; description of job or type of work; dates of leaving employ.

He had worked quickly through ten years of cards when Kevin joined him.

"Are you knocking off work at five?" he said amiably.

"You don't believe much in what I'm pursuing, do you, Conlon?" asked James, though his tone was light.

"Yes and no. At this point I'm willing to go with any idea. But I was wondering if you'd join me in a preprandial drink. You might even like to take your meal in the snug if we don't open the dining room."

"What about the others?"

"Your three comrades in arms are out tonight—told me this morning."

"I'll join you soon," said James. "Let me put in another hour, then I'll find you."

He went on to the next drawer, where the cards were in no particular order. The names in some cases were at the bottom or at the top, and usually written as one would sign one's name. He clearly remembered Kevin saying Mrs. O. had come there as a young girl. Given her age, she would have been a contemporary of Mr. O'Donnell, Mary's father and Kevin's father-in-law.

He looked again at the dates and notations. Yes, O'Donnell senior would have been in charge during the period he was researching. He glanced at his watch with tired eyes. He'd finish with this drawer and take a welcome break. It was at that moment his eyes fell on the next card, the name Sandra leaping off the faded paper. He hesitated for a split second, holding his eyes on the first name, blinking before he allowed himself to look at the surname. Murphy. The name of Murphy sat there, linked to the name of Sandra. He read: Sandra Murphy. High Street, Sligo Town. The date indicated it was forty-three long years ago. He looked at the birth date and did a quick calculation. Sandra Murphy would have been eighteen when she first came to the Lodge.

James felt the muscles in his body grow taut. Taking the card he laid it carefully on the desk, bending the lamp over it. Delaying, delaying, he placed the drawer back in its vacant hole in the wooden case. He adjusted the lamp. He cleared his throat. He removed the more recent employment card from his breast pocket where he'd put it the night before. He placed the two cards side by side, under the lamp, finally comparing them.

He closed his eyes briefly and opened them again. He felt a thrill well within him: the birth dates on both cards were the same.

Kevin looked up from the bar where he was reading a trade magazine.

"A drink, James? Looks like you need it."

"Thanks, I'll have a Hennessy. And it's my twist, you know."

"Rubbish. Your visit here is on the house."

"Perhaps the room and board, Conlon, but I can pay for the rest." His voice was irritable and Kevin let the issue drop.

"Any progress?"

"I'm not sure, but I'd like a change of subject for a while."

"Well, I've taken the liberty of ordering your meal for you. Since it's just the two of us. Speak of the devil . . ."

Kevin sprinted around the bar to take the heavily laden tray from Mrs. O.'s hands. As he lifted off the aluminum covers the appetizing aroma of bacon and sausages, and black and white pudding, filled the air, mixing with the steaming scent of hashed potatoes and of eggs fried to perfection. Mrs. O. returned with a second tray laden with a pot of tea, warm scones and soda bread, crockery jars of jam and butter, and a bowl of baked beans in tomato sauce. She smiled benignly.

"You're like two great schoolboys with your feast." She laughed as Kevin smacked his lips theatrically.

"What are you waiting for, Fleming?" Kevin waved James to the table.

James, reluctant to move from his seat at the bar, turned slightly. "Smells good," he said politely. "Comfort food, I think they call it."

"A queer term for good solid fare," said Mrs. O. in her usual brusque manner. "But I suppose there's truth in it. Reminds me of breakfast when I was a girleen." She left the room as Kevin called out his thanks.

"Ah, God, she's a motherly woman," he said kindly. "I didn't order this, you see. I'd ordered some panfried steaks. But she was right. This is a treat—for me at least." He glanced at James inquiringly. "Doesn't it suit you?"

"Of course," said James freed by Mrs. O.'s absence to leave the bar and join Kevin. They ate heartily and chatted about a recent Ireland-Wales rugby match that Ireland had lost by a failed conversion in extra time. The food and the brandy had somewhat restored James's sense of well-being, replacing his initial uneasiness. But even as they bantered, he was preoccupied. James wanted this issue resolved tonight.

Surely it would be easier to quiz Kevin, but he knew he should address his questions to the one person who could answer them. He imagined her answers. This time the coincidence was no coincidence.

Unconsciously, James patted his jacket pocket which held the two cards. Before joining Kevin for their meal he had wanted to find out if the birth date of Sandra Murphy and the birth date of Mrs. O'Neil—which were the same—matched the birth date of the mother listed on the baby Mary Breathnach's birth certificate. He had checked his notes. All three matched.

"You've found something?" Kevin said abruptly.

"Perhaps, but I'm not sure what it means quite yet."

"You look shagged out."

"Perhaps I'll have an early night. Listen"—he stood up—"I'd like to thank Mrs. O. for the meal before I turn in. Where might she be?"

"Don't bother yourself," said Kevin leaping up, piling the plates on the tray expertly. "I'll bring these down and tell her for you. She'll still be in the kitchen with her cup of tea, I imagine."

James cringed, waylaid again. "I'll help."

"If you wish." Kevin shrugged. Together they loaded the dumbwaiter and James followed Kevin downstairs.

Mrs. O. was reading the *Evening Press,* her swollen stockinged feet propped up on an old worn cushion on a kitchen chair. She started to move but Kevin waved her to her seat.

He turned, unloading the trays from their bays into the double sink, splashing water and detergent in and quickly washing the dirty dishes.

"If you won't let me help," said Mrs. O., "then at least get this man a mug and I'll pour out his tea."

She served the steaming brew and shoved it across the table to James. He nodded. It was comfortable, warm in the kitchen. With the lights turned low, the cavernous corners of the room were shaded and there was a sense of intimacy around the table. Kevin was humming as he rinsed the dishes, laughing too, as Mrs. O. read out some bits of gossipy news from the paper. James himself smiled as she read about a man who'd defended himself in a recent court case. He'd claimed he'd no idea how his opponent in a brawl had maneuvered his ear in such a way that it led to his biting it off, all unintentionally of course.

"Oh, me poor feet," Mrs. O. said suddenly, stretching over to rub her legs.

"Ach, I told you doing all the windows on the third floor was a mistake. Too much in one day. I can get the Walsh boy in—he'll do them all."

"Not as well, mind," she said.

"Perhaps."

"And it'll cost you," she rebutted.

James felt a pressure in his head. How many times before had he been seduced by just such a scene? And then been the one to destroy it on the instant. Why, he wondered, had he found himself in this role over the years? How many times had he hesitated at the brink, such as he was now? Was he an avenging angel, a sword of retribution? No, he brooded; merely a hired hand.

He watched them as from a great distance, the two of them laughing, engaged in a vignette. He'd wished to speak with her alone. But alone or not, the truth was what it was. The truth was also that Kevin Conlon needed Mrs. O. in his life and work. James hesitated.

"Here," said Kevin, as from the same great distance. James heard his enthusiastic voice. "Sean's off, the house is quiet." He smiled conspiratorially. "James, I got a bottle of poteen from one of the stable hands. Did him a favour about a year ago and he hadn't forgotten. He got it from his cousin in Galway."

As he spoke he leapt on a chair and reached to a high wooden cupboard. Pushing aside bottles of white lemonade, he took down one with no label. The illegal pot still form of alcohol known as poteen stood in the bottle as innocent as water.

"Forget you're a lawyer now, Fleming, and join Mrs. O. and me in a glass of white lightning."

This is it, thought James, hesitation behind him. He

173

couldn't possibly take a drink with them, deceiving them in the very act.

His voice like ice, although he'd intended to sound calm, he answered Kevin. "Surely, since Sandra is joining us." He watched as Mrs. O. raised steely eyes to meet his own. Kevin, standing behind her, stopped short.

"Who?" he said, glancing around the room.

"Sandra," said James.

"Oh. Mrs. O'Neil! Lord, for a moment I'd forgotten your name, Mrs. O.," he said as he reached for three small liqueur glasses.

"Yes, Sandra O'Neil," said James, still holding her eyes as she slowly lowered her legs to the floor.

"Indeed, but no one calls me that, as you know, Mr. Fleming," she said firmly.

"No, it's been Mrs. O. for all these years," said James.

"Yes." She glanced at Kevin's back as he poured the drinks.

"And what of Mr. O'Neil then?"

"What of him?" she said sharply. Kevin turned quickly, struck by the change in the conversation, the change in tone. James and the older woman faced each other across the table, hands flat, eyes locked.

"What of him indeed, if he never existed?"

"Fleming, for God's sake!" said Kevin but they didn't heed him.

"What of that either? It was a name like any other." Mrs. O. stared at James.

"Oh, I don't think so. Names mean a lot. The name Sandra now. That meant a lot to me. I'd never heard of your Christian name until today."

"Then you're a poor detective. Any one here could have told you, if you'd only asked."

Kevin approached the table, sliding the glasses across the now great expanse that grew among them.

"And Murphy means a lot to me too," James said in a level tone.

"A common name. I think you found that, Mr. Fleming, in your tours around the town."

"But Sandra Murphy—not so common a combination, would you say?"

Kevin exclaimed. "What is this, Fleming!"

James didn't hear him. "And now, Sandra Murphy Breathnach. I'd say that wasn't a common name at all. I'd say"—he watched as the woman's features coloured a dark reddish hue—"I'd say that was a unique name, after all. I'd say there was only one Sandra Murphy Breathnach, and I'm looking at her now."

"My God," said Kevin as he watched them both. He looked in wonder at Mrs. O'Neil. "What the devil are you saying?"

"It's what hasn't been said here," said James. "It's what hasn't been said since that afternoon Breathnach came down those stairs in your lobby. It's what wasn't said by this woman who laid blankets over the man, and who stood over his body, her eyes closed in prayer." James leapt up. "Or were they prayers? Perhaps . . ."

"Perhaps they were, Fleming," she said with force. "Prayers for a dead man. More than you said for him, I warrant."

"Prayers for your husband, Sandra Murphy." James spit the words out as rage filled him at her deceit, her concealment, for the wild-goose chase he'd been on for weeks.

"This is crazy," shouted Kevin.

"Perhaps," said James, hardly seeing him in his temper. "Crazy as it seems, Conlon, you are looking at Breathnach's wife."

Kevin stood back. "Is this true?"

"What if it is?" she said, not looking him in the face, staring at James. "I'm asking you, Mr. Fleming, to think about what you're doing." Her eyes appealed to him, knowledge in her eyes that he could read, that he acknowledged in return.

He hesitated and she saw it. "Mr. Conlon here has had an awful lot of trouble this year." Her voice suddenly choked with tears, throwing James off guard.

"For heaven's sake, Fleming," cried Kevin. "Whatever's going on here, stop it now."

James watched the woman. "Sorry, we're all a bit excited," he said finally.

A sense of relief filled the room.

She relaxed slightly, taking a sip of the poteen.

He took his advantage.

"Would you have come forward, if Kevin here had been charged?"

She looked down. "But it never came to that, did it? So you can't accuse me of something that never happened. You can't know my heart, my soul, despite your lawyering." Her voice rose in anger. "If it weren't for you and your poking, this whole thing would have blown over."

Kevin shook his head in disbelief.

"It would have blown over, I say. The police haven't charged him. Within a year it would be forgotten. We'd go on as before, as we are going on now." Her voice rose. "Think, man, think what you are doing here. You don't know it all, and you won't want to. Don't press me. There's too much at stake." Anger and sorrow, real sorrow, rang out in her raised voice.

James hesitated again. Perhaps more was at stake than he knew, but he had to know the truth. "I have two questions: the why and the how. Obviously"—his voice was stern, mechanical—"the why is the more important."

She didn't respond.

"Why did you kill Breathnach?"

It was Kevin's turn to gasp. He stared at the woman and at James, eyes bulging. "This is madness, Fleming."

"I agree. Madness to take a man's life—in his bath, for God's sake. Hideous, to somehow poison the very water he would bathe with, relax in. What could he have done that you'd steal his life that way?"

"Impossible. She was with me," cried Kevin, "we laughed, didn't we?" He looked at Mrs. O. "We laughed together at his song, that dreadful singing?"

Her lips curled at the memory and her voice was low and harsh. "I did it bloody my way."

"Yes, yes," cried Kevin, clinging to this, not heeding her tone.

"He wanted to do the whole thing his way." Her eyes glinted, looking inward to some other scene.

"What are you saying? I don't believe it." Kevin's voice was frightened. "Are you saying . . . are you saying . . . no, you stood with me, we joked about that singing, that raucous voice. Don't tell me you knew then that he was dying as we stood there!"

"I wasn't sure. I'd only read about this thing with the mineral salts in a magazine, some years ago." She talked straight ahead, almost musing. "No, I didn't know when I heard his stinkin' voice. In fact I thought the salts hadn't done the trick. I didn't think it had worked until I saw that great mound of flesh at the bottom of the stairs. And even then . . ."

"Yes," said James sternly.

"Even then I couldn't be sure he hadn't died of something else." Her tone was normal now. Narrative. She sipped her drink slowly. "I knew from old days that he'd a bad heart. Even as a young man he'd mentioned it. It stayed in my mind like every other thing about him. And then when I saw the man here, here in my home, and the size of him. It doesn't take a doctor to know with the great fat of him, and his cigars and his whiskey and his heart . . . it could have been a heart attack." She looked at James. "You thought so yourself."

"Yes, I did. I wish to God it had been that."

Her eyes softened only slightly and she looked not to Kevin but to the bottle. He poured out another measure and she sipped it.

"I've no regrets," she said finally.

"I see that. And no remorse either."

"Not at all."

Kevin started to tremble and he sat down, as though the enormity of what he was hearing finally hit him.

"What are you saying, Mrs. O.? Don't tell me it was you who killed him?"

"Yes." She looked at James. "And now it was all for nothing. This man here, your solicitor friend, will make it so."

"What are you talking about?"

"I killed the old souse to protect you, Mr. Conlon, and more than you. I can still do so, if this jackeen from Dublin would only keep his mouth shut." She glared at James.

James stared her down. "Tell us why."

Silence fell. James was stymied. Having put the pieces of the puzzle together this far, he also knew he'd no idea why she had killed her husband, a husband he was assuming she hadn't seen in many, many years. Madigan's phrase leapt into his mind: secret knowledge. One of his scenarios had been that Breathnach had had secret knowledge. But of what? He had to urge her to speak now. She was recovering a certain composure, testing him.

He'd bluff it.

"Did you really believe killing him would keep the secret safe?" He used a sarcastic tone and she glanced up.

"You're a superior lot, aren't you? Of course I thought that. Or I wouldn't have done it."

"What secret?" said Kevin, looking at them wildly.

"I think Mrs. O. should tell you herself, don't you?"

She wavered.

"Tell him, tell Kevin."

After a moment of interior struggle, Mrs. O'Neil shifted in her seat. Her shoulders sagged and she began to speak slowly at first, not looking at Kevin throughout her story.

"You've done more harm than good, you know," she said to James. He didn't move and she saw in his face that he'd crossed his own Rubicon. There was no turning back for him, and now not for her either.

"I don't tell you to grieve you, Mr. Conlon, Kevin."

Kevin was surprised at her softened tone, more surprised by her use of his first name. "I'm sure you're not, Mrs. O."

"It's more than forty years now that I came to work here at the hotel and little did I think then, a young girl in my prime, that it would become my home. Mr. and Mrs. O'Donnell had been married awhile, they were very good to me, and we all of us were hoping to see some childer. But there was nothing happening in that department. Despite her good build—she'd hips made for childbearing—she was sick a lot, and frail. That first summer, it was a hot dry summer, she was ailing. She'd gone away to the seaside where it was cooler. Mr. O'Donnell, and as God is my witness I never called him anything but that . . ."

Kevin looked bewildered. "I'm sure," he said.

Mrs. O'Neil resumed as if he hadn't spoken. "That summer he was lonely, I could see. He was a fine-looking man with black curly hair, blue eyes. I was living in by then, working all hours, here at the old hotel. I remember, now"—she paused briefly as though seeing with an inward eye—"he'd liked me in a new light frock I'd sewn, blue cotton it was . . ." She was musing, lost back in time. "He never said he loved me, but for that summer I loved him dearly. In that way." She shrugged.

"Mrs. O'Donnell came back and, as I had no illusions, life went on as before. I'd no daydreams concerning him. And when I found out I was expecting a child I nearly died. Not for thousands would I have hurt those two, like family to me. So I told him pretty much straightaway. He'd nearly died of the shock. He didn't want to hurt his wife but he was so excited about the child he couldn't contain himself. We talked for hours, mostly as we worked about the hotel and grounds. He came up with a plan. I was in a state myself, and it seemed a good plan. But any plan would have seemed a good plan at the time." James suddenly heard the anger behind her matter-of-fact tone.

"He said I should go to Dublin, have the child there and then he and his wife would adopt it. I could return and we'd all benefit. The main thing was that the missus never know. I agreed and went to Dublin and got a job straightaway. I'd no family, you see—" she paused again, and then recovered—"and it was simple. Things . . . life was simpler then." She glared at James.

"I met Breathnach in a pub the first week I was in Dublin. A little local near the factory where I worked. He was jolly enough and took a great interest in me. I was lonely . . . I was lonely," she repeated to herself, "and I had good times with him. I suppose I was angry too. I suddenly saw a different life. Why give up the baby, why go back at all? Once I was in the big city, Sligo seemed a million miles away. Breathnach courted me hard. I was a fine-lookin' one in those days. And he was quick off the mark. But I said no to sharing his bed unless we were wed. I'd learned that much at least." Her voice was tinged with bitterness.

"It's strange to talk of this now . . . I've not spoken of those Dublin days in nearly forty years."

They all sipped their poteen, James and Kevin waiting for her to continue. As James drank off the poteen the fluid burned his throat and he gasped slightly.

"Jackeen," she hissed.

James caught her eye. He'd been called this disparaging term before: *city boy*. Why was it, he wondered, that in his other cases when he confronted rural people, that he'd also confronted that deep rift between city and country? What was it that gave him the sense that their kind of wisdom was older, their behaviour governed by earlier forms of what they saw as justice?

"Breathnach was a jackeen too." She resumed as if reading his mind. "But, we were wed and soon enough I was sorry. He liked his food and his bed and not much else. Though he worked hard enough. He was an—" She searched for the word—"an arrogant man. A big blow about his dreams of riches and property and power. No, it wasn't long before I was sorry to be tied to him, sorry to have to tell Mr. O'Donnell when he came to Dublin to see me. His eyes were sorrowful that day, I can tell you. He asked about the child and would I be keeping it. And it was then I knew I wouldn't do that to him or the child. I would keep to the original plan. And not long after that Breathnach started to notice, the stupid thick, what was there to see all along. I told him the tale. He was in a rage, but he never touched me after that. I asked him to just see me through till the child was born and then I'd be out of his life. He was decent enough about that, but those last months were hard. I don't think he said ten words to me." She stopped.

James was alarmed. He'd had no idea what was coming, but now he suspected where her story was going. He glanced at Kevin, hoping that he'd be able to take it.

"So the O'Donnells took the child," James said encouragingly.

"Yes, Mr. O'Donnell had told the wife they'd get a baby and she had got this daft idea she wanted everyone to think it was her own. She insisted she go to Galway, to an ancient cousin, and wait there, as though in a delicate pregnancy. They'd take charge of the baby in

Galway and then she'd return to Sligo and all would see the child as theirs alone. She never knew that it was his child. It would have killed her or at least the marriage. He agreed and she spent the months in Galway.

"When the child was born, I felt well and strong, and within a fortnight I went to Galway. Mr. O'Donnell took the child from me at the old train station there, near the weir." And here she sighed, unconsciously. "I went back to Dublin and worked on for a while as a live-in maid. For about a year I didn't see them or hear from them. It near killed me, but I knew I'd be going home eventually. That kept me going. I'd see the child and I'd—"

"My Mary was your daughter . . . ?" Kevin erupted.

Mrs. O'Neil kept her head down. "Yes."

"Jesus Christ! Fleming? Is this true?"

James, almost as stunned as Kevin and unable to verify anything at this stage, merely nodded at Mrs. O., willing her to continue, to get it over with.

"It worked very well, didn't it, Mr. Conlon? No one except her father and I ever knew the truth. Mary never knew, nor Mrs. O'Donnell. Mary had loving happy parents and . . . I was happy too. I saw Mary every day of her life till she went to Galway, to the catering college where she met yourself. The ancient cousin was long dead. The secret was still safe. The O'Donnells died one after the other, as you know. At the end, Mr. O'Donnell asked me if we should tell Mary. I give him credit for that. He was decent to me always . . . according to his lights. But I said no, I'd made my bargain and I would keep to it always." She straightened her shoulders with pride. "I saw then he was relieved in his heart." She stopped speaking, lost in thought.

"Poor Mary," murmured Kevin. And James saw the tears in Mrs. O.'s eyes that Kevin didn't see. She brushed them away.

Kevin spoke at last. "Listen, Fleming, what has this

got to do with Breathnach's death?'' He couldn't bring himself to address Mrs. O.

''I believe that Breathnach was going to use this information—'' said James, still with authority although he was unsure of his ground.

''Oh yes, indeed he was,'' she broke in angrily. ''It was that first day, he saw me in the lobby when he was checking in. I don't know who was the more surprised. He got me alone in the snug not long after . . .''

''I saw you . . .'' exclaimed Kevin.

''I know. You interrupted his pretty speech to me. He told me what he told everyone. He was going to get you to sell this place. He'd get a mighty commission on it too, he said. The men he was working for were rich and powerful. I knew him from of old. He was a talker. But I couldn't trust him either. He was angry and bitter about the past, even after all these years.'' She shrugged, still apparently surprised by Breathnach's feelings. ''He said he'd tell Mary. And you. That's when I made my first mistake and told him Mary was dead. . . .''

Kevin groaned.

''He thought this over for a while, never saying he was sorry she was gone. And then he blurted out his evil plan. He said that despite all, he was Mary's legal father, the birth certificate was there to prove it. His bloody eyes lit up as he told me. He was going to bring a suit he said, to get a share of Mary's property as her father and near relative. Then he said you'd probably go along with it all, whatever he wanted, because you wouldn't want all this coming out about Mary now she was dead. Oh God . . .'' For the first time she broke down, and James knew it was at the thought of the daughter she had truly loved.

''I fought with him, I even begged him, that bastard! I told him a mere slip of my own tongue forty years ago, about Mr. O'Donnell and me, had brought us to this pitch.

If I hadn't told him who was Mary's father . . . He laughed! And he said yes, didn't God work in mysterious ways!

"It was then I decided. When he said that. It was then I decided to get rid of him and his evil plans. How could I ever face Miriam if he succeeded? But I had to work fast. The mineral salts were always here in the stores cupboard. If it worked I was safe. We were all safe."

"And it did work."

"Yes, and we *were* all safe again. Safe except from you."

James was shaken. Kevin was staring at him, accusation on his face.

"Well, I think I know enough for now," James said, assuming command of the situation. "I can't leave it here, you both realize that." He felt the hostility flowing towards him from Kevin and Mrs. O. They didn't respond.

"As an officer of the court I must report what I've learned. I'm going to phone Inspector Cronin now."

He left the room, glad to escape, hoping in a way that Mrs. O. would take flight, suspecting she would not, with no home, no life but the Lodge. He rubbed his jaw and forehead as he spoke to Cronin, quickly summarizing what had just occurred. Silent, stunned, Cronin said at last that he'd come straightaway.

James lingered in the foyer, reluctant to return downstairs, half-expecting Kevin to join him. When he didn't, he wondered at the scene taking place below him. How would those two come to terms with each other now? The thought spun around in his mind.

James rubbed his jaw again trying to loosen the tension in the muscles. He was so sorry. Sorry most of all for Miriam, because he had forgotten her existence.

Chapter Thirteen

For the second time in a week James found himself waiting for Kevin to appear in the grim hallway of the central police station. He was drained and irritable after his session with Cronin, at which he had given a statement of the events that led him to confront Mrs. O'Neil.

Impulsively he left the building and ran to the nearest pub, talking his way in the door since it was closing time. He bought a packet of cigarettes and a box of matches and returned to the police station.

It had been years since he'd stopped smoking, indulging only rarely in a French cigarette. He looked at the packet and broke the seal, taking one and finally lighting it. His head swam at the first inhalation of the nicotine. He breathed deeply and his head cleared.

He didn't want to see Kevin. What he wanted to do was go out and get drunk.

He thought of Sean, openmouthed in the foyer, when Kevin told him to wait up for their absent guests. Sean was unaware of what had transpired that night.

And what of the morning, and what of the next few

days and months? If Mrs. O. confessed, at least there'd be no lengthy trial to drag through the papers. But what of the rhythm of their life, of the hotel? What of Kevin?

James wasn't reassured when he saw Kevin approaching, his face ashen. He glanced away as James stood up, stubbing out his cigarette on the begrimed floor.

"Come on, I'll run us home," said James. Kevin shrugged, following James onto the narrow steep street where his car straddled the pavement.

The silence was heavy until they drove out of the town precincts and then he spoke, willing Kevin to respond.

"What do you want me to say, Conlon?"

"Nothing, I guess."

"Believe me, I had no idea of what was coming. I knew nothing about Mrs. O.'s connection with Mary."

"But you knew Mrs. O. had a child?"

"Yes. No. I knew that Breathnach's wife had a child."

"A girl. Called Mary." Kevin's voice was flat.

"Yes, but . . ."

"But you neglected to mention this to me. . . ."

"I never connected that information with Mrs. O."

"But when you were looking in the files, the records, you were looking for something on her, on Mrs. O." It wasn't a question.

"No. I was looking for anything at all suspect regarding the staff, past or present. I didn't have any one person in mind. I just felt I'd know it if I saw it. When I saw her name, when I realized I had proof that Mrs. O'Neil had once been Breathnach's wife I was only satisfied that I'd solved just that one question."

Kevin shrugged again, silent as they drove up the dark hill that led to the Lodge. They walked wearily from the car park and were greeted by an anxious Sean.

"Thanks, Sean, are they in?"

"Yes, all tucked up in bed. What's up?"

"I can't . . . Sorry, I'll have to talk to you in the morning. Just look after the breakfast, will you?"

Sean nodded, curious, but put off by Kevin's grim attitude.

"I'll be down at five, give you a hand."

Sean hesitated and then agreed, taking himself off.

James hesitated too, as they stood in the foyer. He wanted to talk, certain that Kevin wanted to as well.

Kevin locked the front door and began to switch out the main lights, leaving only the customary smaller lights on. At last he spoke.

"Drink?"

"Yes."

"I think we'll go into the bar," said Kevin.

He poured two double whiskeys and sat down heavily on the bar stool.

"Look, Fleming, it's been a bitch of a night. I feel as though I've just come back from a funeral. I . . . look, I think that you made a mistake."

"You heard her yourself. She confessed!"

"Yes, I heard her."

"Then what do you mean—a mistake?"

"You should have talked to me first."

"Hold on. I wanted to speak to her on her own tonight, but I couldn't get her alone. And, at that point, all I wanted to establish for certain was that she was Breathnach's wife and that she had concealed that fact."

"Or rather, that she had neglected to tell that fact to the police and you?"

"Or you, Kevin!" James paused, suddenly remembering someone else who'd concealed a link with Breathnach. He continued slowly. "I just wanted to find out—no, that's wrong—I knew. I just wanted her to verify it."

"And then what?"

"And then I thought I would try to discover if she had a motive. I didn't think she'd killed Breathnach!"

"But you, at that very point, thought she was a suspect?"

"Yes."

"Then it amounts to the same thing."

James disagreed. "I thought she might be involved, but I didn't think she'd done it. Not until she started to talk."

"But it was a woman's method, wasn't it?" Kevin said staring at him. "Bath salts! For God's sake. You must have known it was a woman?"

"No, I didn't think that, I—"

"And that's just my point. You didn't think. If you had, you would have come to me first when you'd found that card, that name on the employment card. You could have asked me. Perhaps . . ."

"Perhaps what! She killed the man, Conlon. The police believed you had done it. What was I supposed to do? I was committed to clearing you, we were all agreed on that. . . ."

"Were we? I was the one most directly affected. Did I want my name cleared in this fashion? Maybe I didn't. Maybe I don't." Kevin's voice rose.

"What the hell are you saying?"

"If you'd come to me first, it would have been up to me, then, to choose. You know what, you know what?" yelled Kevin, the whiskey sloshing in his glass. "I would have chosen to do nothing."

"You don't mean that."

"The hell I don't. Who are you to tell me? Who are you anyway! You're a stranger here. You didn't know Mrs. O. For Christ's sake, she was like family. And now I find out she *is* family—at the very point the bloody legal system is going to take her away from us." He downed the whiskey and poured another.

James didn't respond. He saw Kevin was on the verge of an explosion he wanted both of them to avoid. James switched on another lamp and sat in one of the armchairs, attempting to defuse the situation but not wanting to leave it hanging either.

"Conlon, I'm sorry about Mrs. O'Neil. I did not expect the revelations that we both heard tonight. Perhaps I should have seen the connection between the name of her child, and your wife's name, but there was no reason to. I thought it was a coincidence." He faltered over the word. He'd seen other patterns, why the hell hadn't he seen that one?

"That's pretty lame, Fleming," said Kevin.

James wanted to punch him, to make him see. But words were his only weapon. "Kevin, does it strike you that she was willing to let you suffer, to let your business and livelihood suffer?"

"So you say. But she told me herself in the police car that if I'd been charged she would have come forward."

"Easy to say now . . ." James smirked, gulping his whiskey.

"I was in the car, you weren't. She loved Mary, and she loves Miriam. She wouldn't have let me go to jail— if not on my own account, then on Miriam's!" He was standing, his eyes bulging, fists clenched. "Go to hell, Fleming."

"What the—"

"Go to hell, and take your bloody snot-nosed Madigan friend with you." Kevin hurled his glass and smashed the ornate mirror behind the bar.

The noise startled them both, but Kevin turned to face James. "Get out, get out of here . . ."

"You go to hell, Conlon," said James, and he left the room.

Some hours later James woke in his room, barely remembering falling asleep in the bedside chair, pen in hand. Now he stood up, stretching his stiff limbs. The room was cold, bitterly cold. The central heating was off and James wondered if Kevin was aware of it. He wondered where Kevin was now—still in the bar, drinking perhaps. He shrugged. It couldn't be helped.

James threw himself on the bed and waited for the dawn. He planned to ring Madigan with the news as soon as was reasonable. That done, he'd be free, free to leave; his work was done here, as was his friendship with Conlon. He thought gloomily of the nights he'd spent at the Lodge, culminating in this one. Had it been Mrs. O that night in the attic when the electricity hadn't worked? There were so many questions still hanging. But the main question had been answered and no one was happy. He'd done his job. Unintentionally well, he thought ironically. It wasn't the first time his professional obligations had ruined a friendship he'd begun to value. And again he thought of the case which had brought Sarah Gallagher into his life. She too had not wanted to know the truth.

They didn't want to deal with the truth, but did he? He examined his conscience. If Mrs. O. hadn't confessed and placed him in the position to act on it, would he have pursued the issue? Could he have walked away had Kevin asked? Could he have let Kevin make such a choice, governed not by law but by some other code: of love or affection or loyalty? Kevin valued Mrs. O., and she was to be valued.

He stood up and paced the room.

What harm would it have done to have left her alone, to live out her days near Miriam, her own daughter's child, the daughter she'd loved from afar? Who benefitted here? He threw his notebook across the room. Yet again, he'd caused only pain and grief. For Kevin, Miriam, Mrs. O., the rest of the staff. Even to himself in a small way. His actions stood apart from him, accusing him, and the result of his actions entered into his soul like small slivers of ice through his skin.

But what of Breathnach? He'd died, and but for an alert medical officer it would have been seen to have been a death from natural causes. If it had happened in Dublin, he might have been buried without an autopsy. What difference would it have made to the grand scheme of things if no one knew, if no one at all knew, he'd been murdered? The man himself didn't even know he was the victim of a murderous attack. He'd felt ill, he left his bath, he'd come downstairs, for . . . what?

For help . . . James recalled Kevin's description. How the man had staggered, how he'd clutched his dressing gown around him, covering his bulk, his nakedness. He'd fallen, sprawling, wet with sweat, with bathwater, naked, gasping, dying.

James shivered at his own imagining of the man's thoughts. In his mental confusion did he know that he was dying? He'd come down for help, seeking out his fellowman, seeking—if not help in his extremity—then the touch of a hand, the sound of a comforting word. Did anyone hold his hand, or whisper in his ear that he was not alone? Did he have, at the end of a lonely life, the horrible knowledge that no one cared if he lived or died? Did it cross his mind that no one, no one at all, would grieve at his passing from this world?

It was horrible to contemplate. James was wide-awake now, sweating at the vision he'd conjured of the man's last few moments of life. And then he saw again, in his mind's eye, what he'd observed himself in the chaos of that moment: Mrs. O., eyes closed, praying. For Breathnach? he wondered. The man's murderer had stood over his body. And she was as cold as ice.

Whatever else she'd done in her life, whatever good she'd done, did not outweigh that single act. She had taken the man's life away, taken his life in her hands for her own ends. She had appropriated the ultimate authority. She had appropriated death.

James was calmer now. He threw open the drapes and saw a weak November dawn. Yes, it was right that her arrest followed on his investigation. He hadn't seen it coming, and for that he berated himself. But he did not berate himself for doing what he'd set out to do. He'd determined to find the man's murderer and had done so. His conscience, he decided, was clear.

James finally got through to Madigan in a short recess of the barrister's court case. As he reprised the events on the phone in Kevin's study it was as though Madigan were on another planet, infinitely remote from the emotions of the past twenty-four hours. He was pleased that Conlon, his boyhood friend, was off the hook. James didn't elaborate on how that friend was less than pleased. Distracted by Kevin's continuing absence, he barely heard Madigan's question.

"What did you ask?" said James wearily.

"I said, it's not over yet. You've got to establish whom Breathnach was fronting for. It was on their account Breathnach was in Sligo. But for them, he would never have been there."

"Never would have died . . ."

"Exactly! This case isn't closed until we've got all the pieces. Get back to me when you can. Regards to Conlon."

Next James rang Maggie who was suitably stunned by his news concerning Mrs. O'Neil. Fortunately she said that there was nothing needing his presence at the Dublin office and James explained he'd be staying on for a few days more.

He hesitated over his next call. There was only one person he knew of who might be able to give him the lead he needed. With dread at the thought of meeting the woman he'd put in jail, he rang through to Cronin and got his permission to interview Mrs. O'Neil. And after a hasty breakfast at a grungy cafe in the town, he met with Mrs. O'Neil with a recording officer present.

James was shocked to see the woman's appearance as she entered the small office. Her round broad face was drawn and lined and her hair, usually in a neat bun at the nape of her neck, was loose and hanging.

James pulled out her chair but she waved him away.

"So it's you," she said ironically. "I would have thought you'd had enough of me last night, Fleming." Her anger, or was it her hatred, was almost palpable.

James plunged in. "Last night we were all dealing with the larger issue of Breathnach's death, but there are some loose ends still. Inspector Cronin agreed I could talk with you—"

"Did *I?*"

"I hope you'll agree."

"Why should I help you of all people? You've taken away my reason for living, and you're here looking for more! Looking for help from me?"

"All I'm interested in is the truth," James flared.

"Why?" Her voice was flat now, even curious.

James faltered. "Because we, none of us, can live with lies."

"Christ, what a load of shite! You say this to me when I lived a lie for forty years and was happy with it. I could be living with another lie now, right there in the Lodge, if it weren't for you. Truth, my foot." She leaned across the table, pinning him with her glittering eyes. "Are you tellin' me that you haven't lived lie after lie, in your time? No, you can't, 'cause I see it on your face. One liar to another." She leaned back in triumph.

"All right," said James slightly bloodied from the encounter. "But I know you love Miriam, and that's no lie. She's going to learn you are her grandmother. Did you think of that? Don't you want to do as much as possible to rectify your position in her eyes? Help me to help yourself. The more you help me, help the police, the more you will strengthen your defense."

"You'd use your own mother to get what you wanted, wouldn't you?" she spat at him, but it was her last salvo. "For Miriam, I'll help you for Miriam."

"Thank you. Now, I want to ask you about Breathnach's story—that he was working for a group of investors."

"Ah-ha, that's what he had told everyone."

"Everyone?"

"Yes, and it was what he'd told me too. At first."

"At first?"

"Yes, but when he got me alone, that one and only time, when he told me he'd use his knowledge of me and of Mary to get what he wanted, he . . ."

"What? What?"

"We had words. I told him he was nothing but a schemer. I told him I didn't believe his cock-and-bull story about the hotel investors. People of that quality wouldn't spit on the likes of him, much less rely on him."

"You said all this?"

"Oh, yes, and more. I told him I didn't believe the story and as a result I wasn't afraid of him, of what he could say. He got ugly then. He said I was right. Oh, he said that begrudgingly, and that the story was a cover. He'd been hired to get some documents, some papers, old papers that people he knew were very interested in."

James wanted to shout what papers, but held his tongue, letting Mrs. O. tell the story in her own way.

"He said there were some important papers in the house. That he'd come to find them, get them, and now, surprise, surprise, he found that I was here at the Lodge. He'd had a day to think it over and he had his plan. He wanted to search the house, offices, attics, storerooms, whatever, and I was to help him. I was his inside man, as the fool said." She gasped with anger.

"Please, go on, this is important."

She looked at him. "Why?"

"Because . . . just go on, please. About these papers?"

"He said Mary had found some documents that could

194

prove dangerous if they got out to the public. He said they implicated someone. Something like that. Oh, he did say that Mary didn't know how important the papers were. Then he mentioned a history book. Hah! I told him that Mary hadn't time to bless herself, let alone write some book.''

"What happened next?"

"He said to shut my mouth. The people he worked for knew for a fact she'd got these papers.''

"Did he identify this employer?" James waited, breathless, thinking of what he knew about the connection between Dunmor and Breathnach.

"Not at all. He just said now it was his job to get them, and they didn't care how. It was then he told me that he'd go to Kevin. That if I didn't help him get these bleedin' papers he'd tell Kevin about me, about me bein' married to him. Tell him Mary was his daughter.'' She looked up at James in horror. "He would tell Kevin he was Mary's father—that filthy pig. I told him that I'd tell Kevin he wasn't anything of the sort, and who did he think Kevin would be likely to believe? And then he said he'd tell Kevin, and anyone who'd listen, that Mr. O'Donnell, Mary's father, was nothin' but a pimp and a whoremonger.''

"What did you say to that?"

"I said I'd help him, but I'd already made up my mind. Even if we found these bloody papers, he would still have this, this . . .'' She hunted for the right word.

"Weapon over you?" James prompted.

"Yes, he could use it at anytime. He could use my secret against Kevin and Miriam. He could go to court with his claim. If not right away, then when? What if he wanted something from me in the future, or from Kevin? What if he followed Miriam? What if he came to Miriam when she was older, when I was not around? What if something happened to Kevin? Breathnach could get at Miriam with his secret knowledge and his claim against her property. If *I* didn't protect Miriam from that pig-ignorant soulless lout, then who would? I was the only one who knew! Me! Me!" She beat her hands on her breast.

James stared at her angry face, her wild demeanor. Was nothing simple? His judgment wavered. For now he saw that she had had what, to her, was a higher motive, a legitimate reason for her actions. She had been protecting Miriam, her own daughter's child, from a very real present and future threat.

He sighed. "Is there anything else you can remember about this so-called history book, these bloody papers?"

She looked at his face, caught by his tone, her eyes dry and bloodshot. "No."

"Just one more question then—for my own peace of mind. Did you plant the bottle of salts and then let Caitlin unknowingly add them to the bath?"

She studied him for a full minute. "Do you think I am that evil? That I would involve a child?"

"No, that's why I asked."

"Caitlin was never involved. When she told me she'd run his bath, unknown to her I went up to his room, bringing the mineral salts with me. As soon as he saw me, he laughed, saying it was good to have a woman servin' him again. I put the salts in the water and made sure they were dissolved. I felt like a weight was off me back."

James signalled her to stop, not wanting her to incriminate herself further, as the officer was recording everything for Cronin. He took his leave, quickly and awkwardly, but armed with enough solid information to go on with.

James could hardly wait to get back to the Lodge. He was energized, his judgment reaffirmed. He'd thought all along that the real estate venture had been a ruse. And now it was confirmed out of Breathnach's own mouth. Yes, he'd been hired by someone "powerful" but not powerful property developers. A history book? Is this where the paper trail had been leading all this time? Did this history book reveal what every other source had been orchestrated not to reveal?

The foyer was empty and so was Kevin's study. He rested his hand on the phone. The idea had struck him earlier. Dunmor had hired Breathnach in the past. What if, for reasons yet to be discerned, he'd hired Breathnach, had finagled that both he and Breathnach would be in the hotel at the same time. What they were seeking seemed, for the moment, less important than his need to find out if it had been Dunmor. He glanced at the phone. Why not? Why the hell not? He'd ring him now, and perhaps startle the truth out of him. He snatched up the phone and dialled.

"Ciaran Dunmor?" said James into the receiver.

"Speaking."

He heard the question in the man's voice. "Fleming, James Fleming, Mr. Dunmor. I'm ringing from Cromlech Lodge in Sligo."

"Ah, yes, Fleming. Something must be up, for you to call me on this number."

"Yes." James was affable. "I thought that you'd like to hear the news directly from me."

"News?"

James could read nothing in his tone and he wished now he could have spoken to him in person. "About the Breathnach case. The media might pick it up by tomorrow, so I thought I'd tell you ahead of time."

"Good news I hope."

"Hardly good for those involved. However, the case is certainly on its way to being closed . . ."

"You've found the murderer then."

"Yes. It is, incredibly, Mrs. O'Neil, if you remember her?"

"Should I?"

"Possibly not. But I thought she knew you and your grandson fairly well. She was the older woman who worked here at the Lodge. She served meals and—"

"Yes, of course, of course . . . my God, that's hard to believe. She struck me as a fine, capable woman. Of course, I can see her now, serving up pints of stout. Her name just didn't register . . . Do you have any idea why she did it?"

"Yes, but it still surprises me. Mrs. O'Neil had been married to Breathnach at one time."

There was an exclamation. "You're jokin'?"

"I wish I were, but it's the truth. She's at the station now, she's made a statement and has confessed. All very straightforward."

"Extraordinary. Extraordinary."

Was there disbelief there, and was there also relief? James responded. "Yes, indeed. It strikes me that people rarely escape their past."

There was no response. He continued. "It's distressing to see her in the lockup. I agree that she was and, I think is still, in a way, a fine woman."

"Yes, yes, she was a great help to Conlon. But now at least he's off the hook."

"He's not happy about it, I can tell you, the way it's turned out."

"Of course, of course. Tell me, you said you'd seen her at the jail?"

"Mmm."

"Well, I thank you for phoning through with the good word. I'm sorry for them though."

"I, too. Mr. Dunmor? I just have one last question."

"I do have another appointment here . . ."

"It's just that, I was wondering if you could tell me . . . Was Breathnach working for you that weekend you were both visiting here, the weekend that he died?"

There was a significant pause. James felt his hand sweating around the mouthpiece. He waited.

"Fleming, I think I've already told you everything you needed to know. It was entirely a coincidence that Breathnach and I were staying there at the same time. We didn't even speak. So that's the end of the matter, as far as I'm concerned. Congratulations on closing the case."

"But it's not closed, Mr. Dunmor."

"You just said yourself the woman confessed!"

"We have to know why Breathnach was here that weekend. He was working for someone. It will be important to Mrs. O'Neil, to her case, that we establish this."

"Why, surely it was an old argument between husband and wife?"

"Perhaps, but there is a question of . . . *coercion* perhaps is the best word to use at this time."

"I'm not sure I understand."

"In order to fulfill his assignment here, Breathnach was coercing Mrs. O'Neil. In effect blackmailing her."

"Regarding what?" The man's voice was strident now.

"He mentioned some documents . . ."

"Who?"

"Breathnach."

"And to whom did he mention this?"

"Mrs. O'Neil. I've been talking with her. At length as you can imagine."

"Are you taking her case then, Fleming?"

"No, but I am still working for Conlon. He and I are about to clear up this issue of the documents," James bluffed.

"I see, I see. Well, I thank you for letting me know. It's a pity about Mrs. O'Neil. She'll be a loss to Conlon and the Lodge. Perhaps he'll sell up after all—to the consortium."

"But that's the other thing, Dunmor. There was no consortium. Only Breathnach's mysterious employer."

"I must go, Fleming."

"Just one more thing, sir. I think I'm on the right track concerning Aileen Dunmor." At this point he'd decided to take a shot in the dark. "I think you'll be interested in what we've found out about her. And the child, of course."

"Child?"

"Yes." Inspiration struck James. "The child, Daniel. He'd the same name as yourself."

"Wouldn't know about that, as I've said before. Keep me informed then, Fleming. Perhaps there'll be something I can do for Conlon. Now I really do have to go."

And he was gone.

James put down the phone. Had he really expected Dunmor to announce to him that he'd hired Breathnach to find some tourist pamphlet Mary Conlon had been dreaming of writing? He'd not succeeded there. Still, he'd thought to mention the coincidence of the name of Daniel. But if there was nothing to that coincidence, he may well have gone too far on the phone with Dunmor. Alienating the "right people" again. His mother wouldn't approve, he thought wryly. If only he could put his hands on those blasted papers!

Kevin was at the desk in the foyer, as James passed through. He looked up warily.

"Fleming." His expression was questioning.

"Kevin."

"Are you checking out today?"

"Look, Kevin, I've just come from interviewing Mrs. O. There's a lot more to this than any of us knew. I'm not leaving, to answer your question. Not until these issues are resolved."

"What issues?"

"Mrs. O. told me about Breathnach and his motive for being here. He was here at someone's behest, but not, as we were led to believe, a group of investors wishing to buy the Lodge! It is essential that we discover who hired him, for many reasons, not the least of which is that there may be mitigating factors that will help Mrs. O.'s case.''

Kevin's exhausted face was suddenly animated with hope. "What are you saying?"

"Breathnach's story was a charade!"

"Then for God's sake, why was he here?"

"He was hired to locate and obtain some documents . . .''

"Documents?"

"He described them as a history book and they were important enough that he was to be royally paid.''

"What! And Mrs. O'Neil knew about this?"

"No, no, Conlon! You see, Breathnach didn't know, until he arrived, that Mrs. O. was still working here. But he was smart and he quickly saw her as someone whom he could readily pressure. He blackmailed her into agreeing to help him find the papers, claiming he would tell you about Mary's background and that he would bring suit against Mary's estate as her father of record. He was shrewd.

"Don't you see? If he didn't succeed in finding the papers that first weekend, he could leave knowing she would be forced to keep on looking in his absence. And at the same time he could still easily return here to the Lodge, as a realtor who'd visited the hotel, but had failed to persuade you to sell.''

"Wow!" Kevin rubbed his forehead.

"Exactly. This situation is much more complex than we ever had cause to suspect. Obviously since Breathnach died before he found the papers, his so-called employers would not necessarily give up.''

"But what papers? And who are these employers, these people in the background?" Kevin was irate.

James chose not to mention his fruitless call to Dunmor, yet another dead end. "That's just it! He didn't tell her, and she . . . well, Breathnach died before he made it clear to her.''

"If only she waited, if only she'd established what he really wanted. If only she'd come to me . . ." Kevin shook his head.

"Look, Kevin, I believe we should move fast. Whoever wants these papers must know what's going on here at the Lodge. There's a real possibility that the break-in the other night was connected. That idea makes me uneasy. But for now, for us, the key fact is that Breathnach said Mary had been working on this so-called history book.''

"Mary!"

"Yes."

"That's crazy. Mary wasn't working on anything. She had a little hobby. Got some small pleasure out of poking around in the attics. Who in God's name would care about that!''

"I don't know. Perhaps she was working on something else? Think, Kevin!''

"I will, but for now the only thing I can say for certain was that she'd planned that little pamphlet about the Lodge, for the visitors here.''

"Perhaps she had it printed and you didn't know?''

"It's possible, but I doubt it. She would have been excited about it, if she'd got that far.''

"Unless she'd done it to surprise you?''

"Mmm, I know what you're suggesting, but no, I think she would have let me read a text before it was actually printed.''

"Well, then, let's assume there's a text in Mary's handwriting. I think we both should start looking for it now.''

"I agree," said Kevin, "but there's something even more urgent I must take care of first.''

Chapter Fourteen

Kevin stood up from his desk and nervously straightened his tie. "I'm on my way to see Miriam at school. I've informed the headmaster and he accepts that the news about Mrs. O. would be better coming from me."

"Would you mind if I came along?"

"No, I don't think so. But why?" Kevin's face was haggard.

"I'd like to ask Miriam a question."

"Let's see how it goes."

They drove in tired silence to the lovely old school, sequestered in its quiet setting. As they climbed the hill to the granite-clad building that served as the administrative offices, James felt his legs grow heavy. With Kevin, he felt a burden of guilt and gloom as he foresaw the effect on Miriam of the news they were about to deliver.

The small room was quiet as Miriam sat at the narrow table, serious and sad, listening without interrupting to the summary of events Kevin gave her. Her expression was difficult to read as her small white face closed. There seemed to be anger there, thought James, but she didn't express it.

When he finished, Kevin sighed unconsciously, reaching out to touch Miriam's thin white hand as it lay on the table between them. But at that gesture she jumped up and, running around the table, her navy uniform hanging from her thin shoulders, she embraced Kevin silently. James stood up, walking to the window, sorry to intrude. Her reaction, he thought, was exactly right. For what words could she say to Kevin, or he to her?

"Daddy," she said at last in her soft girlish voice.

"Yes."

"Don't be angry anymore."

"I'm not."

"I think you are. You see, I don't care what's happened. Now that I know about Mrs. O., I want to talk to her, I want to talk to her about Mummy, you see."

"All right, chicken. I guess we . . ." He floundered.

"Miriam," said James, turning. "Mrs. O. has a few things to take care of, dear, but with any luck she will be released. I . . ." He hesitated. "I'll see what I can do. If she is released, she will need a place to go, to live?" James looked at Kevin.

"She'll come home, to us," said Kevin watching Miriam smile. "It is, has been, her home for nearly forty years. Where else should she go, hmm?" He let Miriam hug him again.

Privately James thought this vision of the three of them in the Lodge a bit grim. He wondered how they would, if in fact they could, live together. And how would they feel when she was sentenced, how would they feel when she left for prison, if the court were not compassionate.

"Miriam, dear, I think perhaps you might be able to help Mrs. O.," said James.

She looked startled, then hopeful. "How?" She stood up straight, ready to take commands like a little soldier.

"Listen, Miriam." James sat down, drawing her back

to the table. "I want you to try to remember anything that your mother might have told you . . ."

"About what?" Her voice was tremulous.

"About some work she was doing, or some research, documents of any kind. Or stories, stories she might have told you about the Lodge in the old days."

Miriam's face was like sunlight in the small cold room. "She told me hundreds of stories, Mr. Fleming, and I remember all of them. I used to help her, up in the attics." At this memory the sunlight faded and fresh tears filled her eyes. Kevin stood up, pacing, and she quickly brushed them away, glancing at his back and then again at James. This time her voice was stronger.

"What do you want to know then?" she said clearly.

"Your mother was working on a pamphlet of some kind. I think it might have some information in it, something very important to some other people . . ."

"Who?"

"I don't know that yet. But if I had her papers, I might be able to find out."

"I see, I think," she said seriously. "You think mother stumbled on something and didn't know what it was."

"Exactly," said James reassured by her perspicacity. "What do you say? Did she tell you anything or give you anything, perhaps, to read?"

"Yes, may I get it now?"

Kevin swung around. "Get what?"

"Mummy let me have a box of her papers, Daddy. She said I could read them and tell her what I thought. She gave them to me . . . to me . . ." Her voice choked but she went bravely on. "I just kept them ever since, along with her treasures. It was like having part of Mummy with me here at school. I've kept them under my bed all this time."

"Yes, chicken, just run and get them."

She returned in moments. "Do you have to take them

with you?'' asked Miriam, hesitating at the last minute to part with her mother's box.

James stepped back, allowing Kevin to glance quickly through the box of mementoes and notes.

"Listen, sweetheart, just take these few things and I'll take the box. But we'll get it back to you in a day or two. Right, Fleming?'' His voice was strained.

"Of course, of course.'' James nodded, agreeing to anything.

Kevin lifted out two small handkerchiefs carefully ironed, and handed them to Miriam. His hand shook as he also lifted out of the deep box a tortoiseshell comb which he'd bought for Mary on their honeymoon in Spain. A small pink satin book lay on the top, a baby book where Mary had recorded Miriam's first words, her first step, her first Communion. Kevin coughed and then cleared his throat. He ran his hand over Miriam's shiny brown hair and then pulled her towards him. James left them alone.

He waited for a long time outside, smoking three cigarettes one after the other. The packet he'd bought at the pub was empty and he balled it in his fist. All of his capital cases had been distressing, he considered, but this one was filled with endless pain, one event after another leading to a renewal of grief and loss for this tiny family.

He thought then of the Lodge standing lonely on its windswept promontory, guarded only and always by the ancient Celtic cromlech.

It had been, he had believed, a great house, a house that represented in itself the history of the country, in troubled times, in prosperous times, both ancient and modern. He had thought it, at first, a wonderful house, standing solid for generations, housing the O'Donnell family from small whitewashed cottage to grand hotel. He'd thought it a house of life, sheltering not only the family, but all who came within its walls, giving comfort and rest.

But now . . . He looked from his vantage point on the steps of the school towards the Lodge on the even higher horizon above him and saw the bleak November view: leafless tress and lifeless grass, the town below them hugging the river that ran through it, seeming to cower as the wind drove from the sea, wild and heartless.

He turned with relief as he saw Kevin step through the heavy double doors, the box under his arm.

"I'm sorry, Conlon," he said quietly.

Kevin shrugged and they ran quickly towards the Citroen as the skies opened, pouring forth a torrent of sleet and hail.

"Will it never end?" said Kevin as they drove slowly, James's vision obscured by the rain.

"I believe the end is in sight," said James.

"Good."

"You know, Kevin, Miriam is a strong, sensible girl."

"She's needed that strength." He cleared his throat again.

"She didn't get it off the wind."

Kevin smiled sadly, acknowledging James's compliment.

As they entered the Lodge, Kevin handed James the box.

"I'd like to get started right away, Kevin. Will you . . . ?"

"Yes, of course, of course, but you'll have to begin without me. I was just writing up an ad for the trade journals. I need a replacement for . . ."

"I know, I know."

"It was all so informal, with Mrs. O., it just evolved, you see. I don't even know what to ask for—a manager, I guess. Let me do this and you carry on. I do want to help you, however. Anything I can do to improve Mrs. O.'s situation, I will do."

James carried the heavy box to Kevin's study, anxious to begin. He set the box on the desk. As he began a general sorting of the contents into individual piles, he considered what he was seeking.

Even if Mary had found proof that a Dunmor ancestor had stayed at the asylum, what possible importance could it have today? The Dunmor family had been in public life for generations. A revelation of this girl's stay in the Lodge wouldn't even cause a scandal. She would be seen in the light of modern thinking: an unfortunate girl victimized by the morals and mores of her time.

The early death of the child would attract some fleeting attention, but everyone in Ireland knew of the great waves of consumption, of tuberculosis, that had plagued the country until the fifties.

But what if the child had not died? He paused. He recalled the last few entries in the journal. The child had been taken away, in good health. Aileen's father was expected shortly to bring the girl and the baby home. Perhaps it had all been an elaborate ploy. Perhaps, rather than attempting to get the girl to agree to an adoption, they had deceived her into thinking that her baby had died? His mind rebelled at this stray thought. Such an act was abominable in its cruelty.

He sat back. He realized that for the last few minutes he'd been speculating on the affect of a disclosure on the current Dunmor family, based on the assumption that there was a relationship between Aileen and the Dunmor family.

"But it's a fair assumption," he said to the empty room. And what secret would threaten the power and position of such a family? What were the most powerful social motives? Greed and fear, as James had learned to his cost. But how did they apply in this case?

Something was at risk. But what? If not life, then

property. But the Lodge was not at risk. Then someone else's property perhaps?

He began to sort through the contents of Mary's box. After he'd been working a mere twenty minutes, Kevin appeared in the study door.

"Come on, Fleming, if you don't eat with us now, that'll be it." When Kevin mentioned food, James realized how hunger and mental fatigue had been draining his energy. Covering the box he went willingly to the kitchen.

It was only a quick meal out of tins with Kevin and Sean, but the food and the good coffee revived him. When they'd finished, Sean hesitantly asked if he could have a few hours off. Kevin smiled, telling him to take as long as he wanted, and he'd see him in the morning.

"God, we're like a bunch of seminarians here!" exclaimed Kevin.

"Hey, at our ages we're more like monks. At least Sean looks like he'll have a night out, a date even!"

"Would you say he's thinkin' of quitting?" Kevin asked James as they finished their second cup of coffee.

"Of course not. Sean doesn't say much, but he's taking this news about Mrs. O. hard. He just needs a change of scene tonight."

"Perhaps, but if we don't get more business, he won't have enough scope for his talents."

With the last three guests gone from the Lodge, there was little cooking for Sean to undertake, little work for Kevin too, but as he said, at least it gave him ample time to help James.

Together they returned to the office. Installed in the outer room, Kevin set to work on one stack of Mary's papers.

"Tell me again what I'm looking for?"

"Let's assume that Mary turned up something in her research for her pamphlet. We're looking for any evidence of that work-in-progress."

"Right," said Kevin becoming immediately involved in the first thing he laid eyes on.

It was easier for James. Every item didn't refer to his own personal past, as it did for Kevin. More focussed, he was able to discern what was irrelevant and set it aside. Working quickly he came at last upon some handwritten pages, layered carefully in the bottom of the box. Suppressing his excitement, he read on to himself.

The sheets of looseleaf paper held notes about the history of the Lodge. Among them was a photocopy of a ledger page in a style he recognized. It was a log of names and Aileen Dunmor's name was circled. A date beside it indicated the year she'd come to the asylum. The bottom of the page held the signature of Sister Jeanne. Somehow, somewhere, in the trunks that he had searched so labouriously, Mary had found what he had been seeking: a list of the inmates of the asylum.

Deeper into the notes James came upon a sketch, a schematic of a family tree. It was perfectly straightforward. At the top was the name of Daniel Dunmor with a birth date of 1800. Immediately beneath this was another entry, also Daniel, with a birth date of 1850. And immediately beneath this was the name of Aileen Dunmor. Father, son, granddaughter.

And there it stopped. Mary had made no entry for the baby, also named Daniel, of whom he had learned only in Aileen's journal. Daniel was certainly the consistent family name for males, he mused. Not uncommon then or now, that the firstborn son carried the male first name in each generation.

Yes, despite the circumstances, Aileen Dunmor had reverted to old ways, naming her son after his grandfather and great-grandfather. But there the line died out. If Mary's research was complete, James considered, then this branch of the family was very much the lateral branch of the current famous Dunmor family of which Ciaran was a member.

But there were two big questions. One was, if the baby (of whom Mary had been unaware) had not died, and at some point was returned to the bosom of the family, then the line might very well have continued. Where was he now, or his descendants? Was Ciaran Dunmor in fact his son? He quickly wrote out the approximate ages of those involved and nearly laughed out loud. Ciaran Dunmor would have been born roughly around the same year as the baby Daniel. So that theory was out.

Ciaran Dunmor's first name, however, was Daniel, as James well knew! James wrote out a skeleton family tree, putting Ciaran and Daniel on a level with each other. He paused to recall what he had read in the journal about baby Daniel's father.

Baby Daniel's father had been Aileen's first cousin! James placed this unknown Dunmor on a level with Aileen's name in his sketch. In direct line from Ciaran he placed the present minister's name, Dennis. And after him his son, Daniel. He considered the pattern of names and an idea struck him. Two branches of the family. It seemed likely that the unnamed Dunmor was Ciaran's father. If he were, was it possible he had also been Aileen Dunmor's seducer and the father of her child?

Was this enough of a scandal to shake the Dunmor family? Unsavoury perhaps, but still not powerful enough to rattle a family as old and wealthy as they.

He returned with a sigh to the documents. There was more text and then a sheaf of photocopies which, James judged from the typeface and writing style, dated back to the nineteenth century. They were small notices in column format. James was impressed: Mary had done a lot of background research. Stapled to this sheaf was a note, "Daniel Dunmor, father of Daniel, 1850, and Dennis, 1851."

That was it, that explained the recurring names! Two

branches of the family springing from the original Daniel Dunmor born in 1800.

He studied the newspapers, reading the heavy-printed headline: Kildare—Unexplained Death of Daniel Dunmor . . . Local police puzzled by discovery of the body in the stables, etc., etc. . . . No leads, but accidental death seemed unlikely—James was frustrated by the lack of concrete detail—survived by his only child, Aileen, his brother, Dennis, and his nephew, Daniel Edward Dunmor. The missing items in the family tree!

James quickly filled it in:

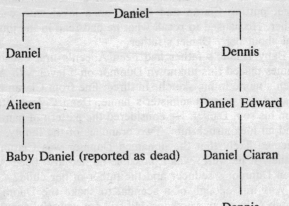

```
                      ┌─────Daniel─────┐
                      │                │
                      │                │
      Daniel                                  Dennis
        │                                        │
        │                                        │
      Aileen                              Daniel Edward
        │                                        │
        │                                        │
Baby Daniel (reported as dead)           Daniel Ciaran
                                                 │
                                                 │
                                              Dennis
```

He filled in the birth dates beside the names. Daniel, Aileen's father, had been born one year earlier than his brother, Dennis. As the firstborn, which James as a solicitor well knew, Daniel was likely to inherit the bulk of any estate from his father. James thought again of the journal, the description of Aileen's home, the rolling fields, the horses, the satin and silks, *the rolling fields!* Who else had mentioned those rolling fields, the wondrous estate in Kildare—that marvelous afternoon tea!

"Oh, my God . . ." he said half-aloud.

"Found something?" Kevin looked up from a paper he had been examining.

"I believe so. I . . . I just need a little more time."

Somehow, James reasoned, the estate had left the branch of the family sired by Daniel Dunmor and had been taken over by the branch sired by the younger brother, Dennis. The newspaper's veiled reports suggested foul play in the death of Daniel but no action had been taken. Was the family so powerful, the wealth so great as to quash a local police investigation? James had no doubt.

As Daniel's only surviving child, Aileen Dunmor would have inherited. And further, if her child had lived, he too would have had strong claim on the rights of inheritance—had he been acknowledged by his grandfather, had a will been drawn. He sucked in his breath and the sound startled them both.

Kevin looked up.

James waved him off. He was writing furiously. Suddenly he leapt to his feet.

"Look, Conlon, I think I've found something. But the information I need is contained in records at the old Registry of Lands in Dublin, among other places. You know the copy shop in the town with the fax machine? Do you think it's still open?"

Kevin glanced at his watch. "Yes, it's open for another hour."

"Right! I'll drive down and fax these details to my office. This way my clerk will have it first thing in the morning, and with any luck she can get back to me on this point possibly by lunch! If she does, it will prove the breakthrough on this case!" His excitement was palpable and Kevin asked no delaying questions but one.

"What in God's name does the Registry of Lands have to do with Breathnach?"

"In a nutshell, Conlon, poor Mrs. O'Neil was the wild

card in this whole situation. I think I've found the information which Breathnach was sent here to retrieve. I just want to confirm it with Dublin first. The thing is, Breathnach's murder clouded the whole issue—not only for us but for the people who hired him. If he'd lived, if he'd found these papers, none of us would ever have been the wiser.''

Kevin looked blank.

''While I'm gone I'd like you to continue with Mary's papers.''

Kevin winced. ''All right, since you believe the end is in sight. What am I to look for now?''

''Anything at all with the name of Dunmor on it, no matter how trivial.''

Kevin assented with a little reluctance and followed James to the foyer. Having seen him out the front door, he locked it sadly behind him. He had seldom locked the door of the Lodge so early in the evening. His thoughts drifted back.

There were the three days they'd closed the Lodge when Mrs. O'Donnell died. He saw her as she was, a quiet woman. A simple woman, he'd thought at the time. She'd liked him and he was fond of her as Mary's mother. And to think, she'd lived a lie all those years. Yet she was, in every way but one, Mary's mother.

He thought then of the week, not so long after, when Mr. O'Donnell died. The large funeral, well attended by the town and the outlying villages. It had been a wet and wild day, that day of the funeral, and Mary had grieved. She leaned on him then. They were so close in those days and every day since.

His vision blurred as he sat once again at the desk, the pile of Mary's papers still in front of him. He reached for one and his hand shook. This was too hard. He held a greeting card of congratulations Mary had received on the birth of Miriam.

Yes, the last time he'd closed up the Lodge so early

was the week that Mary had died. It seemed like only yesterday. He remembered the weather had been harsh, cruel, but he remembered little else. Nor did he want to.

He shook his head, trying to forget, trying to concentrate on the task at hand. He had to believe this was worth it. Fleming had been right up until now. He'd discovered Mrs. O.'s secret. The O'Donnell family secrets would all be out in the open now. No more secrets. He thought of Mr. and Mrs. O'Donnell and of Mary. All the principals involved were gone. But their secrets had lived beyond the grave. And now did the Dunmor family have some secret of their own?

He worked on, coming at last to a stack of correspondence, fastened with a paper clip. The letters were neatly typed and seemed to be copies of letters Mary had written. The one on top was a query to a local printer. Attached was his estimate for printing a pamphlet, giving various quotes on the number of pages and on typefaces, and so on. Yet another was an inquiry as to the cost of artwork to be done from a photograph of the front of the Lodge. Samples of leaflets and pamphlets from local churches, similar to what she'd had in mind, were in this pile.

He was surprised to find included what seemed to be letters asking for funds or backing of some kind. Surprised because Mary had been so very shy, so retiring. Not one, he mused, to ask for money, of all things. Her project had meant more to her than he realized. And he thought with chagrin that she'd shared her ideas only with Miriam, no doubt sensing his own lack of interest.

He read the first letter. It was to an historical association and Mary was attempting to interest them in the history of the Lodge, highlighting the centuries during which it had remained in the same family. He skimmed the next, also written the year before she died. This was to the local bishop inquiring if the tiny graveyard could be formally blessed. Another letter was to a company which made brass plaques, and asked for a quote on a line which read: The Cromlech Lodge, formerly the site of the Asylum for the Bewildered 1900–1920. He smiled sadly. Mary's plans had been ambitious.

The next letter held his attention completely and the smile faded from his face.

It was a letter from Mary to Dennis Dunmor, the government minister. In it she quoted a sentence or two from what she said might comprise the text of the proposed pamphlet. And then she mentioned that Aileen Dunmor had been a patient there in the early years of this century. Acknowledging how famous his family name was, she inquired if the Dunmor family would mind her mentioning their cousin Aileen in her narrative in the pamphlet, commenting that such a mention would make the history of the asylum and the Lodge more real to the reader.

The letter was so naive, he thought, wishing that she'd included him in her project. It was the history of the Lodge she treasured. She hadn't known that other people would not relish it in the same way. Or be willing to let their skeletons out of the closet, even after so very many years.

There was no reply attached to her copy of the letter. He checked the date and it wasn't long before her death. Had Dennis Dunmor bothered to reply? Busy as he most certainly was, he'd probably ignored it. Or had he perhaps handed it on to Ciaran Dunmor? A thought occurred to him and he stood up to get the hotel registers for the two previous years. Had Ciaran Dunmor's first visit to the Lodge come before or after the date of Mary's letter?

The office phone rang shrilly through the silent house. Could it be Fleming with some news already from Dublin? He was anxious to tell Fleming of his find. Mary's letter was possibly what he was seeking—a definite link between Aileen Dunmor, the Lodge, and the current Dunmor family. Ciaran Dunmor was involved somehow, but only Fleming seemed to have a sense of why. But what of Breathnach?

These thoughts flew through his mind as he picked up the receiver, half-expecting James's voice.

"Cromlech Lodge," said Kevin distinctly. A strange voice spoke.

"Is that Mr. Conlon?"

"Yes . . ."

"Well then, Mr. Conlon. If you want to see your friend Fleming alive, you'll bring them papers up to the cromlech in ten minutes' time."

The voice was gone.

Kevin hesitated, but only for a second. He quickly gathered up the papers James and he had been reading and shoved them into his belt, pulling his thick sweater over their bulk. Fearing he was losing precious time, he ran through to the back of the house. Without a backward glance he set off in the dark towards the cromlech that loomed gray against the blackness of the wild November night.

When James had turned the Citroen out of the old stone gates, he regretted leaving his jacket behind. Not only was the night bitterly cold, it was as dark a country night as he'd ever seen. He drove at a creeping pace along the narrow lane, as the mist swirled in the light of his halogens. Down he went, holding the Citroen on the brake, wary of any oncoming car that might loom out of the fog. Just ahead he saw a light, low to the ground, and as he neared he saw it was swinging in a small arc: the traditional signal of the police at random checkpoints. He sighed. Even more of a delay than the poor driving conditions. He put the car in park and waited, but no garda approached. He squinted but could see nothing, only the fog and the mist and the swinging light.

Perhaps, after all, it was another motorist in trouble. He engaged the car and crept forward. Yes, a car was splayed on the verge of the road. He pulled the Citroen in, parked and put on his fog lights. As he stepped from the car he hoped this wasn't a mechanical problem. If it were, he'd send a garage mechanic from the town. . . .

It was the smallest of sounds, a slight rush of the air behind him perhaps, perhaps a footfall on the paved road. Suddenly he knew the movement of air at his shoulder wasn't natural. But it was too late. The heavy club had already connected with the bone behind his right ear. Frightened by his sudden blindness he felt his knees buckle, his bowels revolt. He knew then he was sinking, sinking down. He wanted to call out—Sarah!— but he made no sound.

As James regained consciousness, his first sensation was a tremendous throbbing in his head. He began to lift it, and quickly laid it down, as though his head were an object separate from his body. The excruciating pain made him nauseous and he lay there gasping, his eyes still closed. Slowly he began to flex each of his limbs and they seemed to respond to a direct mental command—slowly, stiffly, but they responded. As he moved he felt the brambles catching, entangling his clothing. He heard nothing and saw nothing as he opened his swollen eyes and peered into pitch blackness.

With difficulty James rolled himself onto his stomach. Pausing to let the pain abate in his forehead, he slowly drew one knee up under him and then the other. He raised himself and rocked back on his heels, swaying with the dizziness this evoked. Suddenly he grew fearful as his mind finally regained some awareness. He froze, wondering if his attacker was still near.

No sound came but the wind rising in the branches overhanging the ditch in which he found himself.

As he dragged himself from the ditch up towards the level of the field and the road, he began to recall the swaying light, a car parked on the verge. James rested on the lip of the ditch and peered down the road. His Citroen was nowhere to be seen. He remembered that he'd started to get out of his car. And the rushing air.

He touched his head, his ear, bringing his hand away, recognizing the sticky sweet smell and texture of clotting blood. There was no one to be seen or heard, no cars, no people. He had a sense that he was, after all, alone.

Labouriously he dragged himself up the hill, concentrating on moving his legs and feet but, as he saw he was nearing the Lodge, his strength returned with the hope of safety, of at least a chair to sit in. He felt for his wallet and it was gone, everything was gone. The car. He sighed. He leaned on the gatepost gathering his powers to move towards the door. Stumbling, then running in a crazy jerky pattern, he lurched at the front door. If they'd attacked him, if they'd attacked him, then . . .

He pounded on the locked door with increasing strength. Calling Conlon's name he realized he'd hardly be heard in the vast Lodge. He worked his way around the house, leaning on the building itself, noting now that the lights on the corners, and those that lit the car park, were out. He felt, rather than saw, the open back door through which he'd passed on Halloween. As he was about to enter, he paused, resting against the rough-hewn wall.

He realized he'd no idea how many hours or minutes had passed. He had no sense of time or place. He heard his own harsh breath as though it came from afar.

The headache was overwhelming now and he shut his

eyes, sliding to the ground, his knees bent like broken matchsticks.

Where was Conlon? He wanted to call out, but feared the consequences. He assessed his situation. From his low vantage point he saw that the gate of the wider yard was ajar, the gate that led to the cromlech field. He stared, thinking fleetingly he'd seen movement, black on black, something hunched, almost animal-like.

He began to move in that direction. Lurching awkwardly, he reached the perimeter of the yard. The cromlech loomed ahead, within reach. He pushed on—a searing pain wrenched down the back of his head and spine and he fell facedown, unconscious, into the muddy clay.

The sound of his own stentorous breathing waked him and he felt for his watch. He hurled it away, the face smashed and useless. Conlon!

At some point the wind had risen to almost gale force and noise filled the countryside. James pulled himself to his feet and watched gratefully as that same wind drove the clouds from the face of the low yellow November moon. Slowly a ghastly but brilliant light lit up the house and grounds, and silhouetted the cromlech on the rise of the field.

There was no movement of any human kind.

He strained to see the cromlech clearly. He strained to see what he thought was a figure, perhaps a human figure, shadowed against the now gray-gleaming pillar, one of the three portals that supported the capstone of the cromlech. Hugging the ground he moved stiffly towards the icon.

He began to run as the shape he had discerned assumed more human form.

Sweat streamed down his face and arms as he ran what seemed like miles. As he crossed the last remaining twenty yards, he heard his own voice calling, then screaming, into the wild wind.

"Conlon, Conlon, Oh, God, Conlon."

He ran towards the figure, recognizing the shape of the head, the back, recognizing the heavy Aran sweater, wondering wildly why Conlon was standing so still, embracing the rough-hewn rock.

Closer, closer, till he put his hand on Kevin's shoulder, his mind denying what his eyes were telling him.

"Conlon."

Kevin Conlon's lifeless body slid down the pillar at James's touch. His face and the side of his head crushed against the cromlech, the coagulating blood drew down the pillar in a dark streak until his body slumped into a kneeling position. James fell to his knees beside the murdered man, embracing him around the shoulders. And as he held him, the poor battered head fell onto his shoulder, and he felt its weight.

Whether he cried out or not, whether he prayed or not, he never knew. And there he stayed, until the lightening sky showed to Sean, returning at dawn, the gruesome scene, silvered over by a hard and gleaming frost.

——— *Chapter Fifteen* ———

James knew he couldn't wait for Cronin and his men to arrive. Cronin would question him and he would be obliged to tell him what he knew. And what he thought he knew. He had to get to Dublin, the element of surprise was crucial.

He glanced at the ashen-faced Sean who was already on his second brandy. He'd had trouble convincing him that they had to leave Kevin's body where it was, that it was critical for the police to be able to see the crime scene intact. But he'd allowed Sean—he could hardly prevent him—to cover the kneeling form with a blanket.

"I need your car, Sean," James said firmly.

Sean looked at James's bruised face, his torn clothes, the sway of his body as he gulped a third cup of black coffee.

"Give me the keys," James commanded.

"Are you mad?" Sean reacted to his tone. "You're not going anywhere. I don't know what went on out there, but I do know you're bloody well not leavin'!"

"I didn't do anything . . . you know I didn't do anything to Kevin." James's voice broke. "But, Sean, for Christ's sake, I can do something now! Give me your keys."

"Jesus. Kevin's still out there . . ."

James felt sick at the thought, recalling how Sean's voice had brought him to his senses in the cold white dawn, recalling all over again the terrible scene, recalling Sean raving and crying out to the far reaches of the gray heavens above them. But no help came. No one heard their quarreling voices or Sean's cries.

"Look, man, you've called the police. Inspector Cronin will be here shortly. We can't help Kevin now. But I can do something . . . I can avenge his death!"

"Get out, then. Get out! You've brought nothing but trouble to this house." He threw the keys across the cold white floor.

James grabbed them, ran to the lobby, and flipping through the phone log, quickly located the number he sought. He rang the small local airport and not for the first time he was grateful he'd memorized his credit card number. Within seconds he had booked a passage on the morning commuter flight to Dublin. There was no time to change but he needed his bag. Running through the house he was horrified to see the havoc, the destruction that had been wreaked throughout the Lodge. Everywhere he looked he saw that anything that could have possibly concealed papers or documents had been opened, broken, overturned, or strewn. It had been done in haste but the effect was nonetheless total. Suddenly, James remembered the journal. Throwing aside the broken desk, the toppled chairs, he sought out the safe in the floor of the office. He tore up the carpet and heaved a sigh of relief, the first that day. The safe was untouched. The murderers hadn't known of it, hadn't known to look. Throwing the carpet back in place, he retrieved his bag and set off in haste.

Fortunately for him, the road to the airport was in the

opposite direction from which Cronin or the police would be travelling. He drove as fast as possible without speeding, watching always in his mirror, watching every car that passed.

In the men's room, with a few seconds to spare, he bathed his swollen face and neck, removing most of the dried blood. Wrapping his neck with the scarf from his bag, he concealed his bruised condition as best he could. His clothes were torn and muddied but there was nothing to do but to brazen out the stares of the staff and fellow passengers. If they thought he was drunk at seven o'clock in the morning, what did he care . . . what did he care.

The flight was rough but uneventful. Scrunched up and squeezed between the armrests of the undersize seat, James was buffeted from side to side as the noisy propellor plane ploughed its way up through thick clouds, sometimes parting them to reveal the small lonely island in the north Atlantic that was Ireland. He actually dozed. When he awoke, the suburbs of Dublin lay beneath him and he was within minutes of the airport.

Maggie hadn't questioned him when he'd called her at home just before his flight took off. Absolutely reliable as always, she'd arranged a driver and car to meet him at the airport, bringing him a change of clothes. And she'd taken careful note of his instructions to his clerk regarding the research he wanted done urgently at the Registry of Lands, and what the clerk should do with it when she found it.

The driver didn't speak beyond the initial pleasantries and if he wondered at James changing into his suit in the backseat of the car, he never said. Nor did he question James's request to stop at a chemist shop and purchase some painkillers.

James's head was pounding still, but gradually his vision was clearing, physically and mentally. The technological power of plane and automobile had brought him this far, but it was as nothing to the power of his feelings of despair, of horror, of incalculable rage that had moved him from the cromlech in that Sligo field to this very point on the highway leading into Dublin city centre, leading to Ciaran Dunmor.

Instructing the driver to wait, no matter how long he was gone, James leapt from the car. Pain in his spine and head caught at him and he paused, then walked more slowly up the flight of granite steps to the door of the Georgian building.

A startled young man, apparently Brendan's replacement, tried to bar him as he entered.

Seeing the alarm on the man's face, seeing the curious faces of the waiting crowd of petitioners, James calmed himself. He adjusted his tie and smoothed his cuffs in his old decorous manner. He cleared his throat.

"I have to see Mr. Dunmor," he said with feigned courtesy.

"He's not here," the man countered.

James leaned closer to the man's face. "I don't believe you," he hissed, so the others might not hear. "Let me see him now, or you'll have a scene on your hands that will make the front pages of every paper in this country!"

"You'll have to give me a minute then," said the man. He disappeared behind the inner door and seconds later escorted a flustered old woman clutching a shopping bag out of Dunmor's private office.

"He'll be with you in five minutes," said the man, taking command once again.

"Too long," said James, fearing Dunmor would leave by another door. He pushed past the man and opened the door.

"I'll ring for the police," said the man levelly.

"Be my guest. Your master won't like it though . . ."

As he'd anticipated, the back door of the office was

225

ajar. Desk drawers were open, ledgers and file folders strewn everywhere. James swung around wildly to see Dunmor in the corner, a gaping briefcase hanging from his hand. For a second his face showed fear.

"Dunmor!" James confronted him. "Dunmor! You can't run now, not from me."

"For your information, not that it's any of your business, I'm on my way to Brussels for an appointment." The man had immediately recovered his composure, his voice strong, clear, dismissive. He continued packing papers from a wall safe into his open bag.

"None of my business, is it?" James had trouble controlling his voice. "Perhaps my mental confusion is delirium then, brought on by the attack on me last night."

"Attack?" Dunmor looked at James standing still near the office door. "Why, Fleming, your face . . . I didn't see it clearly. There's some blood . . ."

"Come off it, Dunmor. You thought I was Banquo's ghost when I walked in here, didn't you? I should be a ghost, shouldn't I? That was the intention. Your thugs probably rang you last night, to say the deed was done . . . didn't they . . . didn't they?"

"Keep your voice down, Fleming," Dunmor commanded.

James moved stiffly towards the centre of the room. Half-leaning, half-sitting, he propped himself on Dunmor's enormous desk. "Why? I have nothing to hide."

"You have something to preserve . . ."

"What, my good name? That's your own problem now."

"No, not your name, your very life." The man's face transformed itself. The rosy cheeks had faded to a mask of gray and white. The eyes glittered and his breath came fast and loud.

"Don't tell me you're threatening me," scoffed James.

"Think about it, Fleming. I'm going to walk out of here in ten minutes. To safety. But where are you going?

226

Back to your petty little practice, to your empty flat. You'll never know the time or the place . . ."

"Oh, now you're God—is that it?—meting out death."

"Isn't that why you're here, because I've succeeded once already? Why think you'd be different?"

"So you deny nothing?"

"I confirm nothing, I deny nothing. Why should I? There's no one here. No mechanical bugs, no tape recorders. And"—he paused as he snapped shut his bag—"you're a dead man."

"Dead men don't tell tales, is that it?"

"It's been said before, Fleming."

"I'm not dead yet."

"You're as good as . . ."

James moved back suddenly as the man came towards him, but he only circled the desk, surveying the open drawers.

"I'm leaving and no one, least of all you, can stop me," he said.

James moved behind him blocking the open door as an escape. "Since I'm dead already," he said calmly, "I'd like to ask you . . . no, I'd like to *tell* you a story."

Dunmor stopped. "What story?"

"About a young man, a decent man, not a lot younger than your own son . . ."

"Keep him out of this."

"As I said," James repeated, pointedly, maintaining control of the situation, "a man not a lot younger than your son. This man led a simple, even unremarkable, life of hard work and affection.

"He loved his wife, he loved his child. A child who is now an orphan. By all that's holy—that child has lost her mother, now her father. The woman who is her real grandmother is now in jail on a charge of murder!"

"Grandmothers! Murder! What does all this have to do with me?"

"Everything. Everything that has happened in the last six weeks, perhaps longer, has been at your behest!"

"Fleming, don't be a fool . . ."

"Oh, but that's exactly what I've been—a fool, a terrible fool. A fool to believe you, to believe in you."

"Who asked you to . . . ?"

"You asked me to. Just like you ask everyone who meets you, everyone who meets your son. Politicians— all of you. You ask us to make the bargain with you, to trust you."

"Leave my son out of this! You don't know what you're talking about. Politics—it's a job like any other. The Dunmor family is good at it. I was good at it. My . . . my son is good at it . . ." Pride swelled his voice. But he moved quickly around his desk, glancing at files, sorting on the instant. James ignored his actions, caught up in his anger.

"A job like any other? How can you say that? You do nothing from one end of the week to the other but wield influence, make promises—"

"Correction, Fleming. I fulfill promises."

"Oh, of course. Isn't that what keeps you in power . . . the wheeling and the dealing?"

"What keeps that waiting room full?" Dunmor waved to the outer office, his voice calm, almost paternal.

"I'll tell you. Greed keeps it full, and fear, and self-interest . . ."

"No, I'll tell you. Powerlessness keeps that room full. Those people have no power. The little people as the papers like to call them. And they are. You've seen them. Oh, the likes of you don't deal with them, as I do. What little people, what regular man in the street, can afford your hourly rates, tell me that? What *pro bono* work do you undertake? None, I'd guess. You're not the type."

"I'm not here to answer your questions."

"And why should I answer yours! I'll tell you, Fleming, you're insulated from the real world, the world of that room out there. I help people, I help people all day long. Do you?"

"That's ridiculous." James blustered.

"You don't help people. You provide a service. A service for which you charge, for which you're hand-somely paid. If not by the person directly involved, then by a healthy percentage of an estate."

"And you're not paid?"

"Am I? Man, you know I'm not. I'm on salary from my son. Before that, when I held office I also made a fixed income, as my son does now, as my father before me."

"And a handsome one by the look of it."

"Come off it. You know our salaries. You know most of us could not survive on salary alone."

"Then you make it on the side . . ."

"Oh," sneered Dunmor, "it's the old graft and corruption line, is it?"

"It's been known . . ."

"Not in my family, by God, and I'd take an oath on the life of my son that none of us has made money out of our public lives, out of our very public service."

"You've made it to this pinnacle of success, you lying bastard, you and your son and God knows how many others in your family. . . . You stand there and take oaths before God, and say this to me, when you are here because you built your whole lives and fortunes on the death and destruction of your own flesh and blood?"

"Shut your slandering gob!"

"Why, because the little people out there, the ones who kiss your feet like some kind of local god, might hear me? Well, they will hear me, everyone will hear me, everyone will know—"

"Shut your mouth I'm tellin' ye!" The man made a move towards his drawer and James stopped, unsure of his quarry.

Dunmor saw him. "You're afraid. You really believe I'd have a weapon here, that I'd use it!" His voice was raucous, laughing in derision.

James recovered. "Probably not. Guns aren't your style, are they? No, hiring people like Breathnach to do your dirty work, to skulk and badger and blackmail to get what you wanted from Conlon, that's your style. Hiring murderers is your style! Hiring scum who nearly split my skull is your style. *Your* style is to hire people you've never seen and never will, to batter an innocent man to death against a stone pillar." He watched but Dunmor never flinched.

"Smash and break a man, and leave him in a goddam field to die . . ." James's voice broke. "To die alone. He was standing, you know, Dunmor. Standing up. Standing up dead."

James moved towards Dunmor who backed away, fear showing on his face. "I'd like to kill you with my bare hands, Dunmor, choke the filthy life out of you right here and now."

"Go ahead, Fleming, your true colours are coming out now. Kill me, and then what would make the difference between you and any common murderer, between you and me?"

"No, no, I won't." James clenched his fists. "I've something much worse in mind. I'm going to bring you down, I'm going to hurt you where it will hurt you most—in public. I'll bring you down, and your son and your grandson with you."

"You?" Dunmor started to laugh. "You'd have a better chance if you decided to kill me now. But you won't. You can't. You don't have the guts. You're nothing but a little middle-class, tuppence-ha'penny lawyer. Who are you to bring me down, or my family? What have you got? Your parents' money? Your superior Protestant airs? A flash car, a little flat? Why, you're small potatoes, man. You always were and you always will be."

"I can hold my head up . . ."

"Hold your head up, is it? Guiltless, are you? You thought you were so damned clever. Did you plan it? Did your hands sweat when you phoned me—on my private line? I bet that made you feel important . . . when I gave you my card. And why? Because you liked me? I doubt that. Because I have power. You were the moth to the flame, and transparent at that!"

James flinched at the truth.

"Hah! I see in your face I'm right. And you talk of my wheeling and dealing. You were wheeling and dealing with someone else's life. With Conlon's life! Phoning me, bluffing me."

"What are you saying?" James shouted.

"Do you think Conlon would be dead if you hadn't interfered?"

"It was you, Dunmor! You killed him as surely as if you crushed in his head yourself. You hired those thugs—"

"Come off it, Fleming. Think about it. You're the lawyer here, not I. I'm just a politician. You're the one who deals in words, in logic, use it now. Would he be alive today . . . ?"

James halted, breathless, the guilt he'd been feeling since he'd come to in the cromlech field flooding through him, vitiating the revenge that had burned in him for hours.

"I said, would he be alive today if you hadn't pushed this investigation too far . . . ?"

"He'd be alive if you hadn't—"

"No, no! answer my question. Would he? Would Conlon be alive? You found Breathnach's murderer. Well done. I'm not sure how you did it. Sometimes you're good at your work, I suppose. You found the murderer. Conlon was cleared . . ."

"But he was sorry it was Mrs. O'Neil . . ."

"Grow up, Fleming. Sure, you say she was in some bizarre way related to him . . . but *bizarre* must be the word. Sure he was sorry. But he would have got over that. Life goes on, as the pundits are so fond of saying. Life goes on"—his voice dropped—"as long as you're still alive."

James felt the words like a slap across his face.

Dunmor saw the effect and he seized the moment. "Mmm. I see," he said in a conversational tone as he sat down behind the desk and toyed with some papers, "I see you take my point."

"What point?" James said dully.

"That if it weren't for you and your meddling, Conlon would be alive now. Did he care why Breathnach was there? Did he really care who hired Breathnach? I doubt it. He had his own life to get on with."

"A life you took!" shouted James.

"No, a life that you risked, as though it were nothing to you. Part of a game of cat and mouse. A life you risked when you pushed this case too far. Into areas you didn't understand. I see it now, I see it now . . ." The man had the almighty nerve to laugh.

"See what?"

"You had no idea what you were doing when you phoned me. I thought so at the time. And now I know. You were fishing . . . bluffing."

"So you admit that after my call you took action, against Kevin, against me."

"I admit nothing. You made a call that, I tell you, was the foolish act of an arrogant man."

James himself sat down. Somehow a lull had come over the room, tension held in abeyance. He rubbed his eyes and winced where the bruises still hummed. What had he thought? That just seeing him would cause Dunmor to cave in, to confess, to collapse in his arms with guilt? His anger and vengefulness had served no constructive purpose. His own guilt was obscuring the issue.

He tried to regain his focus, his anger. He thought of Kevin and felt an overwhelming wave of sorrow, revenge ebbing away. But in its place came a more useful emotion. He looked up at the man opposite him, seemingly filing some papers. A better emotion filled him: hatred, pure and cold and clear, hatred that superseded any other feeling he harboured. It calmed the turmoil in his mind.

"Whatever my role," he began carefully. Dunmor's head snapped up, watching him warily. "I will assume the blame, the guilt. I'll live with it perhaps all my life. My role was as nothing compared to your own. You are ultimately responsible. You caused Conlon's death, you have orphaned his innocent child. I don't believe trying to bring you to law will work . . ."

"Aha! and this from a lawyer. You're a quick study, aren't you?" Dunmor's voice had hope.

"No, the law in this case won't be sufficient. Except perhaps in the details . . ."

"Details?"

"Yes, the nitty-gritty. The kind of journeywork for which I am so well paid, as you said. Yes, the transfer of your estate, your son's, your grandson's inheritance—those little details . . . Yes, the law is very good at that."

"What are you talking about?"

"The law worked well enough for your family in the past. The remote past perhaps. But the laws of inheritance don't change all that much in this country, do they?"

"You're rambling, Fleming."

"I don't think so, Dunmor. I know the law in this regard. And I know a higher law. I know that justice and retribution can be served in other ways than in a court of law."

"A higher court, huh? Didn't know you lawyers thought in those terms."

"Did I say higher? No, I think I meant different."

"Such as?"

"The court of public opinion."

"You'll lose there, my man, I hold that court, I hold that public opinion in the palm of my hand. You can't touch me or my son or our family name."

"I can and I will. I'll bring you down, all of you, I'll bring you down, as God is my witness." James's voice was like steel.

"Is that your best shot, Fleming?" Dunmor stood up as though concluding an interview.

"Yes."

Dunmor patted his breast pocket. "Not without these papers. You have nothing and you know it. You're bluffing again. And look what that cost. Will you now stake your own life?"

"Is that a threat?"

"That was a question, lawyer. You can't trap me with your petty courtroom training. You have nothing. I hold all the cards." He laughed again.

"Then the answer is yes, I would risk my life to bring you down, to see justice done."

"Justice. You're not concerned with justice, man. You've got revenge on your mind. Don't cloak it in ethical terms."

"You talk to me of ethics? You, who have taken Conlon's life away? Your tongue should shrivel and blacken in your head." James moved in his chair as if to get up.

"Listen, Fleming, be realistic. You have no proof of any of these wild accusations. You in your lowly position can do nothing to touch me legally. You think that you could run to the media—they'll eat you alive. One man such as yourself against a family such as ours! We dine with heads of state, we lunch with bishops and cardinals, we golf with financiers. . . ."

"You won't do any of that when the truth comes out."

"The truth? Do you think they care for truth of that kind. They deal in reality, man, same as meself."

"The reality is you're guilty and they won't associate with anyone as guilty as you."

"Do you think they'll care about a Conlon? If they heard of him, they probably thought he'd killed Breathnach. Small potatoes like yourself. Some locals revenged themselves on him for Mrs. O'Neil going to jail—and that's an end of it."

"The police won't buy it, Dunmor."

"The police don't have to. The trail is cold. They'll never find who did it. I assure you of that." Dunmor walked to a roomy closet and removed a cashmere coat and trilby hat and threw them on the chair. The phone buzzed on his desk and he picked it up casually.

"No, no trouble, Michael. Dismiss the others. I'm leaving for Brussels in moments. . . . Yes, I said Brussels. An urgent matter for the Minister . . . Yes, Fleming's here . . ." His face changed slightly as he handed James the phone. "It's your clerk."

James listened to his clerk's voice and keeping his face expressionless, he answered monosyllabically. Dunmor moved about the room, but it was obvious he was keenly listening. James hung up the phone.

"Do you think the bishops, the clergy, do you think the financiers, the power brokers would be interested in your family history?" James resumed. His tone had hardened and Dunmor knew it.

"I doubt it. It's as old as their own or older, nothing exceptional."

"A skeleton in your closet would not interest them?"

"They have their own, I assure you." Dunmor was dismissive as he took out a cigar from its case and took some moments to light it.

"Then the little people as you so condescendingly call

them—would they be interested to know how you came into your great wealth, the wealth that gave you and your son the power you wield today?''

"As long as we can help them with their petty concerns, I doubt it very much indeed." The man's cynicism was overpowering and James fought to find a chink through which to pierce it.

"Let me rephrase it then."

"Ah, in the courtroom again, are we? I see why you never became a barrister."

James ignored the barb. "Let me put it this way. What if your wealth was stripped away from you today? Would your position remain the same? Or your power?"

At last he had Dunmor's full attention.

"Hard to say. Very few in this country manage to climb back the ladder of power after grave financial loss. But my son and I—we're a conservative lot—the stock market never was our source of investment. I know others have been rocked of late, but not ourselves."

"Your money, your son's, is all tied up in the family, yes? In the property, savings accounts, holdings, I imagine?"

"Yes, but that's for all to see. We have no secrets there, no insider trading, no embezzlement . . . we've seen others go that way, to their own cost."

"And the country's?"

"The country always survives, it takes its body blows, it always has."

"Ill-served by its politicians?"

"No doubt, but then that's the way of the world, isn't it? I fail to see what direction you're taking here, Fleming." Yet he sat wanting to know more, curious as to James's confident manner, more threatening than any violence would have been.

"Bear with me, then. I want to relate a story . . ."

"Your first story didn't amount to much. . . ."

"This is a different story, and a very costly one."

James laughed hollowly and it startled Dunmor. "Should I say, an expensive story, but I'll let you be the judge.

"Once, Mr. Dunmor, there was a man who had two sons. He had worked hard, bought well, had good fortune, and was prudent. He'd amassed a huge estate in Kildare, a full stable of valuable horses, and a real fortune of money. At his death, he left the bulk of this estate to his elder son, but left the other well provided for. The brothers were on friendly terms and lived on adjoining estates. Both brothers married well and each had a child, one a daughter, Aileen, the other a son, called Daniel Edwin." James watched as Dunmor's face grew hard and cold.

"I see you know this story . . ."

"Go on."

"When these two cousins were coming of age, Edwin seduced Aileen. Perhaps he believed he could marry her, perhaps it had been as simple and utilitarian as that. But when he discovered he could not, perhaps that's when his plan began to formulate."

"There was no plan."

"How do you know that?" snapped James. But Dunmor refused to answer.

"Since Daniel Edwin couldn't have his first cousin, Aileen, for his wife, he made a marriage of convenience and later had a son himself, a legitimate son. Perhaps he sat there on the adjoining estate envying the wealth, the fortune, as his own father never had envied it, never had coveted it. No doubt, it was an unjust system, but it was, as you like to say, the way of the world. Edwin craved that wealth for himself, for he wanted to gain power as well. You are your father's son, wouldn't you say?" James was sarcastic but failed to rouse Dunmor.

"Poor Aileen was sent away to have her child in secret. Aileen was a problem to Edwin. She was in direct line to inherit all that he wanted and could not gain by marriage. Only she—and her illegitimate son—stood in his way of legally inheriting everything.''

"That son died," blurted Dunmar.

"Be patient, I've nearly finished. Edwin's father died of what we now know to be cancer of the stomach. It was quick, and Edwin became head of his family. He watched from afar as Aileen returned from Sligo, a broken woman.

"So might they have lived. Her father might have lived many years. What a waste, Edwin must have thought. An old man and an unmarriageable girl. The estate would have come to Edwin and his heirs in time—at the eventual death of her father and herself dying a spinster. But he didn't want to take the chance, he didn't want to wait. Just two people stood in his way . . . And then the father was murdered."

Dunmor's eyes were watching James and they narrowed, but still he did not speak.

"The police, perhaps they were bought off. Perhaps that's where it all started, this idea you have that wealth and power can accomplish anything, put you above the law, above morality. For Daniel Edwin Dunmor certainly was neither moral nor—''

"How dare you! My father was—''

"Your father, Dunmor, killed his uncle! Or had him killed. He only had to wait. And he waited patiently as the courts allowed for Aileen to inherit. Picture Aileen now"—James slowed his narrative deliberately—"alone, estranged, without a future. Destroyed in that asylum in Sligo as surely as if they had killed her, because they had killed her soul.

"She died, I know that, only a year after her father. The estate she'd inherited on her twenty-first birthday only a month before her death passed in its entirety to Edwin, your father. . . . Tell me this. Did he kill Aileen too?"

"You lousy bastard!" Dunmor pushed back his chair

from the desk, his face purple, eyes bulging. James braced himself for a physical attack. "I'm telling you. She died, she was a lunatic, everyone said so."

"Who is everyone, may I ask? I doubt more than two or three people ever knew of this story. Did your father tell you, Dunmor?"

"Yes, he did. She was an insane woman, completely mad. She'd inherited—have you seen it?—have you seen our estate in Kildare? In the hands of a twenty-one-year-old mad woman . . ."

"The courts didn't find she was mad, did they?"

"No, but . . ."

"But nothing. Did he tell you how he did it?"

"She bloody killed herself. It's there, covered up, but it's there. My father suppressed it, he paid off everyone, even the church. She was buried from the church . . ." Dunmor was shouting. "That should tell you something about the way of the world. Even the church can be bought. . . . What do you think I believed in, listening to that, knowing what I knew, growing up in Kildare?"

"No, Dunmor. What it was like? Did you walk around your manor house, ride your horses, look out over the fields and think how it all might not have been yours?"

"I was a boy. All I knew was what I was told. Aunt Aileen, she was really a cousin as you say, had been sick and then died young. I never thought about it. Does a child think of these things? Father went into politics when I was a child, in Kildare. He was loved, I tell you. He did good. I am what I am today because of him . . ."

"Yes, indeed you are . . . a murderer!"

Dunmor fell back. "A man of the people."

"Honest to God, I do believe you mean that."

"Of course I do. It's been our life, all of us. Look at my son—there's your answer."

"Yes, let's look at your son. I believe he's due here at any time . . ."

Dunmor's purple face was sweating visibly and he

was gulping air. James feared the man was having a coronary. As Dunmor opened his tie, James started for the phone but Dunmor waved him away, gathering his powers, regaining his voice.

"You asked him here?"

"Why not? He's a part of all of this," James gestured, indicating realms. "Why shouldn't he be here?"

"Because he knows nothing, nothing, I tell you. . . ."

"Knows nothing about what? You've said the records are there for all to see: the inheritance, all legal, Aileen's death, tragic, and so on and so on." James said it all in a singsong tone, like retelling a fairy tale.

"He knows nothing. I never would allow him to find out. My father concealed it all well, and later so did I. As far as I knew there were no records. That is, until my son received that silly letter from Conlon's wife. My son was so disinterested, he merely handed it on to me, thank God, with all of his other social correspondence. At first it seemed a simple matter of retrieving the documents she'd found . . ."

"But why! Why!"

"I didn't want my son ever to know, I did not want to do to him what my father did to me," Dunmor whispered.

"What did he do? Tell me, tell someone . . . you've held it in all these years."

"I knew nothing, as I said. I was a boy, a deliriously happy, healthy, yes, wealthy boy with the world at my feet. My life was good and remained that way. I entered politics and helped my father. He taught me, primed me, I would inherit and he taught me prudently and well. When he was dying I was sorry, but he'd had a long, powerful public life, a good life. I was ready to fill his shoes.

"I was at his side for days as he too died of cancer." Dunmor's voice grew strange as he looked back to that final scene.

"He was dying, finally, one black December day, and he was frightened, raving, calling out in the pain, screaming to God. It shook me to my very soul. I had never thought of him as anything but strong and fearless . . . And now he was afraid."

"What was he afraid of?"

"Of hell, Fleming, of hell. He told me he'd had his uncle, Aileen's father, killed. I had known about that for years. He'd told me when he saw I was following him into public life. He said he didn't want any surprises rearing up their heads then or in the future. He wanted me to know, to be prepared. I'd chosen to live with that. As he had. It was expedient.

"But Aileen. That was different. He'd loved her or so he said that day. It was then he told me about the child, the son he'd had with her. I thought I'd vomit. He actually told me that I had a brother. My God! A brother. He wanted me to be happy at this news! I was screaming in his face. But he wouldn't listen to me, and then there he was, calling for a priest. But I wouldn't get one. I called him a hypocrite. A liar. He told me then he'd loved Aileen. Over and over, he told me. And then . . . and then . . . he told me that he'd driven her to her death.

"Evil! Evil. He'd visit her, talking about the child, blaming her for its death, knowing all the time that the child had lived, that the whole thing had been arranged to deceive her so that she wouldn't bring the child home. He knew the child had been adopted but he never told her. He worked on her mind, day after day. Lying, in secret. He worked in secret like the archfiend himself, until she hung herself in the stables where her father had died, where her father had been murdered by my own father. She hung herself in the stables where I had played as a little boy. Monster. Monster. He destroyed me in the last hour of his life, he destroyed me . . ."

"Did you call for the priest?"

"No. The staff had called for him and he waited out-side the locked door. He could hear my father calling out. He and the doctor. But I had locked the door against them. They stood there calling, and he lay there screaming, and I stood between them. Voices . . . voices screaming." He clamped his hands over his ears as though he could hear them still.

The door suddenly burst open. It was Michael. "Mr. Dunmor, Mr. Dunmor . . . I could hear your voice outside. . . ."

"Get out!" screamed Dunmor.

"So you've known all these years," said James.

"Yes."

"You knew that your father and you had inherited as a result of virtually two murders."

"Yes."

"And you also knew . . ."

"That under the law it could be taken away from us by the state, of course." Dunmor spat the words at him.

"Or by your brother?"

"Half-brother!" Dunmor leapt to his feet. "Where is he? Is that what this is all about? You've found him?"

"I don't have to. The courts will do that. It's over. You know that."

"Not by a long shot. No one knows any of this but you. Years ago I traced that illegitimate bastard. What few records there were, I managed to have destroyed. And now I have the documents you and Conlon found. There's no record of that child . . ."

"Your brother . . ." James insisted.

"Father wanted me to find him, you see." Dunmor's voice changed again as he returned to that deathbed scene. "He wanted to be shriven. He wanted to go to heaven. And me to help him get to heaven." Dunmor laughed derisively. "He wanted me to find this 'brother' and bring him home, to my home." He looked at James coldly. "If I didn't do it then, why the hell do you think

I would do it now? Because of you, Fleming, you miserable little shite?''

"Dunmor, it's over. Everything you did, every step you took all these years to cover the secrets of your father, all for nothing. Hiring Breathnach, Breathnach's death—for nothing. The taking of Kevin Conlon's life—all for nothing. For nothing! Everything you did—all futile. You will lose it all—the house, the estate, the art, the treasures, the investments." James was shrill. "Yes, your power! You and your son and your grandson after you. You will pay for Kevin Conlon's life. But you're old and spent. Your son—" James's spittle flew through the air. "Yes, your son will pay, and you'll live to see the name of Dunmor dragged through the mud. And you will be responsible. You, a murderer, as your father before you. You are Daniel Ciaran Dunmor—your father's son . . ."

"That's enough!" A hard voice called from the doorway, startling both men into a gasping dumbfounded silence.

Both turned to see a gaunt but imposing man standing in the open door. Dennis Dunmor pulled off his fine leather gloves slowly, his expression grave but judicious.

"Did you . . . ?" spluttered Ciaran Dunmor. He turned on James. "How dare you! How dare you ask my son here!"

"He didn't, sir," Michael spoke in a virtual whisper from the door. "When I saw the time passing . . . when I heard your raised voices . . . I believed you were under some personal attack from this man. It did not, however, seem a matter for the police. I took it upon myself to phone your son at his office."

"Get out!" roared Dunmor. Michael left, closing the door behind him.

"A bit of a disagreement here," said Ciaran Dunmor,

as he smoothed his hair, his mask almost back in place. He picked up his briefcase. "I've a plane, you see."

"For where?" his son said tonelessly.

"Brussels, of course. That matter you asked me to—"

"I asked nothing of you." He looked from his father to James. "Is it true, what this man has been saying?"

"How long were you listening?" his father hesitated.

"Too long . . . too long." He walked to the desk and picked up the phone. He handed it to his father who took it, with a question in his eyes. "Ring your solicitor," he said with finality.

Matt grabbed James's hand warmly, ready to slap him heartily on the back. But when he saw the green and purple bruises only half-hidden by James's dark curly hair, he refrained.

"My God, look at you!" he exclaimed as they entered their favourite haunt, the snug at the end of the bar at Doheny and Nesbitt's Pub.

"You should have seen me a few days ago. But the tenderness is going, and the swelling." James smiled a crooked tentative smile.

"Guinness, my man, and lots of it—the best cure for what ails ye."

"Sounds great to me," agreed James, and as they supped their pints, James recounted the details that hadn't made the newspapers.

It was a long story but at the end of it, Matt had only one question. "What was it that you needed to find out from the Registry of Lands?"

"When I read the death notices of Aileen's father, in the stack of Mary Conlon's research, I realized that Aileen would have inherited. I had a hunch and acted on it. The Registry of Lands would show to whom the property went on *her* death. My clerk discovered the date of her early death *and* the record of the transfer of that huge estate to her first cousin—"

"Her seducer, Edwin, Ciaran's father?" Matt finished the sentence.

"Exactly. I had guessed what my clerk confirmed when she phoned through to me at Dunmor's office. It was a paper trail right to the bitter end!"

"It was on the news tonight that Dennis Dunmor is resigning."

"Indeed." James shook his head. "One good thing. Since I've given all my evidence to the state, I'm free to go, as they put it."

"Do you know if they've found the child Daniel? Lord, he'd be in his seventies now."

"They haven't yet, and the whole estate is being held in escrow . . . until they find him or his heirs, if any. The problem is, the Sligo couple who took him in all those years ago left the country shortly after. It was all part of the original plan. They went on to the States apparently. The investigators are having a lot of trouble. But there's a substantial finder's fee! Interested?"

"In another lifetime maybe." Matt laughed as he ordered another round. The pub on this date so close to Christmas was packed with shoppers and office workers making merry.

"You know, Matt," said James, "this case changed me. No, not the case itself . . ."

"The blow to your head, was it? Rattled the ol' brains, did it? Perhaps no harm in that."

"Said in jest, but meant in earnest, Matt. That blow . . . At that point I might have died. And some things passed through my mind . . ."

"Your whole life . . . as they say?"

"Not my whole life, but one major part of it. It's made me think. I might never have what you have, you lucky bastard, with Dorothy and the kids. But I've realized I've left a lot of things undone, unsaid . . ."

"What do you mean, your train trek to Peru?"

"Among many things. I'm going, and soon. Well, as

soon as I take care of some matters first. You see, when Kevin wrote his will, he named me as Miriam's guardian *pro tem*. He'd wanted to discuss the issue with her godparents before he named them in the document. As a result of that will, I am now her guardian."

"Uh-oh," said Matt, truly at a loss for words.

"I'm going back to the Lodge, just for a while."

"What of Mrs. O'Neil then?"

"Mmm, I spoke to her solicitors today, and they say they expect leniency from the court, especially in view of Miriam's orphaned position. The good man I hired as manager of the Lodge is willing to accommodate the situation. Sean's stayed on. There will be a Christmas season there, I'll stay on for that. I'd like Miriam to be able to hang on to the Lodge. It's her hard-won inheritance, and her home."

"It's a tough situation, but . . ." He'd been looking at James as he spoke and he saw the change come over his face. In a blink of an eye he'd gone from his own colour to a dead white to a rush of red. His eyes were fixed on the door.

"There's something else," James said quickly. "I wanted you to meet someone tonight."

"A woman, I can guess. I noted your sartorial splendour earlier." He wondered who could have such an effect on his friend. But then Matt turned to see the tall, dark-haired woman walking purposefully towards their table. They both stood as she approached.

She smiled as she glanced from James, to Matt, to James, then laughing aloud she offered her hand.

James took her hand and turned to his oldest friend.

"Matt, allow me to introduce you to Miss Sarah Gallagher, renowned violinist as you know, and . . . the love of my life."

From the author of
BOY'S LIFE

A new novel of relenting suspense from
the master storyteller of our time.

ROBERT R. McCAMMON

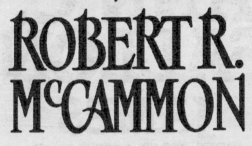

GONE SOUTH

**THE STORY OF A MAN, HUNTED INTO THE
SULTRY SWAMPS OF LOUISIANA, ON THE
RUN FROM A TRAGIC MISTAKE.**

POCKET
BOOKS

Available in hardcover from Pocket Books

522-01